PRAISE FOR JEAN McNEIL

"Jean McNeil's latest is a completely absorbing, eminently readable — to the point of being almost unputdownable — complex, cleverly crafted work, principally about loyalty: what we owe to our country, our relatives, those we love and those who simply cross our path. You won't read many better novels this year." — *Daily Mail* on *The Dhow House*

"Like the landscape she depicts, McNeil's prose combines poetic grace with shadows of menace: behind every flowering bush or luxurious shrub there may be an exotic bird or a poisonous snake — or an armed marauder. The effect is both gripping and unsettling." — *Quill & Quire* on *The Dhow House*

"With dreamlike prose and an intriguing protagonist, fiction- and travel-writer McNeil (*Ice Diaries*, 2016) builds momentum to her novel's surprising final chapters . . . McNeil's storytelling will pull [readers] in and captivate them to the end." — *Booklist* on *The Dhow House*

"Compulsively readable . . . An accomplished travel writer who has been drawn to outposts as remote as Antarctica, McNeil writes descriptions that shimmer . . . We learn the cause of Rebecca's trauma in a scene so brutal and eloquent I reread it several times, astonished and awed." — *New York Times Book Review* on *The Dhow House*

"The sixth novel from Nova Scotia-born writer Jean McNeil brings us a beautiful story about tangled loyalties, self-discovery and the threat of change . . . Her true gift shows in her ability to create deep and complicated characters." — *Winnipeg Free Press* on *The Dhow House*

"The great joy in *The Dhow House*, [McNeil's] eleventh book, is her exceptional ability to illuminate setting and the natural world . . . McNeil's writing is as lush and vivid as the changing hues of the Indian Ocean . . . the sense of place and insight into the mysterious inclinations of the heart linger long after the last page." — *Toronto Star* on *The Dhow House*

"*Ice Diaries* is stunningly written and should be on the shelf of anyone fascinated by the globe's final geographic and psychic frontier."— *New York Times* on *Ice Diaries*

"*Ice Diaries* artfully conveys both the magical allure and the deadly hauteur of this icy world that few of us will ever see." — *Toronto Star* on *Ice Diaries*

"It's a discussion of the Antarctic as a physical landscape — its impact on the imagination — and an exploration of one person's inner world." — *Chicago Tribune* on *Ice Diaries*

"McNeil's first-person narrative of her experience wholly absorbs . . . Most of *Ice Diaries*, however, reads like a novel. It's a paradox: the best novels emulate real life and the best true stories emulate fiction." — *Maclean's* on *Ice Diaries*

"[McNeil's] new book is a welcome literary-minded addition to a category of books dominated by male explorers." — *Metro* on *Ice Diaries*

DAY FOR NIGHT

DAY FOR NIGHT

a novel

JEAN McNEIL

Published by ECW Press
665 Gerrard Street East
Toronto, Ontario, Canada M4M 1Y2
416-694-3348 / info@ecwpress.com

Editor for the press: Susan Renouf
Cover design: Natalie Olsen
Cover images: Will Clarkson, Victor Torres, Tom Uhlenberg/
Stocksy.com

LIBRARY AND ARCHIVES CANADA CATALOGUING IN PUBLICATION

Title: Day for night : a novel / Jean McNeil.

Names: McNeil, Jean, author.

Identifiers: Canadiana (print) 20200403427 | Canadiana (ebook) 20200403451

ISBN 978-1-77041-575-1 (softcover)
ISBN 978-1-77305-705-7 (EPUB)
ISBN 978-1-77305-706-4 (PDF)
ISBN 978-1-77305-707-1 (Kindle)

Classification: LCC PS8575.N433 D38 2021 | DDC C813/.54—dc23

The publication of *Day for Night* has been generously supported by the Canada Council for the Arts and is funded in part by the Government of Canada. *Nous remercions le Conseil des arts du Canada de son soutien. Ce livre est financé en partie par le gouvernement du Canada.* We acknowledge the support of the Ontario Arts Council (OAC), an agency of the Government of Ontario, which last year funded 1,965 individual artists and 1,152 organizations in 197 communities across Ontario for a total of $51.9 million. We also acknowledge the support of the Government of Ontario through the Ontario Book Publishing Tax Credit, and through Ontario Creates for the marketing of this book.

PRINTED AND BOUND IN CANADA

PRINTING: FRIESENS 5 4 3 2 1

MIX
Paper from
responsible sources
FSC
www.fsc.org   FSC® C016245

For the citizens of Europe

"It appeared to us a land without memories, regrets, and hopes; a land where nothing could survive the coming of the night, and where each sunrise, like a dazzling act of special creation, was disconnected from the eve and the morrow."

— JOSEPH CONRAD, *KARAIN*

"I write all day and sometimes well into the night."

— WALTER BENJAMIN, POVEROMO, ITALY, 1932

TABLE OF CONTENTS

TAKE ONE

Each time I set out to make a film I am starting all over again. I remember the films I have made as dreams, fugue states, too intense and painful to bear. But once they are over, all I can think about is: how do I get back there, wherever *there* is.

Any film begins to assemble itself long in advance, on the outskirts of intuition. Being a director at this stage is like being a woman who is only beginning to think of becoming pregnant. It begins as a nudge, an idea of itself first, a galactic child nagging you to yank it out of oblivion.

Four years ago I went to Portbou for the first time and remembered who had died there and what it meant. In that strange place — narrow streets truncated by mountains or by the sea, the devouring, lurid perspective of the place — a new child was born.

I wondered why his life had never been filmed. Biopics are sure winners at the box office and many garner Oscar nominations each year. They are either character-driven and nuanced or high-stakes drama focusing on bringing little-known details to life. I do and don't understand why people want to see fictional renditions of actual — often, let's face it, dead — people whose lives, viewed in retrospectroscope, have a verifiable shape, rather than fictional characters who live as we do, without a clue what is going to happen from one moment to the next. There is a rigid symmetry to the real, at least after it is over. The pieces can be slotted into place, the strategy of fate reveals itself as a chess game played by deities.

But then sometimes you come across a recently extant human being whose spirit feels like a vital presence in the world, still, who is not walking alongside us in another dimension separated only by plexiglass. They are as real as the apple in your hand or the 26 bus weaving down Cambridge Heath Road. They tug at your shirtsleeve and rattle around in your hot water bottle disguised as air bubbles. *I'm alive*, they cajole, these recent, unconvincing ghosts. *Get me out of here.*

When I first float the idea, Joanna says, "That film's been done, dead intellectuals, Nazis shouting 'Raus!' We're living through an eruption of neo-fascism now. Shouldn't you write a story of our times instead of treading over well-worn ground?"

"Well-worn ground is the best kind of ground. How many films can you name about high school?"

"What kind of budget are we talking?" she snaps.

"I don't know. Three million. Pounds," I add, for good measure.

"Too —" Joanna's hand flatlines just beneath her nose, her habitual gesture of the task of balancing artistic inspiration with the likelihood of financing — "low. And anyway, who would watch a film about a hapless Jewish intellectual everyone pretends to understand when actually no one has the faintest what he was writing about?"

I would, I think. And it's too late, in any event. He — Walter Benjamin — is already here with me, his faded serge overcoat, its cuffs rubbed so clean they look like coils, his copper eyes luring me into the dimension of the unresurrected.

When a film begins to press itself upon me, I enter a Red Riding Hood stage. I am a child in a dark wood, or a burning house, or some other archetypal situation. I have to find my way out of the forest/house on fire and the only way to do it is to write a script, then make the words I have put on paper real. Nothing is ever finished in the realm of film, which is to say there is no death. We hum with alertness, we are on the way down, an Orphic descent into a realm of truth where ghosts and other spectators — even you — are watching, forever.

PART I

NIGHT

I

Early January. The pavements are coated with pine needles that have been ground into paste. Carcasses of Christmas trees wait to be carted away to the post-festive charnel house. Some houses still have fairy lights and I find I am grateful to see them, rather than annoyed as I was two months ago, when they went up in early November. The monster of winter is in residence, of course, along with the epic remorse that follows Christmas.

The city levers itself into wintry, estuarine mist. In the half light of midday, bundles of unidentifiable creatures that might just be people propel themselves laboriously forward, curiously elevated, as if they are levitating off the ground, into the fog. The trees wave calligraphically to the sky. At the southernmost finger of London Fields a child wearing a Santa hat roars by me on a plastic car in the shape of a dragon. The man who runs the black pudding and cappuccino stall at the market sits slumped against his counter, reading the *Daily Mail*. "Remainers exposed" is the headline. Underneath it is a police line-up photomontage of the doughty faces of MPs who are not sufficiently zealous about torpedoing the country, we can only surmise.

So we live in Hackney. Why, you might ask? My film school brethren live in Notting Hill, in Battersea. Shorthand explanation: they made more money. Real explanation: they were less besotted with the idea of being an auteur. We moved here twenty-five years ago when we finished film school and made delicate, shifty "European" films, and never left.

Construction cranes rake the skies, where winking planes stitch patterns across the indigo darkness. I walk through arches, underneath bridges, those dank aortae between the neighbour-hoods near our house: de Beauvoir Town, Haggerston, London Fields. We live on the fringes of the latter, between two flat, uncharismatic parks.

Mabati the dachshund (meaning of his name in Kiswahili: corrugated galvanized iron) accompanies me through this Siberian miner disaster film, clattering along on his stubs of legs. I recognize the trees and the streets and the grey parkaed bundles for what they are, but alongside reality is the version I would film, running like a parallel river. This film is about a film director, previously hailed as a visionary, who stands just over the threshold of middle age. The suet hue of the winter sky is the same colour as his heart and he has no idea why, he has done everything right, he has a convincing bio on IMDb, he has made *Voyagers* (2001), *The Grass Is Singing* (2004), *Ryder* (2009), *Everyone Is Watching* (2011) and *Torch Song* (2014). Watch him lurch across London Fields Park in the day-long twilight, bent against the storm of his future.

Yet this is not me, this imposter protagonist. I am not depressed, I see no reason to change or complicate my life. I love our house, a narrow Georgian leakage monster pumping wasted heat through sash windows and unpatrolled cracks in the wooden flooring, fireplace and panelled shutters, stopped only briefly by knock-off Persian rugs bought at the Turkish furniture emporia on Kingsland Road. Our two children, Nathan and Lucy, are well adjusted and happy in their state school, where they walk through knife detectors and on their way home fend off MDMA pimps who try to recruit them into moped gangs.

We have enough money. Joanna and her business partner Neil are the real breadwinners; they now work exclusively for Netflix and Sky, pumping out British content, mostly pearls-and-tiaras nostalgia fare for North Americans transfixed by codified social hierarchies. The money Joanna makes is largely kept from me and goes straight to her broker, where it is invested in renewable energy in South Africa and carbon-capture technology in New Zealand.

Time is ticking. I can hear it inside me. It is less clock than bomb. If I don't make another film I will lose the thread of myself. Ambition is only the terror of irrelevance.

My subject has taken an interest in me. He walks beside me in these submarine hours when Mabati and I orbit the park, trying to read the hieroglyphs the trees have inscribed on the sky. This is when I know I'm on to something, as a writer: my characters don't take over — that's a silly fanciful notion — but they do start to haunt me, becoming friendly ghosts, chaperones, doppelgängers.

"Don't negate this time, however difficult it is to live through," he says to me, loud enough to cause Mabati's left ear to wobble. "Yes, it's cold, it's January, your country has foresworn itself, it's like a living death. But never wish time away. You don't know how much of it there is left."

"You should know," I say. "I've already been alive a year longer than you were when you died."

"Two," he corrects me.

He doesn't really speak like this. *Would you be so kind, gentle lady, as to show me the path to my salvation?* That was how he spoke, all his contemporaries commented on the decorous, Old-World syntax that even in 1940 was considered hilariously baroque. He says this to me in English, although in life his English was shaky and rudimentary, according to Hannah Arendt.

Mabati and I head back to the mothership, 11 Navarino Road. Our wedge of Hackney is criss-crossed by the railyards of the Overground which blazed an orange-coloured trail of gentrification into the neighbourhood — when? I can't remember when it started. Our streets are lined with separate utopias: Paradise Hair Relaxing Salon, Lilliput Daycare, Nirvana Nails. From Google Earth two tourmaline geometries are visible in our neighbourhood — the rectangle of London Fields Lido, the children's square paddling pool sidling next to it. Also visible are smaller turquoise jewels, dropped in the allotment-sized gardens on our street in the back of number 3 or 5, on our odd-numbered side. When your neighbours in London start putting in outdoor swimming pools, feasibly useful only perhaps two weeks of the entire year, and the Range Rovers start stacking up outside, you know you have been oligarched.

London is never only its present incarnation. I cart the memory of what it used to be, like pictures of dead family members, everywhere. Remember when Mare Street was Pentecostal churches and jerk chicken joints and I used to be dragged down the street by crack addicts? London is a spaceship, an opal mine, a broken soundstage of dreams. It is the only city I have ever been in which is more than itself, which has its own agency and intelligence, a giant multi-tentacled alien. It is mythological. I dread the day when I will hear the call to leave, when I no longer believe our fates are entwined. Where will I go then, who will I be? I have made the mistake of hitching my identity to this self-possessed, haphazard city. All around us another London is constructing itself in the sky, tended to by loving cranes bent double, soliciting skeletons of future buildings from the ground, red lights blinking like the eyes of Tyrannosaurus rexes. How would my companion have withstood this future we now inhabit? *The image of happiness we cherish is thoroughly coloured by the time to which the course of our own existence has assigned us.*

When I return home, I smell Joanna's expert arrabbiata for the children, who are no longer children, really, having morphed into teenagers when we were not looking. Joanna is writing on the chalkboard she has hung on the feature wall of our kitchen (fuchsia — the feature wall colour of the moment). *New Year's Resolutions: R's 5oth, March. Turnover on Benjamin, May. A-levels, June. Leave EU — when? U Fuckers: never.*

"Big year ahead," I say, but too late I see that she is plugged into her iPhone with those Bluetooth earbuds. Her mouth is moving as she speaks to Neil, I suppose, or one of her producer colleagues who are all fifty-something women with sharp fringes dressed in floor-to-ceiling Whistles. I watch her rotate around the kitchen, clicking the top onto the blender, whizzing anti-winter flu concoctions that smell like hayfields. She scrolls through emails on her iPad while on her iPhone she swipes through her corporate Instagram.

"A multi-tasking poltergeist has taken over the kitchen," I yell.

Joanna's eyes flick in my direction. She points to her ear and mouths a name which might be Verity or Charity.

I retreat to my study, a room we constructed out of a sinister broom closet space underneath the stairs, the kind of room where weeping Victorian maids probably once drank overdoses of laudanum. Night adheres to the window. The blender's fury is only a distant roar, like traffic on Queensbridge Road. I begin to construct the alternate world I will soon recall from the outer edges of erasure: this world has olive groves, ravines, mountaintop pine trees as unforgiving as razors, slim well-dressed people in graceful Edwardiana and acting in good faith, then in bad faith, then good faith again, like emotional ellipses that never run out. I begin to see a young man with dark hair like ink. I have never met this man, but he is the person who will make my film with me. He feels the tug of my gaze, the call to return to a dimension denser, more real than life.

It is January but this year, 2018, will not unfold as we think it will, its narrative organized into stalwart chapters, January thumbing over into March, then June, then November. Some years are truculent, they have to be coaxed into life. Benjamin writes that to go forward in history we have to reclaim the memory of ourselves, throttle our fear and perfect the vocabulary of our distress. The trick is, as he wrote, to gather the fragments into a larger unity, to put out feelers to the universe, imagine a different destiny. *In these times, when precisely what is happening could not be imagined, and when what must happen can no longer be imagined, and if it could it could not happen . . . in these unspeakable times, you can expect no word of my own from me.*

Events have overtaken our capacity to imagine them. We are tilted forward into light in the form of the coming spring, but for the first time in my life, a menacing darkness clouds the road ahead, as if someone has switched off the sun. Now all hours are three or four on winter afternoons, their melancholy waiting-room light. By then, the day is largely behind us but we have not accomplished what we wanted, we are not sufficiently convinced of our right to exist. We have not used time wisely. Night awaits.

II

S amantha sits down in a haze of blondness — everything about her is blond: hair, beige woollen coat, a sand-coloured scarf. We meet at 193 Wardour Street, the café she likes to take me to so that she can escape her office around the corner, or more likely escape her boss, a flinty maven who has been in the business since the Devonian era.

"I think you should start now," she says.

"I might be promising something I can't deliver," I say.

"Oh, no director has ever done that."

We laugh. I bump the bare filament light bulbs which hang too low in every café and restaurant on the planet at the moment.

Samantha is uncomfortable with my plan to have the young and old Benjamin overlap in the past. The script has the older man meeting his younger self in a semi-hallucinatory sequence. They pass the baton back and forth between versions of themselves in the narrative, leapfrogging decades.

But two actors playing Benjamin means two actors' fees. From the beginning Joanna has been urging me to reconsider. *You're not Todd Haynes and we can't raise $11.7 million*, mind-Joanna says to me now, referring to his Bob Dylan film where even Cate Blanchett has a go at being Bob. *We haven't even got the financing locked down, Richard*, she goes on. *Drop the postmodern posturing and we save a cool million at least.*

Samantha opens her bag and produces her iPad. I am such a dinosaur I still expect people to pull out a paper folder with headshots and CVs, even if it must be ten years now since this was the norm.

"Okay, I know we need the big names. But I met Trevor for lunch on Tuesday. And." She swipes through her folder which, I notice, is labelled *Richard — possibles*.

Benjamin shifts beside me. He still won't raise his eyes from the table. He is thinking perhaps about whom I have in mind to play his lover. The film will concentrate on his infatuation with Asja Lacis, the Latvian theatre director, with whom he had an intermittent affair. (Did they even sleep together?) *Infatuation* is the better word. Benjamin and I share a nervous glance. An ugly word, with its lardy lustre. For a second he looks sheepish, even guilty. "Intellectuals are too susceptible to delusion," he says. "It's got nothing to do with being an intellectual," I say. "It's about having a Romantic temperament. Practical people fall prey to lust, idealists end up infatuated."

"Richard?" Samantha is peering at me.

"Yes, present."

"Good, I thought I'd lost you there." Samantha is swiping so fast I see only a blur of faces. The blur comes to a halt and it emerges — two eyes, a nose, very dark hair. An unusually frank expression in the eyes, which are both dark and light, simultaneously. As is standard, the headshots are in black and white, but the mineral brilliance of the eyes stands out nonetheless.

"Too young."

"He's twenty-two." Samantha frowns. "No, twenty-three."

"Definitely too young."

"You're just put off because he's beautiful."

"Maybe." Although I notice that his beauty does not bully me into submission.

I peer closer. There is an imperfect, transcendent note in his face that I like. His brow is unusually experienced for someone so young. There are already two light frown furrows above his nose. He has a broad forehead, a little out of alignment with the rest of his racehorse features. "He sort of looks like André Malraux. When he was young."

"Or Aidan Quinn. When he was young," Samantha adds.

The face in front of us is future-less. It is difficult to imagine such a face broadening, thickening, collapsing. This face floats free from age or indeed any category — woman, man — as if missing a chromosome.

Beside me, Benjamin shifts. His eyes slide over the photograph.

I lever my face up from the screen. Samantha is frowning. "Richard, do you need glasses?"

"Oh, probably." Benjamin mutters, "Mann, hol dir einfach eine Brille."

"I told you I don't speak German," I tell him.

"What does German have to do with it?" Samantha says.

"Nothing, just something Joanna said to me and I neglected to rebut."

The phantom of a frown passes across her face. She is thinking: has-been, trying to recover his reputation, overly ambitious concept, thinks he is Tarkovsky, etcetera.

She says, "Trevor spoke about him like he was the eighth wonder of the world. He said give it a year or two and he'll have two million Instagram followers."

I look again. It is true, the face lacks the vapidity of perfect beauty. It is rare to find someone who has that brutal perfection but who is also intelligent. Usually they cancel each other out. I am most interested in the kind of beauty I miss the first time I meet someone, or for a long time even, until it hits me when I least expect it and I think, hang on, you're actually *beautiful*.

She sits back. "Richard?"

"Okay," I shove my cup, whose rim of coffee-scum has settled in an exact outline of Australia. "Let's meet him."

I walk all the way home. I have taken to doing epic walks in the last two years. It takes forever, I should get the bus, but these walks are a reclamation mission. I am trying to locate the clue to London's abdication since the Brexit vote. It is hard to say how the city has changed, only that it has, like arriving home to your living room to find that someone has shifted the furniture slightly, only enough to create unease and paranoia. *Did I really leave the cabinet of liberal democracy open?*

Yes, it all looks the same: the British Museum in all its rectitude, the gargoyles of Lincoln's Inn Fields, the ragged-tooth leer of the Barbican, the Gherkin's glass menhir — all still there, still raw and bleak with erroneous power. Now the city is a bullying, rescinding force, like a lover whose lust has turned brusquely to disgust.

Joanna sees me coming home shell-shocked. She thinks it's because of the looming zero in my life.

"Richard, we've only got two months left to plan your party."

"I'm not having one, I told you. Nobody's going to come anyway. I'll be scouting then. I might even be shooting, who knows?"

What I don't tell Joanna: the prospect of my fiftieth birthday with my diminishing supply of old friends plus Joanna's high-roller contacts eating organic Camembert in our living room and toasting my past success makes me break out in a cold sweat. Birthdays are of course a diminishing longing for the inevitability of the future, while everyone around you secretly takes delight in your erosion as they down the Prosecco.

The next morning Joanna stands in our kitchen against the hungry red of its wall, her greyhound beauty stark and serene, like a John Singer Sargent painting: a *Madame X* for the twenty-first century with her agnès b. cashmere jumper, a narrow chin thrown over her shoulder.

She waves a spatula in a directionless spiral. "You're only fifty once. You need to celebrate it." She means: *You're certainly not going to live another fifty years.*

"I will. Celebrate it." My jaw clenches painfully.

"How did your meet with Samantha go?"

"She's found someone."

"Anyone I know?"

"Elliott Sarkissian."

"*Sarkasian,*" she corrects me. "His mother is a very good actress. She's French-Armenian."

"I didn't know you knew about him."

"I read a review of him in something at the Royal Court. Can't remember the name of the play. Everyone assumed he was there because of his mother, but he burnt the place down. He's hot."

I wince at the word. *Hot* for me still means overheated.

"But that wouldn't be in his favour, with you," she says.

"I'm meeting him."

"When?"

"Next week. I wouldn't worry about it," I say. "He's too young and too unknown."

"Why are you considering him then?"

"I don't know. Instinct."

She knows very well that once a script is done I do everything else in a film on my gut. A meeting I have now might only come to fruition for the next film, four or five years down the line. You never know how things are going to pan out in this business. Film is a purer way of living than actual life in that sense: you have to be open to providence. The more films I make, the more I feel the whole thing is somehow in the lap of the gods.

Joanna's eyes narrow — an insinuation is on its way. "You were up very early this morning."

"I was thinking. Apparently it's good for writers to think."

She fishes a Nespresso capsule from its long reluctant sleeve. Intenso — Roma. She must have a busy day. "You look terrible. You should at least shave."

"Thanks."

I hear the thumps on the ceiling that signal the children are up. I have to make my escape before I get entangled with their increasingly elaborate preparations for school. Nathan is doing

A-levels but seems to need a morning bathroom routine worthy of an opera singer. Lucy however is a member of an old London tribe, dedicatedly scruffy, stomping off with hair akimbo to her GCSEs in battered Doc Martens.

A clump of energy forms in the corner of the kitchen. He is there, his high forehead with its plough-furrow wrinkles, the isolated eyes.

"Where have you been?" I whisper.

"Oh, I was haunting some second-hand bookshops on Charing Cross Road. One had a first edition of *One-Way Street*, in German, can you imagine? It was behind a glass case. They want £5,000 for it. Although that doesn't sound like much in Deutsche Marks."

"That unit of currency is long gone I'm afraid."

He has taken off his hat, which sits in his lap, his hair stands vertical in clumps, like molars. His overcoat is dusty — must be the bookshops, I suppose, brushing up against all those piles of Harry Potter paperbacks.

"Where was I?" he says.

"In 1923. I was just writing the scene where you return to Berlin to look for work." He winces. I can't blame him. Who would want to live through that again? In 1923 he was frantically trying to secure an academic position, leaning on great uncles, calling in favours with contacts from Freiburg to Frankfurt. He needed to become what he was in his inner core: a scholar, a visionary. Instead he had to support himself through hackery, sending notes by messenger to aloof editors, doorstepping magazines with names like *The Torch* edited by frenemies, the writer as journeyman, the writer as only one in a disposable army of effete nomadic gunslingers.

By the early 1930s, Berlin is in a dire situation. Inflation, unemployment, strikes — short of war, it could not be a worse time to be looking for a job. Benjamin lives in one room with his wife, Dora, and infant son, Stefan. His friend Wolf Steinle dies of tuberculosis. The death brings back memories of the suicide of Wolf's brother, Fritz, in 1914. "The most beautiful young men I ever knew," Benjamin writes. The death of that beauty is only one tone in the greyscale darkness that seems to be overtaking the world. He is becoming to think the esoterics are right: darkness is real, a force that when unleashed soaks all life in spectral rumour.

Benjamin remembers that version of himself. The sooty smell of his desperation, the growing sense that he may yet fail at life after all. The cuffs of his white shirt are ever so slightly opalescent, rubbed raw with the fanaticism of the late-night scribbler. A graphite note has crept into his eye. It sparkles, a dank beckoning. In the background are the muffled voices of Joanna, Nathan and Lucy. Is it my imagination, or do they sound so much more relaxed, when I am not among them? It occurs to me that they are an autonomous unit. If I were to disappear, they would be sad, I am sure, they would mourn me. But they would also be relieved.

I have always had an intuition when something on the emotional spectrum is coming. I can feel the heat of its approach, as if I've received a text alert from a government agency warning of a hurricane, of unusual seismic activity. Benjamin gives me a baleful look. Perhaps he can feel it too, although it is nothing more than a density in the atmosphere, like a high-altitude wind. Our curiosities are twinned. We wonder if the future will always deliver crisis or simply a momentary rapture or delicate, uncanny lies.

III

"Hi. I'm Elliott."

He arrives like the wind, before I have a chance to form an impression of him. We sit down in a flurry — Elliott and Samantha on one side of the raised, school desk–ish tables. I perch facing the wall. The filament bulb swishes against my head.

"You're too tall for this place." Elliott smiles.

"I'm trying to get shorter but it's not working."

Elliott's smile at my weak joke is like a detonation. For a moment I can't help but join in.

"I've always admired your work — *so* much," he says. "I saw *The Grass Is Singing* when I was fourteen and was blown away. The *light* in that film — I never knew trees could look like that. Like golden ribs."

"Fever trees," I say, and for some reason quote their botanical name, Acacia xanthophloea.

"So," Samantha says. She slides her eyes at Elliott and takes quick, pecking looks, like a chicken. "Elliott's getting very busy. I wanted you two to meet if shooting this summer is going to be on the cards."

"Yes, I hear, and congratulations." Samantha told me Elliott has been nominated for an *Evening Standard* rising star award for his performance in *The Mangrove* at the Royal Court, a play about eco-anxiety in which he takes the role of a young environmental activist.

He lowers his eyes. "Thanks."

"So here's the premise. This film focuses on the last months of Benjamin's life, but we see episodes from his past in flashback, framed within."

I draw Benjamin's biography in outline for Elliott: born in 1892 to a bourgeois Jewish family but assimilated, meaning they were hardly aware of being Jewish, never mind the black cross the word would become, cancelling the existence of six million people less than fifty years in the future.

His father was an antiques dealer. He was a coddled child, sensitive, with the introvert's tendency to overthink situations. Clumsy. His talent was for writing, but stylistically he was ahead of his time. He struggled to get his PhD thesis accepted; he lived the life of the perpetual student, dependent on institutions for his sense of purpose and well-being as much as money, I say.

Then, the war. Benjamin saw the signs early. He left for France in 1932, before Kristallnacht. But like many exiles he had no idea that he was leaving his country forever, that his country would leave him, revoking his citizenship. He had no idea he would never see Berlin again.

For the last eight years of his life Benjamin eked out a living in France writing sketches, journalism, reviews, criticism, the literary equivalent of a minstrel, I say.

I pause to check my sketch is sinking in. Samantha is actually listening instead of looking at her iPhone. There is a rapt note in Elliott's eyes, which in real life live up to the note of deep, even eternal, intelligence I saw in his headshot.

The noise of the café's espresso machine is as loud as a steam train. We all cover our ears with our hands.

I go on. "He was interned in enemy alien camps, he had no savoir faire, no idea how to get along with others in cramped conditions when your position in society and your identity had been stripped away. He smoked heavily, he died at forty-eight but looked sixty, he had a bad heart. He was on the verge of a heart attack at any moment. During all of this he married and had a child but the love of his life was Asja, the Latvian theatre director, who didn't treat him very well. She could not or would not give him what he wanted. She led him on a wild goose chase across Europe, but still he loved her. The nightmare of infatuation, basically."

"Well," Samantha says, "you still certainly know how to pitch a story Richard."

I jump in. "Elliott, I have to be honest here. We think you are a little young for the role."

His eyes flicker. "I'll audition then."

"The script isn't quite locked down yet, but I'd like us to do a read-through. I'm quite informal. We can do it around my kitchen table or at Samantha's office, but either way I want you to be relaxed about it. No audition, no producers in the room."

He sits back. I am being evaluated by someone much younger than me, and so on terms I can't quite access. "I'd work with you on anything." His tone is not obsequious or desperate. He sounds as if he is stating that water freezes to ice, or fire burns. He has a strange elemental certainty.

He leans across the table, folding his thin, lanky frame over it to eat up the space between us. "I love the scene in *Voyagers* when you sweep the camera along the beach at the tide line. It's like the camera becomes the wind."

I can't contain my pleasure. This is exactly as I conceived the shot, and the whole set piece of that scene, when the two lovers (who are actually brother and sister, but they do not know it yet) recoil from the sea as if it is a snake with that dreadful message in its mouth. They know, you see, on some level, already.

"So, why are you interested in this role?"

For a moment he does not answer. Thought shuttles back and forth behind his eyes, figures running behind stage curtains, only their feet visible.

He wanted nothing more than to be an actor since he was twelve, he says. His mother, luckily, is well known. Think Jane Birkin or Kristin Scott Thomas, someone who can bridge the gap between the ruthless, emotionally backward English and the over-refined, self-indulgent French. He does not mention his father.

"I read Benjamin's work in school, for our performance course. The essays. It's actually quite an actorly text — I'm thinking of *A Berlin Chronicle*, when he talks about déjà vu as a sound playing from the darkness of an unremembered past life. I'm interested in his purity."

Purity. The word trills in my head. It must have been a long time since I have heard it.

He goes on: "He has a spectral quality. I can see him — he has this, this transcendent pallor. It's like reading yourself, or looking in a mirror."

He sits back. We stare at each other in silence. People keep pouring through the door from Wardour Street. The slide of the café's front door opening and closing sounds unnaturally loud.

"Elliott is very excited about this role," Samantha says, finally.

Elliott scans my face as if looking at distant hills for a path to the horizon. I can see my reflection in his eyes: a middle-aged director with a three-day-old beard, tall and bony, the stress of coordinating film shoots etched in his crow's feet, a crown of faux-filaments behind his head. For a moment I see two miniature monitor lizards in his pupils. *Christ, that's me.*

Samantha says brightly, "I'll send Elliott the script and we can take it from there."

I stand up to shake Elliott's hand. His grip is firm, yielding but intelligent. When even a person's handshake is intelligent you know you're in trouble.

We both watch him exit the café. He walks with a long, consuming stride.

Samantha frowns. "Are you alright?"

"How long have we been talking?"

"Nearly an hour."

"It seemed like minutes."

Samantha looks at her watch. "Well, it wasn't. I have to be getting back."

"I'll stay here for a bit." I nearly say *to gather my thoughts*, but that would be old-fashioned. "I have some emails to send."

"Of course."

"How old did you say he was?"

"Twenty-three. He sounds like he's seventy-five, doesn't he? It's good to know the young can still have depth, despite Instagram and Facebook's best efforts. Mind your head when you get up or the café will charge me for a new light fixture."

When she has left I experience a slump. All energy pours from me, as if I've been punctured. I don't want to go home. Joanna will ask, *How did it go with Elliott?* I will say, *There's something unusual about him. He's diligent, professional, deadly serious. But he almost doesn't care. It's as if he knows the right thing will happen for him.* Joanna will say, *Some people are like that. It happens at birth, as if the Norns or whoever say to them: You are the chosen one. And they go through life in a golden bubble. Nice work if you can get it.*

I will say, *I don't know that I'm up to it.*

To what?

To anything. How to make this film the testament it needs to be, to what has become of our world. How to survive the spectre of my birthday.

Suddenly Elliott is implicated in my existential doubt. I am intimidated already by his vulnerability, his versatility. Very few people have this innocent charisma.

It can't be that innocent if it makes people want him, says mind-Joanna.

Benjamin does not think much of my phantom conversations with my wife. Shoved out of the scene, he has walked off in a huff to contemplate pineapple-shaped mobile phone covers in the Tiger shop around the corner.

He knows he will soon be resurrected, brought back to life through all the dangerous procrastination of time. Benjamin-Elliott will dream of Troy again, of Thucydides, of the conservative ambiguity of his imagination. He will burst forth into the now-world and witness the handheld panopticons we haul everywhere with us, and the all-day, all-night lantern shows projected onto the lacquered surfaces he will see in each house, living room, office, and will presume are mirror-images of demons shipped from a proximate dimension.

◢

Mabati and I fall into step with each other, even if he has to take ten steps for my every one. All is as it should be. The number 30 bus swings around the sharp angle of the diamond of Hackney Downs. The Georgian houses that rim the park's perimeter are lit only in their upper rooms. At this time of year I feel I am captaining a submarine, moving between mid-oceanic trenches where pulsating purple jellyfish send strobe lights into a bleached, depthless darkness.

Benjamin has deserted me, since I met Elliott. Perhaps they have gone off together. I have a sudden image of them walking near, frustratingly within earshot but much more interested in each other than in me.

"You must go to Tiergaren, to the Herkules Bridge," Benjamin says, "you would have loved the flowerbeds, a labyrinth of hyacinths. They only came out in early May. In Berlin the spring is later."

"I love flowerbeds," Elliott says, solemn.

"The lake froze in those years. Women would whirl like ribbons on the ice. People say children cannot remember anything from before they were three but I remember it exactly. I would sit with my nurse on a bench and watch them."

"Weren't you cold?" Elliott asks.

"Ha! In those days children were not treated like porcelain." Benjamin squints, as if seeing Elliott for the first time. I can't tell if he is trying to resist the authority of his youth, his potential.

"You know," Benjamin says, "you look a bit Russian."

"Everyone looks Russian, if you look at them long enough."

This makes Benjamin roar with laughter. *"Everyone looks Russian . . ."* Poor Benjamin has to fish his handkerchief from the depths of his coat pocket. I see a flash of embroidery on its hem — his initials, *WB*.

Elliott and I exchange a glance. *Is he for real?*

"The sound of the skates" — Benjamin hurls his head back, nose to the air — "it's a unique sound, don't you think? Like horses drinking water, but very quickly." He addresses himself to Elliott. "I didn't know how safe I was. Don't make the same mistake."

The phone rings in my pocket. A mobile number I don't recognise blooms on the screen.

"Richard?" The voice is familiar, but I can't immediately place it. "It's Elliott. I hope you don't mind me calling you direct. Samantha gave me your number. I'd like to come over tomorrow, if that's possible, and read for you. I really want to do this, I know I should wait for your call but I don't want to lose the chance, or for time to pass and us both drift toward something else."

"Yes, Elliott, of course." I muster enthusiasm out of my wrong-footedness. "That would be great. What about two? The kids will be home at 3:30. They can be noisy."

"That's not a problem," he says, as if he needs to reassure me, and not the other way round. "See you then."

Elliott materialized out of the cold afternoon, his head sandwiched between a huge pair of noise-cancelling headphones, like an airport runway worker.

"Welcome to Draft Manor." I pulled aside the velvet curtain we keep strung behind the entrance door. "All guests are welcomed with a complimentary hot water bottle and duvet."

I looked down to find his hand there. I shook it. I remembered the firm yet delicate handshake from our first meeting. He had long fingers that curled around mine; they looked not entirely like fingers but something more alive — lilies, sea anemones.

"Can I get you something to drink? Tea? Coffee? Decaf?" I went into the kitchen. Joanna was with Neil at a meeting. Lucy and Nathan would be home soon enough, thumping through the door with the mashed-peas-meets-antiseptic smell of school clinging to them.

I left Elliott to browse the study. When I returned he was staring at the photo of my father stroking Siwezi (meaning in Kiswahili: not possible). This image usually causes people to pause — a man fingering a grown male lion, whose head lolls adoringly in his lap.

"I read you grew up in Africa."

"Where did you read that?"

"Wikipedia."

"Ah, totally accurate then."

"What was that like?"

"It was —" I found myself adopting the same posture as one I have written for Benjamin in the script, whenever he is thinking deeply, neck folded back, mouth open to the ceiling. "A kind of heaven, although flawed. I didn't know that at the time. I still haven't recovered from losing it."

"How do you mean, losing it?"

"My parents sent me away to school."

"How old were you when you came here?"

"Twelve. I moved to Italy first. I didn't come to Britain until I was eighteen."

He blinked. "I didn't realize you were Italian."

"I'm not, but my mother is. Well, I am Italian on paper, and I speak it well. That doesn't appear on Wikipedia, I take it."

"How did you feel about moving here?"

"I think I was in shock for a year," I said. "I couldn't understand why anyone would live somewhere so hostile. I was outraged that people had to put money in gas meters in order not to freeze to death."

For the first time in many years, a mental picture of me at first contact with Europe formed in my mind, a bronzed photograph, like one of those nostalgia filters on Instagram. A hale, rangy twelve-year-old who grew up running barefoot along dirt roads avoiding scorpions and puff adders, shooting guineafowl with a catapult, his skin burnished by a boyhood spent outside and, also, by a note of dusk that comes from blood rather than the sun.

Elliott's eyes swivelled around my study, landing on the potbellied rendition of Alfred Hitchcock crouching on the mantelpiece — my win at Dinard for *Voyagers* — now covered in the lightest film of Hackney benzene. Then the black-and-white photos of my childhood on the far wall, of my father and grandfather with their neighbours, Maasai herdsmen lined up as if for inspection wrapped in shukas, all with the same blunt, horizon-awed stare.

His silence as he stared at these images was a question.

"My father and grandfather," I said.

"You mean —" He pointed to Lenoi, whose hawk nose I have inherited.

"Yes, him."

"But your father looks —"

"White, yes. His mother was, the first European woman to openly live with an African at the time."

Elliott turned his lighthouse toward my face, scanning it anew. "You've got quite an unusual family history. So many countries and cultures."

"Yes, I'm the original citizen of nowhere, to quote our present prime minister."

The thunk of the door closing signalled Nathan and Lucy were home. They put their heads around the door with total disinterest until they saw Elliott.

"Hello, who's this?" Nathan said.

"This is Elliott. He's up to be the lead in *Benjamin*." A quick flash of apprehension on Elliott's face forced me to add, "We hope."

"Cool." Nathan's head slipped back and Lucy's replaced it immediately around the seam of the door, eyes horizontal and alert, like a two-headed serpent. "Hello, Elliott. I hope you get the part."

"Thanks," Elliott said.

"Okay, children, we have a read-through to do. Elliott, let's go to my study/broom closet."

Joanna appeared in the hallway, on her way in from outdoors, attached by Bluetooth to her iPhone. She plucked the earphones out and rubbed her hands together to warm them before offering one. She looked, as she often does, much younger than her forty-seven years in her slim overcoat, three-quarter-length trousers which show off her ankles and terminate in beige platform Converse All-Stars.

"Elliott, so lovely to meet you. I've heard so much about you. I'm so glad you're up for this film."

Elliott took her hand and shook it earnestly. "So am I."

I must have looked alarmed at this scene out of *Downton Abbey* and their precision at its delivery. They were both so on point. "Richard?" Joanna asked.

"Yes, we're just on our way to my study."

Joanna was very good. My line gave her a diversion to look at Elliott, to soak him up. I watched her scout the elements of him: the delicate, not wholly or not only masculine, bones in his face, the decrescendo of his cheekbones. His lightness, which is not the same as thinness, although he is that, as if he is made of air. *Sprite*. Her conclusion, which was foregone: too young, too fey.

My study was the usual Shaker disaster scene: raw wood cabinets and stony chairs upholstered in pages of scripts gathering dust, in copies of books providing random inspiration — Benjamin's writing collected in *Illuminations*, Arendt's *The*

Human Condition. I cleared one of these chairs. Elliott sat, his eyes restless, scanning the room with that forensic gaze of his.

"I like your study. It's very classic. Like those Huguenot houses in Shoreditch."

"Yes, I find the spartan look inspiring. It speaks to me."

A smile played with his mouth. "What does it say?"

"I believe it's *write this bloody film, Richard, or you'll be burning me to keep warm this winter.*"

We started the scene. In it Benjamin is reading the essay he is in the process of writing to his friend, Gershom Scholem, who is aghast at its direct attack on another writer, the satirist Karl Kraus. The essay is an attack on the early days of national socialism, then — in 1931 — brewing in Germany. I read the part of Scholem, who immigrated to Palestine in 1923 and who remained a lifelong friend to Benjamin.

Elliott assumed Benjamin's unhappy posture of the writer, the endless wrestling with words and meanings, hunched over in his chair like an upside-down question mark. He read the line from the essay I quote in the script: "'A society that is in the process of building houses with glass walls, and patios extending into the drawing rooms which are no longer drawing rooms, of private life that is openly dismantling itself . . . man is becoming a different creature, a monster, a new angel.'"

My eyes found his hands. Elliott had the right fingers for Benjamin — seemingly delicate, but actually in possession of a lean muscular power. A dancer's fingers. He was a rope casually knotted. There was something of the noose about him. I caught only a glimpse of a flour-white ankle for wrist, blue veins tangling across them in minor tributaries, the way he inhabited his body, as if it was gifted to him only yesterday. I could already see him in the plan-séquence, the unravelling of beats, the last chapter of Benjamin's life unfolding in bittersweet pleats.

He looked up. He saw perhaps the fixity in my gaze. I thought, *This person has the capacity to look into people, as if he can see right through the porridge of cerebral cortex and eye jelly clear to the back of your head.*

"It's good."

It was true. His rendition was serious, mimetic, not leaden. He managed to convey the excitement of thinking.

A door flings itself open. *Film is about figures in a landscape*; so said my first teacher at film school. The figure — the character, the actor — has to embody this landscape somehow, they have to convince you they are of it, have been formed by it.

In a realm just behind Elliott's face, that mobile angel unaware of the novel horrors kept in its wings, a figure stands adrift in a landscape — Benjamin in Antwerp train station before the war, buying cigarettes, or fast-forward eight years, Benjamin asleep, bundled in his overcoat in the Drancy transit camp, where he has been dragged despite speaking perfect sibilant French in the early days of the occupation.

It's very difficult to write about writers. To understand their work you have to quote from it, and so much rhetoric can make a film didactic, like watching a lecture. Yet the writer's life is in the work, always, so much more than the living — that realm they have abdicated, in order to exist. The negative power of the writer is to turn their lives into art.

"I'll do a bit more work on the scene," I say to Elliott.

He rises and reapplies his baggage handler earphones. At the door he plucks one from his ear. "It was so nice to meet your family," he says. I have the sense he is not talking about Joanna and the children, or not only, but the photographs on the walls. They have confirmed something for him, a question he has entertained about me which he has not shared, or not yet, has been answered.

We hesitate on my doorstep. The Japanese maple in our front garden looks at us expectantly, its branches asleep, anticipating spring. I will soon have to make a decision, to offer him the part or carry on looking and risk our production schedule. Putting a partly European funded film together has consequences, now that the UK is a limb about to be severed from the body that has sustained it for forty years.

"I'll be in touch," I say. With that, Elliott bounds down the steps.

Later, I am in my study when a smell of ginger enters the room, faint at first, tangy, unmistakable, then it is wafting, everywhere. The fume of another soul is perceivable in its smell, we just don't have the faculties to pick it up.

"You're back," I think — or even say out loud.

He sighs. "The face of the lover first appears in a dream, but we do not know its identity, or we do not remember the dream."

"So you like him."

"It is getting crowded in here. It is like a conference on philology at Baden-Baden."

It's true, I have brought Elliott into my internal landscape so quickly. "I can't evict him now," I say.

He comes to rest, a floating episode, in the chair in the corner of my study. He takes off his hat. His hair looks ill-considered today, like moss. The hourglass face emerges from underneath it: the square, blank forehead, the arrowhead nose. He is thickening, becoming more real with each day we approach the beginning of the shoot.

A plane roars overhead, unusually close. We crane our necks to the roof. His eyes search the sky outside the window. "So much noise from above, now," Benjamin says. "In my life all planes were trying to kill you."

I say, "You know, I think I might be hallucinating you."

A wounded note floods his eyes. "Everything is a hallucination."

Benjamin bends toward the window, a dark Cyclops looking out onto an elegant street, trussed in its sudden mansions. Twenty years ago they were squats, and now they could buy an olive grove in Andalucía or a farm in Nova Scotia.

Benjamin dissolves through the window. I am coming to realize he is not convinced about me at all. He will resent me for my slippages in the rendition of his life this film will be, my slowness to accept my own limitations. I fear I won't capture the grain of glamour that clings to the memory of his life, the bitter current of him, despite his stolidity, his apparent ordinariness. Film and literature alone have the ability to get to the core of the emotional truth of living in a treacherous zone of phenomenological fact. Elliott has the same force field as Benjamin I realize. The room hums with his presence of his absence, long after he is gone.

IV

Elliott and I take our coffees to one of the upper floors of the Royal Festival Hall. River light floats through the giant windows.

We find a sofa on level five. We are seated for only a minute when a woman wearing a black pouch bristling with programmes approaches us. "Excuse me, sorry to bother you, but do you have a ticket for today's performance?"

"It's 4 p.m.," I say.

"Yes, but there's a matinee in the hall and a performance at 7:30 and I'm afraid this area is reserved for ticket holders only."

"This is a public building. We're allowed to sit where we like. We are not bothering anyone."

"I'm sorry, sir, but we keep this area free for ticket holders now."

I sense a losing battle. We rise and find a spot two levels below. On our way there I bore Elliott with how much I loved the Royal Festival Hall when there wasn't a single café or restaurant inside and you didn't have to buy anything or have a ticket and its areas were not zoned off like nightclub VIP lounges.

Elliott listens to my monologue, head lowered in that abashed posture, as if I have admonished him for not having been on the planet during the Golden Era I am banging on about.

I say, "I think I'm being haunted."

"By whom?"

"I don't know. There are so many candidates. The country I thought I was living in, the fact I'll be fifty in a couple of months. The film."

"How so?"

I decide to be frank. Why do I feel I don't have to strategize with Elliott? I simply trust him. Or is it because I need a confidant too keenly? My life is solitary, apart from Joanna and the kids I have no one, until I assemble the ragged family required to make a film. There is nowhere to dissipate my emotion. I feel I am living on an inner island.

"Well, for writer-directors at least, it's like this: the film wants to exist. It's impatient for it, and now it's harassing me to bring it to life. It knows it will be immortal. Every morning when I wake up it is sitting there in my head, waiting to be animated. *Are you up to that?* It's not too different from parenting. The film is as wary of you as your children are. You hold too much power over their existences, but they are the stronger entity."

Elliott nods gravely through all of this. "Did you always want children?"

"Joanna did the wanting, and I found she was right."

His mouth twitches, as if I have delivered a minor blow.

"How have you been getting on with your reading?" I ask.

"You know, that line in his final essay, about the private life dismantling itself, the new angels. It's so prescient. The glass house of Instagram, people giving their lives away for fleeting doses of approval and dopamine. It's like he foresaw the technological age."

"He did. He knew that when the public had become the realm of the private and vice versa, and both saturated in images, our inability to think straight in the hall of mirrors we have created for ourselves would be destroyed."

Elliott shakes his head. "The Weimar Republic. It was just phenomenal — what an exciting time. How could reality change so quickly? It's terrifying."

"We're living at the end of the Weimar Republic right now, the twenty-first century version."

"Aren't you frightened?" His eyes widen.

"Yes, absolutely. But fear can be an engine in the creative life."

He studies me for a moment. It is the same evaluative glance I see more and more in the eyes of my children. However much he might admire my films, perhaps for Elliott I appear as a mad uncle. An intemperate eccentric.

"So why Benjamin?" he asks. "Instead of a contemporary film? You know, the lost generation, young people's futures ruined through lack of access to Europe, oligarchs takeover Westminster, children going hungry in the sixth richest nation in the world?"

"I could do that, yes. Maybe one day I will."

I tell him the story of the genesis of Benjamin. How Joanna and I and the kids were staying with a friend, a film director,

Catalan, who specializes in elegant literary noir thrillers. They have a house twenty kilometres from Figueres, in northern Spain, in Dalí-land — a landscape of basalt and few trees, olives, leeks, good wine, etcetera.

"Well, one day we drove up to the French border on a whim and I visited the monument to Benjamin and poked around the town. It was a month after the Brexit vote and Joanna and I had gone together to the memorial but only one person can descend at a time. I felt I was going down into my own death. The structure is a kind of tunnel. When I walked out of it I doubled over, the sense of exile was so strong I could not gather breath in my lungs. I said to Joanna, 'Brexit will do this to us. It will make us refugees in our own land.'"

"What did she say?"

"She said, and I quote, 'Richard, you are being melodramatic.'" I said, no, it's déjà vu, I'd always known this was going to happen. British people are so arrogant and assured of their right to rule the world. Now we are going to find out what it means to be a pariah, and poor, courtesy of the Tory dictatorship that currently passes for a government. I said, 'This is what history does, if it is unresolved. It boomerangs back, and this time it knocks you out.'"

It is dark outside. We can no longer see the river. We look at our reflections in the giant screen of the windows, sitting side by side on a chocolate-coloured sofa, separated by a respectable distance. Elliott is a comma curled over his coffee, hare-wide eyes, squid ink hair, his bludgeonless beauty. There he is, my double, gargoyled in the window, in the darkened eye of history. A human piece of driftwood, as Joanna once said, when she could still muster fondness for me.

We smile at each other, pre-emptive, apologetic smiles. For a moment we are adrift. This is our first elective meeting, not tied to the premise of the film. We just agreed to meet for a drink, that's all. I haven't told Joanna. Elliott might feel the lack of purpose, how exposed it leaves us, and shifts violently in his seat. He is not made for stasis. What would it be like, to be so hungry for performance? I am in awe of actors, their lunge for the moment. I can only resurrect it, skirting it, adding water and flour to thicken the instant.

I shudder involuntarily. A flume of ice moves through me.

"Are you okay?"

"I don't know." I am rattled. I have never felt anything like it. The chill had started in my chest, in a space I wasn't even aware existed. Like a dark, neglected room. My heart had actually stalled, I think, at least for a second. "Maybe I'm coming down with the flu."

Elliott frowns. "Well, let's get you some lemon and ginger tea."

"No, no. Nothing a glass of Sauvignon Blanc won't cure."

This at least makes him laugh. Watching the supernova smile erupt on his face, I have a strange feeling of accomplishment. I have known Elliott for only a few days, but somehow the atmosphere between us has become dense, very quickly, like the outskirts of a storm. I think of that line of Benjamin's, in "Fate and Character": "Character is unfolded in them like a sun. Complication becomes simplicity, fate freedom." Elliott has a reversal in his being, deep down he can turn himself inside out and become something completely different. It is beyond being a chameleon, it is a more profound transformation. I think he might have the power as an actor to put ideas into circulation, not just to give a performance.

I say, "You're thinking."

"I'm thinking about you." Spots, leopard-shaped, appear on his neck.

"Now I've embarrassed you."

"No." The thin ropes of muscles in his throat tighten. "I learn things when I'm with you. It's odd. I feel like I've known you a long time."

Elliott is studying me. He will put store by how I respond.

"Me too," I say. "It's a good sign."

The press of people around us becomes tighter. We've been talking for three hours. The evening's classical concert is about to begin.

We walk over the Hungerford footbridge against the tide of people headed for the South Bank under an estuary sky. Riverboats, their lounges raked by disco lights, glide on the inky river, passing underneath us so close we could abseil down.

We part at Embankment Station. He puts his hands in his pockets, turns his face away and I think he is about to move toward the barriers. I have my goodbye forming in my mouth, but he turns toward me.

"My agent said I should take this job in LA. I'll have to be there next month."

"Next month? You mean February?"

He nods. Someone jostles me in their race for the barrier. "You have to do what you have to do," I say.

"It's very helpful, talking to you. It always is."

"I'm good at talking. It's the basic rule of filmmaking: ninety years of talking trying to convince people to give you money, ten seconds of actual filming."

He lurches away. I watch him disappear down the stairs, into the Northern Line.

Villiers Street is packed and a black cab putters along behind, scattering pedestrians like a sheepdog working his flock. The street is one of the few that hasn't changed. It still has that seedy, guttural ring of the original London, before it was lined with mirrors.

Beside me, a smoky aura congeals. He is back, with his disappointed moustache, his air of a solemn angel. He walks alongside me, gloveless hands in pockets, resolute. Dressed in black and white, he looks like a clarinet. "Why is everyone staring at illuminated notebooks?"

"Oh, those are smartphones. The internet."

"The internment? Are they all prisoners?"

"Yes, we are. We all now have these personal stupefying panopticons and tracking devices we carry round."

"No one is looking where they are going, yet they don't seem to crash into each other, like flocks of birds." He slides his hat down over his eyes. "After this I am not coming back. The next time I'll be talking to a robot, no doubt. It's all too Fritz Lang for me."

"Don't go away," I say.

"*Humph.*"

In the Covent Garden piazza, a screen has been installed above the Apple Store. It broadcasts a zebra pattern — black, white, black, white. Multi-ethnic models appear, brandishing the latest tracking device, a 1980s Benetton advert meets *Brave New World*. I swing round to see what my internal Benjamin makes of this, but he has departed.

I don't want to go home. An infinite restlessness takes hold. I want to walk the city until the sun comes up on the other side of night. But that would be thirteen hours from now. I know because of the World Clock website, which gives the time of sunrise and sunset, the length of day and night, the difference in minutes as the planet rotates, the astronomical, nautical and civil twilights. How reassuring, that we know on 29 March 2019 as Britain supposedly leaves the European Union the sun will rise at 5:43 a.m. and set at 6:28 p.m., that astronomical twilight will begin at 3:46 a.m., that solar noon will take place at 12:05 with the sun overhead at a 41.9 degree angle.

At home, this is what awaits: Joanna spinning between devices, flicking glances at the clock to see if it is late enough to call Murat in Los Angeles to discuss the apocalyptic teenage rapier fighter series they are cooking up together. Joanna with her terrifying competence. At some point I have been lapped by her, like a Formula One driver whose maintenance crew have discovered an inside edge in tires or aerodynamics and I can only watch Joanna/Lewis Hamilton pull away. My life is backlit by hers; she has assumed a CinemaScope depth of field. The three years that separate us are suddenly significant in a way they haven't been since our twenties. I will go over the half-century line first. What awaits on the other side? Maybe a disappearing act. Now that I have survived this long, I don't know what to do with my life. Perhaps after survival there really isn't much more to detain us here.

In forty minutes I am in the Georgian paradise of de Beauvoir Town, the soles of my feet stinging. A newsagent, a flash of a front page: "Nuclear war now closer than ever before, say experts." "Medical students urged to volunteer in worst-ever NHS winter crisis." In the off-licence I sweep past the white wine chiller cabinet in a brief frenzy of determination, but then turn back and pluck a guilty bottle of Vouvray from it. It's a Pinot Grigio catchment area; the owner stocks the French stuff exclusively for me.

The fist which has recently appeared in my chest opens its palm wide and clutches my lungs. A searing hinge, like a door on fire, swinging, runs through me. I drop the bag with the wine with a clunk on the pavement.

A child surrounded by a haze of skunk lopes up to me. "Hey man, are you okay?"

"Yes, fine, thanks," I stutter. If I breathe in his air for any longer I'll be stoned.

A strange fizzing takes hold of my heart, as if soda water has been poured through my veins. I stagger in the direction of Draft Manor, whose alert eyes oversee me. I am afraid, but fear always galvanizes me. I think, *I need to make a film that will be more than a resurrection.* It will be as if Benjamin never died, as if he lives in all of us, as if his death is all our deaths, but how to invoke the levity of his thought, of his life, even as all of us in this country have been abandoned to exile? Could we please go back to having a story with many possible endings and not a requiem? The nation state is a prison.

I heave myself up our front steps, my favourite line of Benjamin's booming in my head. It is a variation on Nietzsche: "If a man has character, he will have the same experiences over and over again."

V

We are having a typical breakfast: Joanna at the counter, fingering through an elaborate Excel spreadsheet for the next episode of her series *Winchester*, me at the table thinking about all the ways things can go wrong.

My WhatsApp pings.

"Who's that?" Joanna's tone is deliberately casual.

I hold the phone two feet away so I can see the screen — Trombone Arm, as Nathan calls it, an instrument played by middle-aged people who refuse to acknowledge the need for reading glasses.

"Elliott."

"Didn't you say his agent told him to cool it?"

"Joanna, nobody says *cool it* anymore."

Hurt, fleet as a stream of photons, streaks across her face.

Would you like to meet my mother and me for a drink next week sometime? She's doing a play at the Duke of York's. She won't drink preperformance, but we can have a coffee. Three coffee cup emojis, followed by a thumbs-up.

That would be great, I text back. No emojis.

"Don't answer immediately," Joanna barks. "He'll think you have nothing better to do."

"I don't." I rise.

"Where are you going?"

"To work on the script."

"Good. You'd better get it locked down, Richard, it's nearly February."

I shut the door against the cooling wind in my wake. What meteorologist could measure the atmospherics of a marriage? I say I am going to my study to write, but it's become more of a wound-licking station lately. I'm not sure when I cast my wife as head of production and myself as chief scriptwriter on this film called *Marriage Is Hell*, but we have assumed those roles nonetheless. Worse, I have excelled in playing Richard Cottar, talented but scatterbrained artiste, a person who slinks through life like a wounded hedgehog, in sharp contrast to my lion-spearing ancestors.

The scene I am working on and that has been troubling me lasts less than a minute — it is a vignette, properly speaking. Benjamin is in the Bibliothèque Nationale, sitting at a desk in a waistcoat and three jackets.

It is the winter of 1940. In less than six months the Nazis will overrun Paris. The winter is cold and the coal stove in his apartment inadequate. He has taken to working all day at the library, then continuing when he gets home, writing all night sometimes, swaddled underneath three blankets. He is writing against the clock, against history, that is obvious, even to him.

I close my eyes, and a face hovers in my mind like mountains burnished in the aftermath of sunset. Elliott's face materializes, serene, intelligent, vaguely interrogating, like a medieval angel. When, historically, did faces lose their immanence and become mere apparatuses for the conveying of expectations? His face — Elliott's, not Benjamin's — has begun to insert itself quietly, between my every thought. Or perhaps it is not his face, or even a face, but a repeating image, a pattern.

◢

Elliott and his mother await in a hotel bar in Covent Garden. I pause across the street, steadying myself. The hotel's windows and doors are swathed in heavy brown curtains to keep the draft at bay.

I take in the lime exterior and bordello windows. Two triangular braziers stand sentry by the door, their naked flames speak of castles, Elizabethan plotters carrying torches down dank alleyways. Sleek people exit and enter its door effortlessly, watched over by a man in a narrow top hat. Cabs pull up, cabs pull away, landing at its door with a flutter, a pack of corvids. There's an impatient, burnished smell — not of money or conviviality, but talent. London is possibility, that is why I stay here — the feeling that just by being in its precincts, anything can happen, and we are all eccentrics just one step away from our grand destinies.

Inside, I spot her immediately: a long-necked woman, her wide-sprung actress's face a lily in the dark. Elliott sits beside her in a dark brown chair, fingering but not eating bar snacks.

"Hello," I say, forcing my shoulders back from their usual vulture posture to stand to my full height.

His mother — I panic because I have forgotten her name, and want to look at my phone, where Elliott has written it in his text — stands. She is nearly as tall as me. She grasps my shoulders and kisses the air around my ears. "Richard Cottar. I've looked you up."

"I hope you didn't believe everything you read on the internet."

"Not at all. But I'm hoping you'll tell me the truth."

We assume our positions in a triangular arrangement with me in the apex chair. I look from Elliott back to his mother. I find him like a blueprint beneath the surface of her face. She has a wide, well-made forehead, commanding. Her blue-green eyes are set quite far apart. There is a saintly, static quality to her face; Elliott's on the other hand is fully plastic. He never looks quite the same twice.

"So, Elliott tells me you are very influenced by French directors."

"Yes." My look says, *Who isn't?*

"There are so many candidates."

"Ah, well. François Ozon, Nicole Garcia, Maurice Pialat, Olivier Assayas." A pause. "Truffaut, of course."

"And why is that?"

"Because they all see emotion as being at the core of life and are able to bring out its sublime quality without overromanticizing it."

His mother wears a white shirt and black jacket. At her throat is a silver necklace. From it a horseshoe pendant dangles — for luck, perhaps. "And where did you study?"

Manners — as is often the case — override the allure of asking, *Am I being interviewed for a job here?*

"Bristol for my first degree, then NFTS. Those were the days when you didn't have to start plotting your career in nursery school."

Elliott shifts in his chair. He might be wondering if this meeting was a good idea after all. The young never imagine that things can go wrong.

"I think you can understand my concern at Elliott playing this part. It is a load to place on such young shoulders."

"I agree. That's why we are still discussing it."

"So you haven't cast him?"

"I don't think I can talk about Elliott as if he's not in the room with us." This is a habit of parents, everywhere, I can't help but note — even when present their children are somehow remote, more ideas than beings.

Elliott agrees, it seems, because he says, "I am actually here, this is not a convincing hologram, although that's coming down the line."

His mother shoots me a suspicious glance, then another conspiratorial one in my direction. "I'm not sure when this generation became so declarative."

"I like it," I say.

"I don't think it's entirely honest," Thérèse — finally I remember her name — says. "That's the problem."

Elliott sits forward, elbows on knees. "Why am I not being honest?"

It is her turn to fidget and sigh. They have each other's gestures. "Because you've been brought up in a ruthless system of emotional capitalism in which you feel you have to perform yourself constantly in order not to fall behind in a sham meritocracy. But let's not have an argument here."

Abruptly, she stands. "I must go, I've got an hour before I have to be onstage."

Elliott and I also rise, knocking the table with our knees so that his mother's half-drunk coffee spills over the edge. "I'll see you later on," she says to Elliott. Her tone is blithe, contingent. She winks at him.

As she is about to pivot away I see her back tense. She turns toward us, her Greek amphorae profile, the anguished forehead that must serve her so well onstage. "I do hope we will see each other again."

"I hope so too."

We sit down. Elliott takes his mother's vacated chair, sinking into it with a sigh. "She liked you, I think."

"I'd hate to see how it goes when she doesn't like people."

I feel slightly dizzy. I realize I haven't eaten since lunch. That happens when I am writing — I lose all sense of the here and now.

We transfer to the restaurant, where we eat gravlax and rye bread. I order a bottle of champagne, which is out of character. The drink makes me expansive. I tell Elliott stories I haven't told anyone in years, and which I may never have told Joanna, about the puff adders in our garden in Nairobi who killed an entire litter of newborn Dalmatians, the only time I ever saw my father cry, and our dog Simu (translation: telephone), their mother, who was not bitten but died of grief. I tell him about the sunset over the four knuckles of the Ngong Hills and the fluting trill of the Abyssinian nightjar, how I was so homesick the first year I moved to Italy I really did think I would die.

As we talk our fellow barflies scan us, their eyes sliding and snagging on Elliott — whose face could be male or female, at certain angles, and which has that youthful solidity of spirit still, sitting not more than three inches away in his distressed jeans and snow-white trainers — then darting to my face. *Older man with his rented love.* They sense an unfamiliar current of intimacy between us, unsalacious, almost abstract.

Elliott looks at his watch. He sees me seeing him do this, sees me straighten my back.

"Do you have to go?"

"No, no."

"What is it then?"

"I just —" He closes his eyes for a long time, opens them. "I feel guilty. I blew someone off. Someone I was supposed to meet." He purses his lips.

"You mean, now? Tonight?"

"Yes."

I put down my fork with a clatter. "You should have told me. We could have met another night."

"No, it's not that — serious." He leans on the word.

"You could argue nothing is that serious at twenty-three."

He accepts my rebuke with a flinch. Now it is my turn to feel a shot of guilt, bitter as vodka. "I'm sorry. It sounds as if I'm not taking your experience seriously. I don't really think that."

For the first time since I have met him, he gives me an openly wounded look. "Why did you say it then?"

"I don't know, I was shocked, I suppose." I don't say: it's payback, for arranging to spend time with someone other than me.

The noise is too loud — ordinary clatter, a door opening and closing, laughter of bankers, who form an interim monoculture while we wait for the theatre people, the punters and the thesps, to come back after their shows finish.

I feel a palpitation of some kind near my heart, and wince.

"What's the matter?"

"Just a twinge." But my mouth is dry. I gulp my water. "This person whom you blew off, is it a man?"

He sighs, quick as a spasm. "Yes. Someone I'm not sure about."

"Then it's fine not to leap into anything."

"I want to be in command of myself. I don't want to be dismembered. By love," he adds — as if that needed clarifying.

"It's very hard to avoid that completely. I'm not even sure it's a good idea to try."

He sits on his hands. "I don't want to go home."

"Where do you want to go?"

"Can I stay with you?"

I let out a long breath. "You can sleep on our sofa, although you'll have to fight Mabati for the privilege. Unless you mean me personally."

"I do mean you. Personally."

I had expected him to deny or evade it. For a second my stomach rattles and the now familiar fist re-grips my heart. I think I might throw up. This isn't what I was expecting. But yet it is.

◢

"For God's sake, Richard, what's the matter?"

"I can't sleep. I'm going downstairs to put on some coffee."

Joanna flips over in the bed and thrashes like a fish. "It's 3 a.m. You only got in at midnight."

"I might as well write if I can't sleep."

She has heard my sharp intake of breath. She springs bolt upright, like a vampire.

"Don't worry. It's just a muscle twinge."

"Where?"

"My shoulder," I lie.

"Left or right?"

Joanna's sister is a doctor. Joanna herself did two years of medical training before switching to a degree in literature and film.

"Left."

"You've got to go to the GP. Tomorrow — I mean today."

"It's nothing."

"If it's in your left hemisphere, it's not nothing. Please, Richard, you're almost fifty. You can't be cavalier with your health." Her voice is unusually beseeching.

"Alright, I'll go. Although I won't be able to get an appointment for two weeks. That's if I'm lucky. The government has a new strategy, haven't you heard? They've started killing people to make it easier to sell the NHS to American insurance companies. They're banking on the plebs dropping dead first."

She actually laughs, like the old Joanna, before she became moneyed and powerful. "Are you sure you're not coming back to bed?"

"I'm too restless. I'm going to re-draft some scenes."

"I think you should have herbal tea instead of coffee. Just in case."

"Okay." We both know I'm heading for the Nespresso machine.

I descend the stairs. I like the house at this hour. It is freezing, and somehow becomes what it must once have been, a gaslit Victorian mausoleum with maroon wallpaper, home to unknown families who have left no trace but whose existence I perceive. In the middle of the night I sense it most, that the house is actually owned by others, and I must ask their permission as I move along the corridors that link the cold, slumbering rooms.

I put on the electric heater and make a hot water bottle. The script is already open on my laptop. The title page stares at me: BENJAMIN. "What do you want?" I ask it, out loud. *Show some moral courage*, it responds. *Screenplays don't write themselves*. I am not worried I am speaking to a Final Draft document, and I lied to Joanna, I don't feel restless, it is much worse than that. I feel shaken inside-out, a pocket relieved of its burden of change. The fluttering in my left shoulder has moved to my stomach. I feel elated but also close to tears.

Elliott and I finished the champagne and gravlax and found ourselves outside the bar, shoved onto the narrow pavement amid the late-night Covent Garden crowds. Taxis on their way up Seven Dials brushed against us like furtive ravens. A woman being strangled by a purple feather boa tottered down the middle of the street in yellow three-inch heels.

Elliott shoved his hands into his pockets. "Thank you, Richard, it's been good to talk."

"If you were any more grave you'd be a tombstone."

His face went suddenly pale. The colour really did drain out of it. For a second he looked like a child.

I said, "You know, age difference gets to a point where there would be something almost obscene — I'm sorry to use that word. I know it happens all the time between older rich guys and younger women, but it can never be right."

"You mean it's age and not orientation? It's not because I'm . . . another man."

"I don't know. I haven't had a chance to think about it. I'm not even sure I think of you as *another man*. You don't realize how young you are, and that's a blessing."

I stopped to check his expression. The intent note which was always present in his face was more persistent. It occurred to me this might be his rendition of fear. I was not used to feeling such sudden and unflinching empathy for people I hardly knew.

"Look, Elliott, just to be clear: I'm directing you or about to direct you. Your mother gave me a look as if she already suspects me of unhealthy intentions, although hopefully only professional ones. I can't live with suspicion or lies or any kind of emotional dishonesty at all. I'm just not built for it."

He frowned. "So you're not a hundred percent straight."

"In my lived experience I am, so I think that makes me straight. Maybe I've just never been asked by the right person. Although if you need someone to ask, you could argue that's the answer to your question."

I thought, *I'm taking stabs in the dark here, emotionally. It's dangerous, when you can't see where you're going and you're just . . . trying to grasp something.*

"Where is your father?" I asked.

"He's dead. He died when I was fifteen."

"I'm sorry."

His gaze was clear, untroubled. I thought, *He believes he has fully absorbed his father's death, but it will come back to haunt him, it is haunting him now. Perhaps he is trying to dispel his ghost through me.*

He kicked one spartan white trainer against the other. "You probably think that's why. I want a father figure."

"Directors are always in loco parentis. Even if we're terrible at parenting in real life." I tried to smile a wince away. But Elliott, ever-observant, caught the change in my expression.

The carousel of people around us began to circle faster, young women in three- and foursomes in praying mantis shoes on their way to a Leicester Square megaclub; a man in a Burberry trench coat and a trilby hat, an apparition from a Graham Greene novel; burnished young men in pipe-cleaner trousers and narrow shoes; winter-weary people detecting the ever-lengthening days, sunrise at 7:43 now —

"Richard?"

"I'm fine." My head was spinning. *You're probably just drunk,* unsympathetic inner-Richard tells me-Richard.

"You're still casting me?"

"Yes."

Elliott hoisted himself to his full height. We shook hands, such an earnest, affable gesture that we both burst out laughing. Then we went our separate ways.

VI

"The darkest January in northern Europe since records began." The *Guardian* reports that in northern France they have had only three hours of sunshine all month. The days do not seem to be lengthening as they ordinarily do. This year darkness seems to hover.

In two weeks I will go to Kenya to sign some documents for my father's estate and see my cousin who dealt with the practicalities of his death. This promise of ten days of tropical sun keeps me going through the murk.

On the last Friday in January I find myself on the Overground from Hackney Central to Imperial Wharf. The dinner will be on a houseboat in Chelsea belonging to Ivan Holborn, one of Joanna's equity investors, a hedge fund man with interests in the 'stans — Kazakhstan, Kyrgyzstan, Uzbekistan and the other one whose name I always forget. His money is a key piece of the puzzle in our financing. Without it, there is no film, so Joanna has stitched us — Elliott and me — up. To quote her: "Since you and Elliott have become such good friends, you might as well be finance ambassadors."

"*Finance ambassadors.* Why are you talking that wealth-management claptrap? Are you worried he'll pull out?"

She doesn't answer immediately, which means yes. "I just think it would be politic."

"Where exactly does Ivan's money actually come from?"

"Where does any money come from? The stock market. Christ, Richard, do you want to make this film or not?"

"So much I'll take money made by the draining of the Aral Sea, the extinction of snow leopards, mercury poisoned fish and wholesale larceny, I guess."

The Overground is lined with exhausted Goths on their way to West London parties. I glide sideways in the orange-and-blue cylinder through the stations where I have never lived: West Hampstead, Brondesbury, Kensal Rise. Willesden Junction's warehouse roofs shine platinum in the night. On the train I debate what I will tell Elliott about Ivan. He will guess his essential dodginess. Perhaps it is best I am upfront.

He is waiting for me at the exit of the station.

"Hey," he says, American-style. Maybe he is practising for his upcoming stint there.

"Ready to convince the money men?" I had nearly said *seduce*, but decided against it.

"As I'll ever be."

We both pause for a moment, aware we are relying on heartiness to get us through this first moment, the moment after which we have made a mutual decision to put our last conversation behind us. I had expected him to apologize and had my generous, tolerant defence at the ready: *No, Elliott, it's my fault. I was a bit abrupt, I'm sorry. I've been working on this draft at all hours, I get up at 5 a.m. every day and I'm kind of losing the plot.* But no apology comes, and I struggle not to feel deflated and erroneous.

We walk without talking through bullying streets of gated new-build communities empty of pedestrians until we reach Lot's Road. I am seized again by the sensation in my chest. It feels like a mini jackhammer, strutting at my aorta. I stop.

"What's the matter?"

"Just muscle twitch I've been having."

"Have you seen a doctor?"

"No, I haven't made an appointment because they'll book me in for May 2020. That or they'll just put me on the new crematorium conveyor belt the Tories have built. Resource-waster that I am."

This triggers a smile, a return to his almost invisible calmness. "You know you should just pay and go private. Jump the queue."

"I can't, I believe in the NHS."

"I know you do, but you have to think of yourself."

"Now you sound like Joanna."

Suddenly, I can't muster the energy to propel myself forward into the dimension that awaits: the houseboat, rich people, the whole diorama of coercion. This happens sometimes. I become aware of the blunt force trauma of the future, the sequence of one moment after another which must be withstood. Perhaps because I am not manufacturing them, moments, actual, real, lived time, come to feel like an enemy occupying force and I just don't have the energy to resist their troops anymore.

Elliott carries on for a pace or two. Then he turns, framed by two of the four white cylinders of what used to be the Battersea Power Station and their crown of red lights. He is thin, I see again, too thin for a leading man, and tall, although not as tall as me. He still has the gangling, protean quality of children, and a sloping, salamander curve to his eyes.

I breathe in, then out, deep scooping breaths.

"I just have to gather myself," I say.

Elliott's face is a mask of concern. I don't want him to see me like this. He is depending upon me to do the heavy lifting at dinner, but he is not yet experienced enough in this world to know how exposed I am by the raw power of money.

We arrive at the boatyard. Broad-bellied riverboats list onto the mudflats at low tide, joined by an umbilical cord of mini-gangplanks.

"Okay," I say with false courage. "Let's do this."

We are there quickly, and just as quickly are inside, where three dark-haired women shake my hand. As I hand my coat to a young woman in black (the caterer, perhaps) Ivan gives me a quick rundown: Matilda is in finance, Lucy is an independent producer with a couple of credits to her name, Lucia is a Spanish actress who has been in everything — TV, film, documentary. I should know her, but I can't place her face. The women all give Elliott the same look: neutrally avid.

A thin man with the unmistakable mien of the moneyed loiters by the glassy bow of the boat, his back turned to us. "Tony," Ivan calls. "Come and meet Richard."

Tony turns: a black shirt, grey trousers of some matte

metallic fabric. Blond hair, close-cropped. He is muscular but slim, like an expensive candlestick.

Tony does not do introductions it seems. He paces toward me, handshake-less. "So this film, it's an autobiography?"

"More a biography, but not in a straightforward format."

"Why this man? I've never heard of him. Why now?"

I launch into my pitch. "Benjamin was made stateless by the Nazis, along with thousands of others at the time," I say. "He was a refugee. We're living through the worst refugee crisis since the Second World War, and it is fraying the fabric of civil society and presenting serious challenges to our democracies."

Tony's eye slides in the direction of Elliott. "And that's your lead?" He seems to be about to say something else, some qualm I have already thought of, but desists. A suspicion about him attaches itself to me, a burr, a pincering small insect.

Ivan calls us to the dinner table. Elliott is enfolded into the triangle of women. He casts them earnest, steadfast looks. The houseboat lists slightly to the left, so we sit on a downslope. Outside are onyx mudflats and, beyond them, a gleaming gallery of luxury apartments on the south bank of the river.

With Elliott safe in conversation with the women, I am left with Tony and Ivan, who are daguerreotypes of each other: Tony in a silver shirt whose discreet shine signals its expense, and black trousers, Ivan in reverse costume, silver trousers and a black shirt.

"I hear you're known for your intimate directorial style." Tony's voice is cool, a plank of pine.

"All arthouse directors have intimate relationships with their actors." I try to sound casual, but I am also telling him to back off. "We have the same vision for the film, that is how I work."

Dinner is served, starlet fare — seared tuna, a salad, no carbs — but hunger deserts me. The scene begins to take on the feeling of a half-forgotten dream. I feel an abstract anguish, a pulpy feeling I have to quash immediately or I will throw up. What is the matter with me? In the window's reflection Tony and I dangle long-stemmed wine glasses that look like chalices. Elliott is visible only in profile, talking to Ivan. The three dark-haired women look like bottles of imported spirits: amaretto, Courvoisier. As for me, I do not compare well with Ivan and Tony, who are as sleek and thinly muscled as cheetahs.

I send a glance in Elliott's direction. He sends me a hearty look back with just a grain of concern within it. The complicity between us is instant and not at all conniving.

The boat's list has softened; the Thames must be rising. I no longer have to hold on to my wine glass to stop it sliding down the table. Elliott touches his left elbow with his right hand, he shifts in his seat, his hair falls over his forehead and his features seem to elongate, as if he is melting.

An air of history has accumulated. This is not an ordinary dinner party; something will be decided here, on this barge theatre in the Thames. I hope it is that Ivan will not withdraw his funding, and we close financing. I am eager to inhabit the hellish nirvana of shooting again. My whole being is oriented toward this coming summer, sipping espressos while the crew sets up a track. Together we will coax moments from the cool tomb of oblivion.

The dinner concluded, the women and Elliott sit on one side of the houseboat, a tight cabal on nautical sofas. I am on the other, flanked by Ivan and Tony who, I very belatedly realize, are a couple. They do not touch each other, they don't exchange colluding glances. My realization is slow-witted, based on the lanky electricity that passes over men, sitting between them, and carries on going.

Ivan is composed, even coiled. He is a man who has never had a serious doubt in his life, I think, a Jay Gatsby — the phrase of Fitzgerald's leaps to mind, "the colossal vitality of his illusion." Tony is more circumspect. I wonder why they are interested in this film, apart from Joanna's persuasions. But then producers are almost always mysterious — benevolent oligarchs who float into your life on the wings of fate before destroying your film.

"I have a good feeling about this film," Ivan says, administering the poison.

"That's good," I warble.

"It's a fantastic script, Richard, how you weave between the past and the present, the way it becomes so apparent that ideals are the first casualties in any fascist takeover."

"It will be an important film," Ivan joins in. "We'd like to see it up for a BAFTA."

"So would I."

From across the room Elliott sees me pincered between the daguerrotypes. He shoots me a look of profound sympathy. I can only purse my lips in return. *Let's get out of here*, I mentally telegraph him, but Ivan is holding a bottle of sambuca, I see with some dismay.

Later — I'm not sure how much later — the evening comes to a close at last when the three women levitate as one and announce they must hail a cab. Elliott and I bounce to our feet. "We should also be going," I offer.

We burst out of the houseboat and clatter down the gang-planks to the street. We stand, waiting for a taxi, hands in our pockets, the river glittering behind.

"That went well, I thought," Elliott says, a game note in his voice, although his face is tired.

"Thanks. I hate singing for my supper, but it has to be done, from time to time."

We take a cab to Embankment. On the journey we do not speak, the first time we have fallen into silence in each other's company. Elliott looks out his window and I mine. I have the riverside view. London becomes a litany of landmarks we must tick off in order to get home: Houses of Parliament, check, Tate Britain, check. We don't know when we will see each other again. Now that he will be signed to the film within days, there is no other pretext for us to meet. I am gripped by that odd sadness, of losing something you never possessed in the first place.

I remind myself I have only ever loved women. No man has ever captured my attention on that instinctive, gut-clenching level. There have been abstract infatuations, like Benjamin. If I had met him in the flesh, would I desire him? Hardly, but that is the general problem in my existence: I have not been able to translate the euphoria I feel while making a film to my emotional life. I simply have not mustered the density of desire required, or is it because I just haven't met the right person? In truth I have always thought of desire as a bitter elixir.

I am too aware, that is the problem. When you can't fool the self there is no one left to fool, but no intrigue, either. The life assembled from blind spots, that was Walter Benjamin's. Mine have been pummelled out of me by the age of psychiatry. This oblivion seems to be unavailable to Elliott's generation for a different reason. They are adrift in a different sea, so overly aware of themselves yet trapped inside a rigged system that is not fascistic by name but which smoothly cancels their futures under the cover of democracy. I fear for them.

At Embankment we go our separate ways almost without speaking, scattering into the spaghetti tunnels of the Tube lines that converge there: Bakerloo, Northern, District and Circle, separate veins into the thousand dispersed thudding hearts of the city.

◩

Some years are definitive. A life is like a short story that way — for years, even decades, we rumble on, married to the same person, living in the same house, buying the same brand of Greek yogurt while the children grow steady like seedlings, doing the same job.

And then, without warning, the story pivots, the moment coalesces. All is revealed and nothing will be the same again. The realm you thought was stable is revealed as itinerant, capricious. I already know these two years — from the Brexit referendum in 2016 until . . . when? 2018, now, maybe, but who knows, the nightmare could go on forever — will be that short story, with the special twist in its scorpion tail. My favoured title for it: "The Rug Pulled Out from under Our Feet."

For Benjamin, the events of 1923 and 1924 would change his life, although this is not apparent in the first week of January 1923. Germany is in profound economic crisis, provoked by the occupation of the Ruhr by French and Belgian forces, precipitated by Germany's default on its repatriation payments from the First World War. A general strike is called.

He travels to Heidelberg, Freiburg, Munich, Frankfurt. Benjamin craves the shelter of porticoes, dust mites, of eleven narrow libraries. He joins his family at a sanitorium in Breitenstein. There, he shares one room with his wife, Dora, and his four-year-old son, Stefan.

Snow blankets the region. The hush it casts over the gargoyles and lace curtains of the building is like being in a tomb.

He cannot get his PhD accepted, he cannot get a job. Both academia and journalism are closed to him. A close friend, Wolf Heinle, languishes on the threshold of death, his lungs perforated with tuberculosis. Heinle's death, on February 1, Benjamin will feel as keenly as if it were his own — more so, as he has to go on being witness to it. Life is a vise, a surly handcuff. He has realized this too late to be able to mount any defence.

That is the only good thing about dying, Benjamin thinks: you never have to read the epilogue. He disapproves of epilogues, their cloying proto-Freudian afterwardsness, their winking tone of "I told you so."

The winters are lessons Benjamin fails to learn. He endures them, waiting for spring and the possibility of travel. He is the only member of his family afflicted by wanderlust; his mother is content to live in the foursquare streets of Charlottenburg forever.

In the spring of 1924 he will leave Germany with two days' notice, due to a new decree by the bankrupt government that German citizens can only travel abroad if they deposit a substantial bond for their return, and travels to Italy, leaving Dora and Stefan in Berlin — I am not sure why other than he loves to travel alone. He will go to Pompeii, Salerno, Ravello, Pozzuoli on the Amalfi Coast. He will spend five and a half months on the island of Capri.

There he lives among a clique of people who either are or will be famous, a group he characterizes as an "itinerant intellectual proletariat." Bertolt and Marianne Brecht are there, in a category of their own, drawn by the island's vertical glamour, its bohemian life under the white bone of the Mediterranean sun. It is the days when the intelligentsia all know each other, they rotate in and out of the same houses, bars, beds, a Jazz Age *La Ronde*. They collide in the German café and pub, the hideously named Tomcat Hiddigeigei, and in the evenings discover their zeal for passeggiata, even in the heat. They will remain on the island into August, when malaria comes to the coast.

But for now, it is winter and he is jobless and directionless. He takes Stefan outside to play in the snow and watches him run ramrod into a bench, coming to rest clumped and crying in his blue serge coat. He comforts his son, collecting him in his arms and wiping away his fat, hot tears with a single gloved finger. The abyss is everywhere: inside, outside. It seems scripted in the curlicues of winter cloud in the sky he sees reflected in Stefan's eyes.

Out of despair, he begins to write short prose pieces that look at the human effects of the larger economic crisis: "Breakfast Room," "Gloves," "Germans, Drink German Beer!," "No Vagrants"; "To the Planetarium!" These combine microportraits of everyday life with meditations on social conditions. He looks inward and outward at once, discovering his internal rear-view mirror. His eye is enlivened by despair. He perceives the kaleidoscopic, fragmented nature of reality. His depression perhaps restricts him from writing long prose, and these sharp blasts from the now have an appealing, found-object quality. They are eventually collected in *One-Way Street.*

In the scene, Elliott will perform the moment — unrecorded, maybe unrecordable — when Benjamin's attention is snagged outside his own internal drama. On a walk from the sanitorium into the town that he undertakes to amuse Stefan, they proceed slowly, his son's red-mittened hand gripping his own, stumbling every so often on a tuft of buried frozen grass. Stefan's tarrying allows Benjamin's eye to land on things he would otherwise have skated over, such as the *Post No Bills* sign on the side of the town hall. Benjamin performs one of his feats of lateral thinking and will turn this admonishment into a manual for writing, he decides, composing it in his head just as he perceives the cold finally sinking into his toes through his tired, nailed-sole winter boots. Number four will be "Avoid haphazard writing materials." Good advice indeed.

Stefan squeezes his hand. "Papa, I'm cold."

"Yes, I know. Let's head back."

The snow has begun to fall with renewed intensity. Elliott and little Sam, who will be playing Stefan (and who is the son of one of the parents at Nathan's school), turn back. The final seconds of the scene are shot wide, the camera watching as their figures are dissolved into the white winter.

VII

The only useful thing about early February is that it is light at five o'clock. Good old planet, I tell Joanna, still doggedly spinning on its axis.

We sit in the kitchen, oppressed by its hungry red walls. Who was it who told me that red makes you hungry? No wonder every time I go to the Rothko Room at the Tate Modern I always leave starving.

"You were late coming in last night," Joanna says, in that odd tone again. Her words sound like cold caramel, like a substance she had to soften in order to make swallowable. "How did it go with Ivan and Tony?"

"Well, I think. They were captivated by Elliott."

"Good." She gives me another of her narrow looks.

Being in a long marriage is like taking a polygraph test 24/7. It is not impossible to lie (you can try) but small parasympathetic nervous system ticks will trip you up. Although Joanna knows I am too much of a workaholic and too obsessed with film to do anything so ordinary as cheat on her.

I rise. "I have to pack." In two days' time I will go to Kenya. While I am away Elliott will fly to LA. I won't see him for three weeks.

"Richard, forget about packing. When is your appointment with the doctor?"

"Ah, no."

Joanna rolls her eyes. "Don't tell me."

"I'm sorry, Joanna, I just forgot."

This is not entirely true. The practice now hounds you with so many text message reminders forgetting a doctor's appointment is now a fond 1970s memory, like telephones with dials. I had rung them to say I was busy and would reschedule, but now it will have to wait until I return.

Joanna looks at me, really looks at me, for the first time in months. Her eyes are grey and slope down at their corners, very slightly, which gives her an atmosphere of éminence grise. She is still thin and girlish with her twenty-inch waist and her black jeans that end in a pair of chunky trainers. She does not look like my wife, but an actor's consort, a fashion stylist, one of those LA women you see on Instagram wearing Ray-Bans and gripping a Starbucks skinny latte.

"I've got a meeting this afternoon with Federico at Canal+," she says. "He's worried about Brexit."

Her change of tone signals an admission. She was not going to tell me this.

"Why would he be worried about Brexit? It's only going to spell the end of our lives as we know it."

"*Not* funny. He could pull the plug. If the Tory psychopaths manage to push us off the cliff edge he's not sure the European Convention will cover the reinsurance for the shoot in Spain and Italy."

"Is that really possible?"

"It's a grey area, technically it's both of us, but no country has ever been so idiotic to leave the European Union before, so we are all in terra incognita."

This is true. I have only ever shot films in a country which was the member of a twenty-eight-country-strong trading block, frictionless borders, frictionless VAT refunds, co-financing agreements. Now we will be snarled in acres of red tape. Not for the first time I wonder if that's the psychopaths' political strategy, to tie us all up in bureaucratic knots so we don't have time to take to the streets or even vote as they hit the delete button on the country's future.

"Yes, but there's still time to sort it."

"No, there isn't. We need the script locked down. This trip of yours is very ill-timed."

She's right. If I don't finish the final draft in the next two weeks we can't go into preproduction and we might not be able to film in the summer. The talent might not be available, and the whole thing could fall apart. The determining forces of my life are becoming more demanding. A thickening is taking place. I'm not in control of it. For the first time in many years I detect the slinky premise of fate.

"I can't not do it, Joanna. It's my family.'

"So." She turns her flinty negotiator's gaze on me. "What will I tell Federico?"

"That the script is nearly done. Tell him whatever you think will work."

"Are you still prepared to defer?"

We have both agreed to waive our fees, mine as director and hers as one of the executive producers, to stay in budget. "I told you, I'll do what it takes. We both will."

She sits down. "I'm frightened by what's happening, Richard. Our lives are being unlaced." She bites her lip, something I haven't seen her do in years. "What will we do about the children? Nathan's going to be doing his A levels just as the lorries are parked up to Croydon and people are stockpiling baked beans. Nathan and Lucy won't be able to do their junior year abroad. We'll all be trapped on this shithole of an island for the rest of our lives."

A tightness grips my stomach. If Joanna is worried, we all needed to be worried. She is the original Iron Lady. I realize I have come to think of my wife as Theresa May — joylessly competent, but less catastrophic than the other options.

A photograph affixes itself to my consciousness. This is happening more and more often: visions are becoming consecrated, too soon, in the now: Joanna, her once luxurious caramel hair. Eyes quick, intelligent. She is a greyhound, slim-ankled, alert, a runner in all senses. Joanna will go on and on, round the track of our lives. She is beautiful and relentless.

But like me, she is changing. Her edges are dissolving slightly. This is the true nature of ageing: a kind of erosion, we become less emotionally scattershot and more in control of ourselves, but we are no longer juicy.

"What are you doing tonight?"

"Writing. Tomorrow I'm meeting with Elliott."

"You were just out with him at Ivan's."

"I know where I was last night. I'm going to Kenya, Elliott's going to LA, poor him, so we won't see each other for a while. I want to project a few ideas into his head before he's overtaken by shooting whatever mumblecore dirge he's been cast in."

"You're spending a lot of time with him." Her voice is precise, delicate.

"We get on. Thank God."

"Does he have a crush on you?"

I jump out of my chair, so abruptly Mabati scatters in fright. "I don't know, Joanna. He probably wouldn't tell me if he had."

"Do you have a crush on him?"

"I think he's a phenomenal actor."

"That doesn't answer my question."

"I've never had a crush on another man in my life."

"That still doesn't answer my question. I'm asking about Elliott, not *another man*."

I shake my head and close my eyes. On my eyelid is an image of venetian blinds, then, slowly emerging from them, Elliott's face. "It's not about that."

She stands, suddenly satisfied. Or maybe because her phone is ringing. I hadn't heard it. She takes the call and I flee the house with Mabati. The night holds open its arms. We pitch headfirst into its clamour: barking, police sirens, the ordinary thunder of traffic on Amhurst Road, my heart, that inner metronome, dogged and convinced. The dog and I breathe in unison, anointed by the night's dark rapture.

◢

"This place is wild."

I follow his gaze as it rakes the room. Couples of varying degrees of ambiguity are stationed on the tables around us; there is not one male-plus-female pair staring into each other's eyes. At the table next, a thin, dandyish man with round spectacles is accompanied by a short, cloud-faced young woman — his daughter? Next to them two identikit women with rigid fringes wrap talon-like nails around martini glasses — sisters? In the corner, a duo of elderly men in country jackets of matching bile-coloured tweed eat in monastic silence, a West London Gilbert and George. Everyone looks garish but vulnerable, as if their garb is only a decoy for a bitter wound. There is a higher concentration of such eccentrics in London than most places, for reasons yet unknown.

He leans forward. "I'm going to tell you a secret."

"Oh yes?"

"I'm glad to be going to the States. I want to be a long way away from England. It's the first time I've ever thought that. I think it might give me some perspective on what's happening here, politically."

"I don't know, Elliott. The States and Britain are going through the same transformation at the moment, that's the way I see it."

"What do you think is going to happen?"

"I wish I knew, but I don't think liberal democracy is coming back in the form that we've known it. They say history doesn't repeat itself but as far as I can tell it's lined up to be a copy of the early 1930s — the exact same scenario Benjamin faced, in fact. A vain and divided left, an organized right wing riding high on the misplaced grievances of the working and lower-middle classes. All that's missing is the ideology."

"They didn't have Cambridge Analytica contend with in the thirties."

"No, but they had Nazi-supporting newspaper barons — Germany was full of Steve Bannons and Tucker Carlsons. They all knew how much they stood to gain from the displacement of war and the erasure of Jewry. Now all we need is for mass unemployment to come along and we have the complete run-up to fascism picture."

Elliott absorbed this, expressionless. "I don't want to be powerless for my entire life, a piece to be moved around on a chessboard."

"A hard fate to avoid, as it turns out."

"Are you happy you're going to Kenya?"

"Yes, but for me it always means I go backward in time."

"I wish I had somewhere to go back to."

"Weren't you brought up in Paris?" I ask.

"Yes," he looks surprised, as if he himself had forgotten. "Until I was eleven and we moved here for my father's job."

"What did he do?"

"He was" — a small intake of breath — "a development consultant. That's how he died, in Angola."

"You didn't say he died in Africa."

"Is that significant? I suppose it is, you're African after all." His voice was suddenly blithe, his face shuttered. He'd changed an internal channel. "He was advising the government on diversifying the economy. He specialized in technology. The car he was being driven in was shot by robbers. Mistaken identity. The robbers were after an oil executive who took the same route every day and whose licence plate was only one letter off the one my father was being driven in. It happened in Luanda, in the middle of the day. The driver was also killed."

He tells the story in a detached mode, as if on automatic. He has told it many times before, perhaps: to therapists, school counsellors.

His hand lies midway between us on the table. I have to resist the urge to take it. "I'm so sorry."

His eyes have thickened. When they finally agree to meet my gaze again they are two woollen blankets. "My mother thinks I still haven't recovered from the shock. But it was eight years ago. And now — now somehow with this political mess, it's all coming back to me. I feel just like I did in the months after he was killed. Like I'm being split in two."

He leans forward and grips my forearm, hard. "I don't want to be separate from Europe. Now that I have to choose, I realize I am European, really. At least it's clarified that." He releases me. "The first time I voted in my life, and it went against me. I haven't voted since."

"We are being fooled and exploited. But you still have to exercise your democratic right."

"I'm afraid that's what's in store for me — manipulation and lies. For my entire generation."

"I wish I could tell you something reassuring."

Elliott's gaze snags on the framed prints on the walls of the restaurant. They are from Holbein's *Danse Macabre*. In them, a skeleton or skeletons accost a series of important people — a knight, an abbot and abbess, even the king — in their daily activities to drag them unceremoniously to their deaths.

"It's the original decadent bohemian bistro," I say. "It's been here for decades."

I look at the prints, then back to Elliott's face. Framed against the verdigris walls with his blacker-than-night hair and drastic features, he has the fastening reality of the Holbeins. Faced with the greater power of his beauty, the prints shrink into caricature.

"Richard." My name, in Elliott's voice, sounds different, a bell rung lightly. "What are you thinking about?"

"I'm thinking you'll be back soon," I say, whether to reassure him or myself I don't know. "Turnover is late May, it's confirmed. We'll wrap by August." I recite our timeline like a magic formula: by talking about it I will make it happen.

Our starters arrive. The food tastes like dust in my mouth. We talk, animated, we claw at either edge of our table, our faces bathed in the low magma of candlelight.

This is not the first sign I have that evening that a strange force inside me is active, that I am being guided from one plane of existence to another. I don't trust the way my eyes have become attuned, almost anxious, for Elliott, how his eyebrows have become hieroglyphs. His fingers play with the cascade of wax on our candlestick bottle. His expression is studious, as if he has set himself a test.

"How did you and Joanna meet?"

"In the cafeteria in film school. You know that story about the couple who met on Tinder and who weren't looking for anything serious but who ended up married? That's us, analogue version."

"And how long have you been married?"

"Twenty-one years this year. But we were together for three years before that."

"Why did you wait?"

"Marriage wasn't fashionable in the nineties. When we did marry it was for tax reasons mostly, and the children."

Elliott withdraws his arms and elbows, folding them back into his lean frame. I have the impression something has just occurred to him, but he will not share his thought with me. "So you didn't believe in marriage, as an institution?"

"No, not for a second. But it believed in us, it seems. And here we are, more than twenty years later, against the odds."

His eyes darken. "What odds would those be?"

I resist the urge to say, You'll find out. It would sound like sour grapes. And he might not, after all, ever marry.

After dinner we walk along the Embankment. On the corner I do something I haven't done in twenty years; I go into an off-licence and buy a packet of ten cigarettes.

"I didn't know you smoked."

"I don't. Want one?"

"Yeah, sure, why not?"

I light his cigarette for him — I've also had to buy a pack of matches. We walk along the river, trailing smoke. "I hardly ever see the Thames and here we are again." I say. We both shiver a little. "It's too cold to stay here," I say. "We need to get a cab."

"Let's go home. My mother's away. It's not far."

"Kentish Town is far."

"Let's just go." His hand tugs at my sleeve.

"Joanna will think I've been mugged."

"Text her that we're going for a drink after dinner."

I shake my head. Elliott sees it, I think, but doesn't understand the nature of my shame. "Then don't text her," he says.

In the taxi we speak little, only to comment on what we see out the window in the slipstream of the London night: the beached battleship of Trafalgar Square, rickshaw drivers in Soho, purple shag carpets covering their loveseats, the sudden quietude as we glide north, past the magnesium pool of Mornington Crescent, where a feeling like emergency and veneration hits me in the lungs.

His mother's house is a grey gargoyle on a thick Camden street. We get out of the cab. I think, *I'm drunk, but not drunk enough.*

He fumbles with the key in the front door. "Sorry," he smiles over his shoulder. "I'm nervous." His nervousness spikes my nervousness. I could turn around and run — I should — but my feet follow his into the hall like obedient dogs.

We are hit with a blast of radiator and oriental rug. I follow him into the abyss of the corridor: rugs, blocky furniture, darkened rooms suddenly thrown into wailing light as he hits the wall switch — "sorry, that's bright" — and then finds the dimmer.

I scour the walls for evidence of his father, or brothers and sisters, but can find only a small photograph on top of an upright piano. In it, his mother, her wounded dragon features softened by youth, sits on a beach gripping Elliott — I can only imagine it is him — in her arms.

"My father took that picture," Elliott says, behind me, so close I jump.

"Do you have any photos of him?"

"My mother did have one on display, of us all on holiday in Tuscany one year. But she took it down. I don't think she can bear to look at his face, even now."

"Grief can do that," I say.

"That's why I was looking at your photos of your father. There are so many of them in your house."

"My father was very photogenic, always surrounded by lions and monkeys." There is a strange fizz in my stomach as I say these words. Usually I only feel this when I am lying.

"Let's sit down." Elliott encircles my wrist with two of his fingers, a delicate manoeuvre that nonetheless feels like having handcuffs clapped on me. We collapse onto a sofa stuffed with cushions. A squeal makes us leap up. Two eyes belonging to a Staffordshire bull terrier peer out from between us.

"Mortimer, what are you doing there?" The dog is so ecstatic to see us it manages to simultaneously insert its foot into my mouth and whack Elliott in the eye with his tail.

An unidentifiable sound — a sort of hiss, like chameleons make when fighting — comes from the kitchen.

"What's that?"

"Just the ghost."

"You have a *ghost*?"

"All houses of this age do."

"You're not worried? Who is it? Why is it hissing at us?"

"A woman. Don't worry, she's not going to give you trouble. She only makes that sound when new people come over. She just doesn't know you yet. She's quite a good judge of character, I think."

I cast a leery look in the direction of the kitchen. "Well, that's good to know she's looking out for your best interests. I think we might have a ghost too, although I've never said so to Joanna. It's a very subtle feeling of someone looking at you, of being watched."

He considers this for a second. "Maybe we are just a film for them. Entertainment."

"Yes, exactly," I say. "We are a film they are watching, forever."

Elliott jumps up and heads toward a cabinet. "So, whisky?"

"That depends: whisky with a *y* or an *ey*?"

"Hmm, fussy. I think a *y*. Something with *Glen* in it, anyway."

"Okay, why not?"

"Don't sound so miserable about it."

"I'm not miserable, I'm *resolved*."

This makes him laugh, which feels like a triumph. *What does language communicate?* Benjamin asks me. He is not present physically at the moment, only as a shadow in my mind. *Precisely nothing. We think we are communicating through language but actually we are in it. It is a mental entity.*

I feel language draining from my mind as I sip the Glenmorangie. Hours pass, or perhaps minutes. We lay our heads against each other on the back of the sofa. I haven't touched another person's cranium with my own in so long but it feels natural, we are Siamese twins. I know I will have to sever us, when he asks me to stay, or when the clock strikes 2 a.m., whichever is earliest. If I get home to Joanna by three I have a chance to explain. After that, I'm done.

"Can I ask you a question?" He keeps his gaze focused straight ahead.

"Well, there are two answers to that: yes and no."

"Okay." He swallows. "I'm just going to go ahead with it. What is the most intimate subject you could make a film about?"

"As in, intimate to me?"

"Yes."

"I don't think I want to tell you that."

He is hurt, I see. He never considered the possibility I would not confess.

I resist the urge to apologize. I do so want to tell him. The alcohol pulls me down, into disclosure.

"I would make a film about a married couple who have not had sex in seven years. Who were once very involved with each other but who have drifted away, like continents on separate tectonic missions."

His moth of a mouth curls at the corner. "Only you would phrase it that way."

"I think you rate me too highly."

"Come on, Richard, no one talks like you do." He pulls himself up to sit straight. "How does that happen?"

"For one, I don't think long-term physical lust is possible."

"Some people seem to manage it," he says. "I've met people who are still in love with and desire each other."

"It just didn't happen that way, with Joanna and me."

What I do not tell him: I remember our encounters, before the children were born, as pure lust. Then they became emotional, then sentimental, then practical. In the last year when Joanna and I still touched each other we turned toward the other, hands groping, eyes shut, like moles.

"What do you feel for her now?"

"Love, respect. Gratitude."

"Well, that's not so bad."

My scalp nestles into the back of the sofa. It is happy there. "Yes," I say, "it could be much worse."

"But you're unhappy about it."

"I feel I've failed, as a man. As a husband."

Because I *have* failed — to have sex, to even initiate sex. It's not so difficult really. You just make a decision and get on with it. What am I afraid of? That Joanna would push me away? That I wouldn't be able to get an erection? That it would feel like scissoring through cardboard? No, I fear losing her respect. Having a terrible sexual encounter, a failure, between us, like a grain of dust in the eye.

"You have to think of your own desires," Elliott says.

"No I *don't*. Everyone's always thinking about their own bloody desires. I have responsibilities, Elliott, it's not all about me. And anyway, my only desire is to make films. I don't know what I want, apart from that."

Although don't I? I want to finger the boundaries of another person, trace the outline of their body, perhaps. I am not sure I want to go too deeply inside anyone else. Women's boundaries are pliant. I've never been interested in those of men, they make such rigid shapes in the world. But now, in Elliott, I see another kind of perimeter. The cut of a person unusually pitched against the fabric of the world. We are all scissors, slicing our paths, but he is more himself than most people are. If I desire him at all it is on this abstract level, to be a colluder in his geometry, to be a co-conspirator in the shapes he is making in the world.

It is not sex I want, or maybe I do, but it is a decoy.

I sit forward and put my head in my hands. "I can't drink like I used to: all night, mixing cocktails, wine, whisky, or whiskey with an *e*. I have to go."

"Okay. I'll call an Uber."

I can't muster the courage to look at him, so I speak to my knees. I had rehearsed a speech, about love and cinema, which might have gone something like this:

RICHARD: You're aware I feel a strong affinity with you. I'm always humbled to have a friend who is not the same generation as me. It's one of the best experiences you can have in life, to have that connection. It's love, or could be, but filmmaking is about taking that love and turning it into something else, sublimating it into cinema.

ELLIOTT: You mean if you act on it, then that sublimation can't happen?

RICHARD: Possession transmits itself through the camera. The viewer can tell that some line has been crossed.

ELLIOTT: You mean the camera is only a metaphor for the desiring gaze we turn on each other?

RICHARD: And which viewers turn on you. They can't have you — or at least not all of them can, who knows, someone will. But they are in the same position I am in, we don't possess you. That line has to be maintained.

I say, "I'm afraid. There it is."

His face looms larger and larger until it is inside mine. Two lips prise mine apart. A presence enters me.

I sink into the moment. Deep inside me, in a previously arid chamber, a once-placid creature stirs.

It is he who makes the decision to pull away. As he does, a ribbon of my being unfurls with him. I try but I can't tug it back.

His eyes are wide. "I didn't know I was going to do that."

"Well, that makes two of us." The air around us closes. "I don't know what you've done to me."

He takes this as a rebuke, which it is in a way.

His coming absence yawns before me, my own too. "So we'll keep in touch while we're away?" The thin note of anxiety in his voice.

"We'll be ten hours apart. Don't WhatsApp me at four in the morning."

"Sure thing." Elliott looks relieved that I am speaking to him as I always do, half fatherly, half curmudgeonly.

The Uber comes, a Lexus with blacked-out windows. The night is a crow. I fly home, the seat beside me taunting me with its emptiness. Until now I had been complete.

◢

In the morning Joanna is up, getting the kids ready for school. On their way out Nathan and Lucy nod at me in that milky shy way they have adopted since I've been working to finish the draft, as if they are living with an eccentric uncle who can't be too interrupted or too indulged.

Joanna gives me a long look. "You got home late."

"We went through the whole script." I feel instant scalding shame. I haven't lied to my wife in — perhaps ever.

"So, how did it go?"

"I think he's prepared to go ahead on the basis of an escrow."

"Has he talked it over with Trevor?"

"Yes, Trevor's going to advise him to do it." Another lie. I don't know what Elliott has discussed with his agent. I turn my face away. This kind of negotiation is Joanna's job, normally. I am only doing it because Elliott and I have become friends, as Joanna puts it. Plus, any decent director these days is also a good producer.

"Did you tell him you're deferring?"

"No."

"Good. It's best he doesn't know that."

Suddenly the idea of having a secret from Elliott seems not only wrong, but obscene. Some niche of my being has pledged its allegiance to him.

"You look tired."

"I couldn't sleep. I put on the heater and wrote."

"Good." Joanna's head snaps up and down in her version of a nod.

"I'm just going to go to bed."

She gives me a quizzical look. "It's eight o'clock in the morning."

"I know. I need to lie down for an hour."

Her voice pulls me back into the kitchen. "Richard, I'm really worried about you. When are you seeing the GP?"

I stand and face her. She is wearing a charcoal cashmere turtleneck. Her shoulder-length hair is down, which is unusual. She wears it in a power bun most days. Her chin looks pointier than usual. She has changed at some juncture in the past weeks, but I cannot put my finger on the nature of the transformation.

"Tomorrow." Another lie. "They squeezed me in."

In bed I close my eyes. On the inner screen of my eyelids is a silhouette of Elliott's face. His angular features, his marine eyes. I see his eyes and he does not look at me as much as wash through me, back and forth, tidal. I expected a man's mouth to be formally distinct, to have sharp angles, an unpleasant famil-iarity, outcroppings. I must have closed my eyes during our kiss, because in my mind's eye a purple miasma began to form and billow like ink poured into water.

Before, when our heads were still innocent and touching on the back of the sofa, I'd said, "It takes character to be a man. People are depending on you. Men have the power, yes. You have rights but also responsibilities. No one talks about that."

"What responsibilities?"

"To show the way. To be dependable."

He was quiet for a minute. "You *are* dependable. The films show the way through."

"Through to where?" I said. "That is the question. I worry they are just images, we are stuffing the world full to the gill with images, they are what keep us quiescent. Film had the capacity to be revolutionary, but all this endless teenaged dystopia and blood-lust longform television is just too much opiate of the masses."

"I think images show us what is possible."

"I used to think that too."

For a moment I saw myself on Elliott's bony sofa, the man — the person — I had become. For so long now I have been trying to avoid a particular fate, that of the burnt creative. You see them all the time, at screenings, at private views in galleries, in the house seats in the theatre, come to see their mates onstage. They may have watery eyes and blotchy skin from too much Pinot Grigio, and no matter how expensive their hairdresser their hair is electrified, yet dull. But the singed quality is not physical but metaphysical, the light within them is grey and livid at once, a flame fed on helium. Sometimes I wonder if evolution got it right, if we are really meant to live beyond fifty-five.

"Richard?" Elliott's eyes are lambent with midnight.

"I want this film to be light, somehow. You are that illumination. There's already enough darkness in this world."

Life needs something of me, really needs me to step up to the plate, at last. I am being called to attend to historically important matters. But I am not fierce or indomitable, I am not the man Elliott thinks I am, there is a weakness in my fate neither he nor I can guess. I can't even say what it is about him that captivates me, apart from the obvious: his intelligence, sensitivity. He is also kind, I think, a quality in short supply these days. There seems to be no language for it, only a harmony, a music I have never heard before. I know these two weeks ahead when we will be separated will be a test, for both of us, they will determine the name of our unspoken language, they will bear witness to or liquidate our magic.

◤

EXT. DAY. A PLAZA IN CAPRI TOWN — MAY 1924.

The plaza is bathed in roseate light. It is almost empty apart from ASJA LACIS, 33, a Latvian theatre director, and DAGA, her daughter, 8, wily, even a bit feral, who accompanies her. Asja wears a slightly gaudy striped dress.

BENJAMIN appears around a corner leading onto the plaza. He sees the woman, stops and retreats back into the shadow of the street. From here he watches Asja and Daga enter a shop. He waits a moment, composes himself and strides toward it.

Asja stands behind a counter. Daga's head comes up only to the first row. Inside are piles of cakes, sweets coated in sugar and several banks of nuts.

SIGNORE FERRETTI, 50, unusually trim and fit for a man who owns a sweet shop, looks at her expectantly.

Asja's broken Italian hits Benjamin's ears like shards of broken glass. "Vorrei comprare un po'. . ." She stumbles, unable to find the word. She peers at the nuts behind the counter.

The pained expression all people wear when they hear their language mangled fleets over Signore Ferretti's broad, otherwise allowing, face. *Scusi?*

In that moment Asja becomes aware of Benjamin's presence behind her. He makes brief eye contact with her. He addresses the shopkeeper. "Buongiorno."

"Buongiorno, Professore."

Asja barely turns around this time. She tries again. "Vorrei un po . . ."

"Puis-je vous aider, madame?"

Asja turns and glares at Benjamin. Her eyes are the watery colour of very light jade. He sees a flash of recognition from deep within her eyes, even though he is sure they have never met before.

"Je voudrais acheter du amandes."

"Aha, madame. La signora vorrebbe comprare delle mandorle."

"Ah! Mandorle."

They all nod, in delighted agreement. Daga frowns at the ridiculous adults.

They leave the shop, Asja first, Benjamin holding the door for her. Belatedly he realizes he has not bought the bread he went in to purchase. The bread, his wife and his son in Germany, the doilies of his mother's house, his governess, his ink-stained fingers, the ashtray stuffed with ugly cigarette butts have all somehow been erased by this woman in her dress that looks like the striped awnings of butchers' shops.

Outside, the morning light is fierce. It will be a hot day. The three take refuge in a wedge of shade.

Benjamin offers Daga a sweet. He is quick to make friends with children. Bertolt and Marianne Brecht's children burst into delighted laughter whenever they see him.

Daga scowls. At eight years old, she is already impatient with her mother's friends, who all have the rigid yet dreamy mien of the intellectual.

"Allow me to help carry your packets, madame."

Asja wordlessly hands him her paper bag of almonds. They walk down the street. The Mediterranean glitters below them.

"I've heard of you."

"Oh yes?" He does not look at her.

"I was staying with Bertolt. He left last week."

Benjamin manages to drop the package of almonds. He bends to pick them up. He is flustered, bending over with difficulty, like a much older man.

"Sorry," he says, over and over. "So sorry."

◰

Screenplays are written in the present tense not because of the obvious reason that they will recreate reality, replaying and resurrecting deceased and fictional moments. Rather film recognizes that what we understand to be reality is always happening, over and over again. Each moment is only a random triumph among a ribbon of iterations. How much of eternity is decided by the inflection of an eyebrow, a pause, a rancid note in the voice, the sound of the red-capped robin chat outside the window being audible or not.

Benjamin walked into his destiny when he decided to help a garishly dressed woman buy a packet of almonds that morning in the Piazzetta on an island in the searing Tyrrhenian Sea. He knew it was not just a case of his curiosity having been piqued. He knew the present tense is a prison but simultaneously a self-renewing creature that sheds its skin every seven years. He wrote on that reptilian frequency; his books and essays were skins he needed to discard to keep going. He feels the serpent of the now, the rough epidermis as it scales his leg; too late does he appreciate how intent it is upon rapture.

VIII

We file on board the plane and my viewfinder shrinks to a porthole. The plane, an ageing British Airways 747-400 series, shudders in anticipation before the engines are put full throttle. We are pinned by g-forces. Then, with another series of tremors in which I clench my anus — as if that would will the plane into the air — we are aloft. After the plane has gained enough altitude to convince us that we are not going to slam back down to earth we all open our eyes, blinking and astonished.

I will spend two weeks in Kenya, no wife, no family, to attend to my father's considerable estate. He has left his farm in Usain Gishu to me in his will, and I have put it in the trust of my cousin Mike, who runs a major safari company catering to Americans with an *Out of Africa* vision of the experience, to the extent that when his drivers collect them at Nairobi airport they are instructed to put the theme music to the film on in the car.

Kenya is the country of my father and his father, who was Black. But it is not an easy country and no longer mine, riven by a kind of factionalism which in the local imagination is explained as ethnicity, but which is really a stream of unquestioned allegiance, or, to Europeans who don't know any better, tribes. It *is* tribal, that's the problem; it seems to be encoded into the very fabric of the place, because it is a made-up country. The British invented it. Before that, there were only Nilotes and Cushites, Maasai and Luo, Kalenjin and Mijikenda.

The announcement comes on. "Today we have two choices: chicken or fish."

Good, I think. They're doing food. We're definitely not going to crash. Or at least not yet. I can have a gin and tonic.

I rubberneck over to the window, whose shade the person sitting there has miraculously left open, and see the English Channel, no more than a wide estuary from this altitude. Another stab of panic. Why am I doing this? My father's death has put Kenya behind me for good. I wasn't going to become a filmmaker there, I wasn't going to find my subject there, Walter Benjamin isn't there — possibly he never gave the continent of Africa a thought in his life. Elliott isn't there.

Then, fast-forward. (I have a personal superstition against filming flight scenes.) In Nairobi the air is familiar: thin, garbed in diesel, montane. But sweet too. My bones jangle when I come back to Kenya — it happens anywhere on the African continent actually — because they know they are home. The BA flight lands at night, the runway lit by the airport equivalent of one hurricane lamp. The terminal has the dingy lowering light of

Greyhound bus terminals in the States in the 1980s. (I know, I was there.) We are all exhausted but elated as we wait in the abattoir-like customs and immigration shed, as if in leaving Britain at this time of year we have escaped not only winter but revolution, or war.

Once outside, the highlands air dries my skin instantly. To convince myself I am really here I think, *My father is buried here, my grandfather, and his before him.* This now powerful and independent country, where there is a near constant flow of light, feels unstained by the bleak intentions of Europe. I always feel freer anywhere in Africa, or at least safely out of sight from the gimlet gaze of history.

For the next two weeks I undertake family tasks, signing documents, authorizing probates, shuttling between cousins who have made it so big in banking or safari companies they have actual Salvador Dalís on the walls. I bask like a lizard in the sun in their plantation-house compounds, ignoring the factor 50 Joanna thrust into my suitcase.

My father's inheritance will be snarled up in Kenyan probate for too long for me to use it to finance *Benjamin*. My cousin Mike has handled the process through his lawyers. His father, my father's brother, will look after the house and garden after ownership formally passes to me. Mike and I need to discuss the arrangements. He telephones me to suggest we meet at Westgate Mall. I am taken aback — this is where al-Shabaab killed 67 people on September 21, 2013. After a long refurbishment, it reopened last year.

"Can't we meet somewhere else?" I say on the phone. "What about Sarit Centre?"

"No, man. Westgate's safi. It's quiet, good for talking."

"It's quiet because no one wants to have a cafe latte in a tomb where sixty-seven people were gunned down."

"Pole, didn't quite catch that. Bad connection. See you there, he?"

I haven't seen Mike for ten years but I recognize him immediately. I am always amazed how little ordinary people change, as opposed to actors, who are unrecognizable from one minute to the next. A stout man in a checked shirt and chinos comes toward me. He has sandy hair and wears desert boots with *safari* emblazoned on them, the default footwear for Kenyan men of an outdoors inclination.

"Richard, man, it's been too long. You never keep in touch. Not even on Facebook. You're famous now, he?"

"No, not quite famous. Just well known."

"Yeah. Well, we thought you'd want to go up country and have a last look at the place."

"I don't think I have time on this trip," I say.

"It's only four hours by road."

I resist the urge to say, *I know how far it is, I did that trip every week for four years when I was at school and countless times before.* Although in those days it was closer to five or six hours. The Chinese have improved road construction in Kenya lately.

In the café we swap pictures of our children. I haven't seen his in many years. He has a boy and girl roughly Nathan's and Lucy's ages. They are both at private school in South Africa.

"So that's Nathan," he peers at the photo. "Got a bit of the nusu-nusu, doesn't he?"

"We all do, Mike."

"That's right, in the blood." He pinches his forearm,

puckering his skin and letting it go. "But some it comes out in, and some it doesn't. Strange, no?"

The watch Mike wears catches my eye. It is dull platinum and has four dials. Along with running a safari company Mike also owns a helicopter firm that ferries Kenyan politicians and businessmen around the country in smart black-and-white buzzing bees, as well as two houses, one in Karen, the exclusive suburb where the leftover whites insist on huddling, one on the coast, a few shell companies in the Caymans and a flat in Fulham.

"I heard you were working on a film about a Jewish —" He hesitates, likely wondering if he has used the right term, if it is acceptable any longer to refer to people with that adjective sticking out in front.

"— writer. Yes. Walter Benjamin."

"Why don't you tell an African story?" He hesitates, possibly remembering I have already done this, in *The Grass Is Singing*. "Maybe it's time to come home," Mike says.

"I'd like that, Mike. But I don't know where home is."

His lip twitches. "Shame," he says.

I would so like Kenya to be home. But that would be sentimental and foolish. *Home is where your paycheque is* — this is Joanna's favourite saying, which she picked up in America.

"We just wish we'd seen more of you, over the years," Mike says.

"I know, Mike. But my life is elsewhere."

"Yes, we all understand. UK is where the action is in your world."

With this statement Mike is referring to a number of things: the fact I did not come back to Kenya for my own father's funeral among them. Mike, his father and my other cousins buried him, or rather burnt him. He wanted a Hindu burial by the river, and that is what he got.

"What about the teeth?" I ask. "Did you solve that?"

My father had two gold crowns, which someone in the undertaker's firm removed with a pair of pliers.

"No. We made enquiries. But it's likely the guys who did it are long gone. You know how it is here."

I nod, although I don't, not really. Not anymore. A vision of my father stroking Siwezi's matted mane appears unbidden. There was a time in his life when, should anyone have approached my father, for good or for ill, Siwezi would have swiped their faces off with a single swat of his paw. But Siwezi was long dead when thieves were prising the gold from my father's molars as his corpse was being prepared by the edge of the Sosiani River.

"I mean, Richie, we know you had your differences."

Where were you? This is Mike's question, unvoiced. I am fully aware my family here found it completely unnatural, like the failure of the short rains in October last year, a catastrophe in this part of the world, that I did not come. Lately the gods have forgotten to dispatch these rains, along with errant sons, and the world is burning alive underneath us.

A memory of my father returns to me, fully performed, like a scene from a film I have made but forgotten. I am twelve — no, thirteen — years old. One afternoon I bring home my friend Alex from school for the first time. Alex is tall and blond, the son of a neighbouring farmer. He is the hale, wheaty white boy this part of the world used to specialize in producing, the corrupt issue of colonialism. He could not help that he was perfect. He was good at rugby, he was good at school, girls loved him. He would go on to establish a satellite television empire across East Africa.

I watched my father lead him around our garden, introducing him to his pet chameleons, the three warthogs he also kept, the go-away bird who nested in the umbrella thorn outside my bedroom and whose rough caw I woke to each morning. Even the go-away bird preferred Alex. As he and my father perambulated the garden a golden penumbra formed, a mobile sunset they carted around with them. That was the kind of son my father wanted, and he never hid this fact from me: a self-contained, masculine boy who brought home rugby trophies and went on camel treks to the Matthews Range on the weekends.

I find some resolve, finally, to rejoinder. "You never come to the UK, Mike, why is that?"

His mouth makes a sour shape in his face, a small square axe. "Nonnie and I don't like UK, you know that. Too many rules. As soon as you set foot there it's all *do this, don't do that.*"

"Yes, it's called society."

My father's body lay by the riverside for a day. He was washed and attended there. A Hindu funeral is not an uncommon funeral in the region, even for people who have never been to India. Sometime in the twenty-four hours when he lay in the small wooden hut where bodies are prepared and which is chilled the old way, with blocks of ice, I see a pair of hands forcing open rigor mortis lips and clamping pliers on gold teeth. I cannot get this image out of my head.

"What do you want me to do?" I say.

My cousin blinks, very slowly. He is affronted by my directness. "We want you to do the right thing."

"And what would that be?"

"Sign the papers. You're never going to come back to live here, are you?"

Mike wants me to leave my father's house and garden in trust to the family, rather than sell it. But if I sell, I will be able to finance my next film after *Benjamin*, whatever that might be, and perhaps even the rest of my life. Nathan could go to university in the States, as he seems to want to do, mystifyingly. Joanna would respect me more, now that I had nearly as much money as her.

My father's garden is the only thing I have an attachment to, even if it is ferocious. The fiscal shrikes; the puff adders; the pair of chameleons, their slit-eyed faces like Steven Spielberg aliens; the go-away bird, its floury fluffing in the thorn tree; the Hadeda ibis, so loud in the mornings I never owned an alarm clock until I went to live in Italy the summer after my twelfth birthday. They all line up to interrogate me, accompanied by the drastic sunrise of the highlands, the equatorial schedule, the celestial flicking of a switch from night to day which has made me unfit to inhabit these crepuscular zones I have been trying to live in ever since.

Childhood is a scar. Everyone knows this, but we will not admit it. A wound you tend for the rest of your life.

"You're so successful now, Richie," Mike says, his watch clunking on the table as his wrist turns over and he stands to leave, its hollow sound not so different from the reverberation that follows a rifle blast. "We're proud of you."

We are stuck in traffic, in Mike's Defender, being driven by his driver.

"You're back," I say silently. "Why have you come all the way to Kenya?"

"The heat is infernal here. How do you stand it?"

"By not being overdressed for the equatorial regions."

Benjamin wears a fedora and black overcoat, a shirt and tie underneath. He says something like *humpf.* Then, "I'm counting on you."

"Yeah, join the queue."

In Nairobi the traffic is an infinite detonation you are powerless to stop. With the driver's ear cocked toward the weird quarter-African in the back seat I can't afford to talk to poor dream-Benjamin, who has wandered clumsily into this underworld of fumes and hunger. We look up to see Marabou storks still perched in the umbrella thorns that line the Mombasa highway, dressed in their filthy black-and-white suits, arboreal undertakers.

"Do you miss him?" Benjamin asks from the seat beside me.

"Who?"

"You know who."

"I'm seeing in double vision. I think I am looking at this city with my own eyes but actually it's his eyes I am seeing with, now."

"You should send him messages with your impressions. The young are ruthless because they have options and too much future. He will forget you otherwise."

"I've made a promise to myself not to contact him for a couple of weeks. I want to let whatever he has done to me have a chance to dissipate."

From his jacket breast pocket a monogrammed handkerchief peeks. Benjamin is turning over a piece of paper in his fingers.

"What's that?"

"Just a souvenir." He proffers it to me: *Monaco Grand Casino, December 1935.* "My sister and I gambled once. I lost a thousand francs. My legendary luck."

"Yes, well I'm about to put two million dollars into a trust fund rather than my bank account out of sentimental attachment to my African upbringing and emotional coercion on the part of a cabal of super-rich cousins. Shall we find a roulette table?"

The traffic breaks into tributaries at the new Langata bypass. None of these roads existed when I was growing up here. The city has turned into an unruly, churlish metropolis, the New York of East Africa.

"Yes, I miss him," I confess to Benjamin. "I miss his easy company, the way he has just discovered the history of Bolshevism — for some reason they forgot to teach it at school. He is a bel esprit. He is humble, open. I didn't know it was possible for that kind of character to exist anymore. He seems to like me. That's the miracle of the situation."

Benjamin is cleaning his glasses. I notice again how well made his face is, neither oval nor rectangular, his intelligent eyes. He has Emil's — his father's — certain nose.

"He likes you because you've lived for decades on the other side of what he cannot see, which is perspective, authority, accomplishment, hard-earned respect. You are offering him a role that could transform his career. He can see how fair and committed you are to your craft, how much you admire and value actors. He wants your integrity. For himself."

Benjamin pauses while a cashew nut seller presses a bag of warm nuts through the open window. "Help the man out, for pity's sake," he snaps. "Buy a bag of his nuts."

It is four o'clock. I close my eyes. The light has no subtlety here. I have escaped the dungeon of winter but the contrast is too great: downtown petrol stations and their attendants in smart blue uniforms, tired 1950s window displays, frayed miniature palms potted along the avenues, a donation from some sheikh in Dubai.

"What's wrong, sir? Is it the air?"

Mike's driver looks at me out of the corner of my eye. I find I have buried my face in my hands. I am sunk in doubt that I am wrong about Elliott, the suggestion he does not have his own integrity, in my inability to think of myself for once, to act in my own interest and take my father's money and run.

"The heat," I say. " I'm not used to it anymore."

The driver smiles. "Yes, you people in Europe, you all wilt in the sun. You need to develop some black skin."

We drive under a sky so blue it should be patented: Kenya blue. There is a dark note within it, as if you could peel it off and access the thermosphere, the last layer of oxygen before space. So many Europeans were seduced by this place, its perfect evolutionary climate, loamy fields from which four yields of anything — flowers, string beans, tea, coffee, peas, papaya, sorghum — can be coaxed each year. The charms of abundance. It made my white forebears unfit for any kind of stricture or privation. God forbid my father would have to get on the Piccadilly Line or do his own washing. His voice still ricochets around my head: *What's the point of putting a shilling in an electric meter and*

begging for gruel in that mean city, Richie, when you can wake up
warm here every morning and have ice cream delivered to your door?

"You'd hate it here," I tell Benjamin. "There's nothing of Europe."

"I wouldn't be so sure," he replies. "We are both drawn to the seductive beauty of nature. It seems a source of inspiration, but like all beauty it siphons the discontent that is your fuel from your mind. Look at me, hauling myself into the Russian winter, just for a woman. What was I thinking?"

"I love that story," I say. "In 1926 you followed Asja to Moscow. You were initially entranced to see Communism in the flesh but also taken aback: the shop signs point at right angles into the streets, as 'old inn signs do,' you write. The shops were like taverns; it is 1926 but the nineteenth century had been arrested. Despite your intellectual communism you were confused to find these shops were not about commerce, but distribution."

Poor Benjamin, more bourgeois than he thought, fingers pinched by the dense January cold, much colder than anything he has felt before, even while growing up in Berlin and its prairie surrounds. See him returning to his lodgings at a spartan hotel. He has been to lunch at Asja Lacis's house, which she shares with her husband, Bernard Reich. She does not welcome Benjamin's presence; she is not into ménage à trois. I imagine her as big-boned but beautiful, in a truculent, intolerant way. It is hard to understand what Benjamin sees in her. It is a political, which is to say intellectual, infatuation.

As we climb from the benzene-dusted streets of the city centre into the forested gardens of Karen, my thoughts are tugged away from here and my overcoated companion. It is no good, I can't not think about him. I have tried fondness, I have tried disbelief. It is as if I've filmed him already: Elliott-as-Benjamin walking down the corso in San Remo, his dark suit exchanged for a plain linen ensemble, his whole being shot through with a mysterious and vaguely dangerous light. He has been resurrected into the Mediterranean and tonight he will eat spaghetti alle vongole and drink a lightly sparkling Cinque Terre wine; his thoughts prove buoyant too. He is almost happy.

IX

O n a dank evening soon after our respective returns we meet for a drink in the Wolseley. I love its Viennese spaceship interior, reassuring and womb-like with its cobalt marble and waiters whose hair is gelled until it has the consistency of an Elizabethan ruff.

He breezes through the door and ignores the maître d' when he sees me. He drags his chair out. I stand. We embrace, the table between us. He sits down again in a flurry, a bird coming to land.

"What can I get you?"

"Let's have a glass of champagne."

"Why not?" I order two Pommery Brut Royals. "So." I try to drain the anxiety from my gaze. "Here we are, back."

"From a long way away," he says. "Both of us."

"I know. I can feel the distance." It's true. Somehow our real selves are still in other time zones. They missed the flight, and have to find alternative transport to get back to us.

Framed against the dark marble and its gilt trim, Elliott looks less like a person than a portrait. Yesterday he was sitting for Titian and today he's fixing me with his five-hundred-year-old blue gaze. I think again how his face has the inevitable quality the camera loves. People think that actors have to be beautiful and angular, but the necessary element is something more subtle. I'm not sure anyone knows what it is.

"So, how was California?"

"We worked sixteen-hour days, the director was an alpha male, every single person on set looked like they spent their lives in the gym. I was the weedy gothic English kid. Textbook English-actor-in-Hollywood experience, probably. Cheers."

We clunk our champagne glasses. "How about the accent?"

"Easy. You just have to flatten your vowels."

In the spaces between what he does not say and what I don't ask is the shape of his off-set experience: a girl or a guy, his fellow actor or actress, perhaps, a sharp, combustible infatuation. Or maybe not. But he *has* changed. He is not the same person, and I can't put my finger on how or why. I have lost the thread of his existence, like a spool or roll of tape that has wound itself tightly and you cannot find the loose end.

"So how was Africa?"

"Africa is a continent of fifty-three — well, fifty-four now, counting South Sudan — countries. I was in Kenya."

"Okay, point taken: Africa is a continent and not a country. How was Kenya?"

"It was — a parallel dimension."

"You wish you could live there, don't you?"

"I do and I don't."

"Why don't you go back?"

"Because everything is here. Home is where your paycheque is," I quote Joanna's line at him.

A careful, protective expression streaks across his face. "What did you think about when you were there?"

"My past, my father, my mother, our lives there. You."

His gaze drops to the table with a clunk. He either was or was not expecting the truth.

"I was trying to figure out if I'm attracted to you or attracted to the fact that you're attracted to me," I say.

He retreats into his chair and runs his hands along his skull, as if to calm himself, or simply to subdue his hair, which has a habit of trying to escape his head. He sighs and I realize he is about to deliver a blow I don't have time to defend myself against.

"I jump in the pool, as my mother says. I'm impulsive, reckless. I'm just taking stabs in the dark, emotionally." He gathers himself internally, sits straighter, as if summoning a rectitude. "I don't want to jeopardize our working relationship. I want to do this film."

"That's — agreed, Elliott. We're doing this film together."

His face immediately tumbles into — what? I can't read the expression, it transits his face too quickly. Most of us register perhaps one emotion on our faces at a time. Elliott's is an orchestra: annoyance morphs into despair, followed by stabs of abashment, then a stunned, affronted shock.

Relieved to be released from further confessions, we take in our fellow barflies, expensive-looking people, matrons with salon hair, and a duo of men at the adjacent table, one of whom actually wears a cravat and seems to be interviewing successive thin women who turn up on the half hour.

We decide to have something to eat somewhere less expensive, even though we are both unsure if this is the right thing to do, if we are dragging out an evening that ought to be terminated.

We leave, acknowledging the doorman's exhortations to mind the step down to the pavement, and join the throng on Piccadilly. We cut through Air Street, then Glasshouse Street to Golden Square. I hope to take us to Andrew Edwards on Lexington Street but they are full. We settle on Ember Yard, where we perch on stools and eat tapas. I listen to his on-set stories. He was kept at a distance by the young American actors. He found them cliquish, full of in-jokes.

"It's an emotional jungle in your twenties," I say. "One is easily stung by those situations."

"And you're not?"

"That's one of the consolations of age, I don't have to suffer them anymore."

"You talk to me as if I'm an equal. It's taken my experience in the States for me to value that. Our director is an indie legend over there, but he was all, 'Dude, can you look a bit more dumbstruck.'"

The restaurant is too noisy, packed by people who look as if they've come into Soho especially in their cashmere jumpers and Docker trousers. I have a long history in this part of London: nights drinking on the pavement outside the French House with my crew; festival apparatchiks; even, in the early days, Joanna. The agents and the post production houses' offices are still here, but are now outnumbered by the Snapchat headquarters and asset-management firms.

I am overtaken by a feeling of loss. It rears up in front of me, a solid wall of water.

"This city is slipping away from me," I say.

His look is certain, a little unkind. "Maybe it was never yours in the first place."

We say goodbye at Tottenham Court Road Tube, another quick embrace into which we list like crippled ships.

I say, "I think I'll walk to Clerkenwell and get the bus from there."

"Ok," he says, solemn, looking down at the ground, then up. "Okay."

The streets fall away behind me. Museum Street, Theobald's Row, the Farringdon Road junction, St. John Street, Clerkenwell Road with its stream of shops selling furniture that looks like it belongs in 1950s airports. It is cold, still, but that early March incipient note of spring colours the air, even at midnight. One 55 bus streams past, then another. I allow myself not to take them. I avoid my reflection in windows as I walk, and he keeps step with me doggedly, this Richard-the-rest-of-the-world-sees. He is still tall and thin, a younger, less stooped, darker-skinned Julian Barnes. This Richard is well off, or at least comfortable, although it wasn't always so. In the early 1990s, before he met Joanna, he was renting bedsits in undesirable precincts like everyone else, Archway, Clapham North, getting mugged on the way home late at night by shapeless hooded men with tattoos on their knuckles. The city was hostile, alien, but somehow more friendly to this Richard's existence than it is now, with his Margaret Howell trench coat and his Alessi kettle.

The past is becoming the future too quickly. Maybe this is what it means to get old: to look around you and think, *This is not my reality. How did it get here?* This century still feels new to me. It has brought with it a ruthlessness that has entered human interactions and which I'm not equipped to deal with. As for London, this city has taken my blood. It has eaten my youth and deposited a layer of toxic subparticles on my lungs in return. Although I did have luck and London had a stake in generating this — my filmography, my very good agent, my marriage. As for Joanna, she would never have agreed to "rot in some chocolate box village" — her words.

But lately, for the first time, I have been thinking: maybe thirty years in this city is enough. I have — we have — options. Joanna and I could get creative industry visas for the U.S. and move to LA for a while. We could even go and live on my father's land in Kenya, although expat life would drive Joanna stark raving mad.

What is keeping me here, is it you? I silently address the city. The real reason wafts into view: the faces of my children. Joanna and I could always deposit them in university halls and scarper, and we might have to do that in the end. "I don't think I can stomach this," Joanna has said, over and over, since the referendum. She means Brexit, the Tory party, what they have stolen from us. "I worry it's a secular Kristallnacht, twenty-first-century version," she says, "and we're going to be the mugs who stayed too long until it was made impossible for us to leave." I don't know if it is *Benjamin* that is turning our thoughts in this dark direction. "They're not hauling us away in the middle of the night to deportation trains," I tell her, to which she replies, "Yet."

When I finally arrive the house feels asleep, but I know that everyone is parked in their rooms in front of digital aquaria.

Even Mabati is giving me the cold shoulder; he knows I have absconded on an emotional level and doesn't even stir at my arrival.

In the darkened hallway I pass the black-and-white photograph of my father and Siwezi. My father raised him from a cub when he was only twelve years old. George Adamson himself gave him advice on how to do this, which from what my father told me amounted to the following: feed him freshly killed chickens and don't ever try this with a leopard. Siwezi was dead by the time I was born, but my father's house was full of photographs like these, stills in which you can still see the amber vacuum of those predator eyes which my father swore filled with love whenever the lion saw him.

I see this picture every day out of the corner of my eye as I enter and exit my house, my father, preserved beyond time in the moment. Two apex predators, the tanned child and the tamed carnivore on that sunny escarpment day, looking back at me from the future.

◢

There's a literary evening near you on Saturday night. Want to come?

I text back: *What's a literary evening?*

In response Elliott sends me a link to a webpage. Something about an interview with Alan Hollinghurst at Sutton House.

I could come to yours and we could walk there together. There's a catch, though. You have to dress up.

As what?

A character in his novel The Line of Beauty.

I remember the novel, that I couldn't finish it. The book is set in the 1980s ostensibly but felt dated, a hangover from *Brideshead Revisited*: straw boaters, striped jackets, the thin patrician legs of the English governing class encased in caramel-coloured trousers, velvet Pasha loafers on their feet. I couldn't get a grip or interest on any of the characters, who seemed to be drifting through their lives in a very un-neoliberal fashion, although Hollinghurst was an elegant, Jamesian writer, that much was clear.

I text Elliott to say I can't do the costume.

He arrives on foot to collect me. He has also abandoned any pretence at simulating toffs. He wears a long charcoal grey over-coat with a suspiciously dense thread count I haven't seen before. He sees me peering at it. "My mum gave it to me for Christmas. What, it doesn't look good?"

"No, it looks great." I don't tell him it is the same brand of winter coat Joanna wears. Clad in it, he looks like a pencil, but also like my wife. For the first time I see the similarity in their features: the arrow-shaped face, a thin elegance, intelligent eyes always scanning the moment, looking for the real story, which is to say the latent electricity beneath it, and an air of certainty which comes from a place beyond personality.

We bisect London Fields on one of the lit pathways, the lamps throwing individual moons. Blocks of council flats with squares of yellow windows prowl the perimeter of the park, ocean liners on a dark sea.

Benjamin wrote that when we walk in urban environments we carry ghost cities in our mind. I think of the indie record label that used to inhabit 10 Martello Terrace, the pub where wizened men in flat caps used to chain-smoke over pints of Best Brew, derelict mansions now actual mansions inhabited by people with second homes in Southwold. I spot two reassuring drunks at the edge of the park, shouting and brandishing tins of Tennent's at each other, Staffies orbiting them on chain leashes.

Elliott walks resolutely, determinedly, hands thrust into pockets. He accepts my periods of silence as we walk. He does not try to fill them.

"I'm thinking of how it used to be around here twenty, thirty years ago," I say eventually.

"When did you move here?"

"In 1993."

A smile, semi-secretive. "That's before I was born."

"I'm aware of that."

We allow this fact to muscle in between us, our accompanier. To have a friend so much younger, who didn't exist when a large part of your life was already complete, is perhaps a manner of reaching out to infinity or passing the baton to the reversal which will come, in time — when Elliott will exist, and I will not. Not unlike having a child, then.

"What was London like then?"

"Desolate. You had to think twice about walking to the pub at night, or going to the pub at all for that matter. They were all full of hard cases. Then you'd get jumped by a crack addict on the way home and dragged down the street for your wallet."

"Did that happen to you?"

"Yes, more than once. Joanna thought we were insane, bringing up the children here. It was like a Martin Amis novel. The schools were terrible and we had no money. When Nathan came home from school at six saying 'boh'le' instead of 'bottle'

Joanna insisted we transfer him to a private school in Highgate. On scholarship, by the way."

His body seems to dissolve into the air, his head a bright exclamation point floating through the darkness. We arrive at Sutton House via a street of disapproving Georgian houses with BMWs parked outside. The house is a Tudor mansion, crammed with ghosts but no central heating. It was the residence of Cromwell's secretary and a waystation for courtesans when they came to London to visit the Queen, and still has the furtive air of assignations, the density of whispers in a small, quizzical courtyard.

We open the door and step into a set populated by extras from the latest BBC big-budget costume drama: young men wearing white blazers with the insignias of rowing clubs on their lapels, pipe-cleaner trousers and brogues, saturnine men in tuxedos, young women in proto-Tory evening wear.

Elliott and I wander about in this Other England. In one room there is a life drawing tableau. Two naked men hold a fireside wrestling pose, like Gerald and Birkin in *Women in Love*, while a circle of attentive draftspeople sketch hamstrings. In another room twenty people sit around a table embellishing screenprinted posters of Margaret Thatcher. A photography studio is erected in a corner room where a flame-headed woman with green eyes glares at the camera.

Elliott and I retreat to the courtyard. Puffs of our breath accompany us. We are followed, not subtly, by the gazes of men, enveloped in them like silken threads. I wonder if it will ever come to feel like a cocoon. There is a pattern. Men glance at Elliott, then away, astonished, then back, bolder. They register me only in so far as I am attached to him.

We look at each other too in the buttery Tudor light, searching for clues to our estrangement.

I say, "I should go."

"I'll come with you."

"No, stay, I'm just being an old person."

"No, I'm done here." The finality in his voice, the bite on the word *done*, rankles. As if he was looking for something or someone specific and failed to find it.

We lurch into the night. Released from the 1980s Edwardiana and the reeling drunken tossers in boaters, I take a deep breath of the present. Elliott looks over his shoulder, as if we are being followed. No one emerges, but I feel the press of gazes on us nonetheless.

"How will you get home?" I ask.

"Can I come back to yours? I could use a cup of tea."

"Of course." It lasted only a sliver of a second, my hesitation. Still he caught it.

"I won't wake anyone up, I promise."

Our steps ring sharp in the night. They seem to bounce off the shuttered houses.

"What did you think?" I venture.

"I liked it, although it's straining to be properly bohemian, and it's a bit tribal." His face darkens. "Too much sexual vanity. I don't feel at home anywhere. Not at straight gatherings, not at gay ones."

For the first time since I have met Elliott he looks genuinely unhappy.

Our house looks as it always does at night, expectant but recalcitrant, unable to give up its secrets. I push the door open. We take off our coats and pile into the kitchen. He collapses onto the sofa, legs in front of him, ramrod straight. "Do you have a hot water bottle? It was freezing in there. I guess Tudors didn't have central heating."

"Two," I say and hold them up. One is brick coloured, the other the blue-green of Prozac pills (although they are a long time in my past, thankfully). "Red or blue pill?"

"*The Matrix*." He grimaces. "We're living in it, aren't we?" He does not seem to expect an answer.

Over the rumble of the kettle I say, "This isn't what I imagined as an end to the evening."

"Did you think I was going to stay there and cruise?" A sharp, hurt note in his voice gives me pause. I am very good at reading the weather reports issued by actors, but Elliott is more mutable than most. "I don't know why men create such sexual factions," he says.

"You could find someone who doesn't do that."

He folds himself deeper into the sofa. "That's the hope. But where is he?"

"Straight people have the same dilemma. But there's a bigger pool to choose from, if you're in the lucky position of being able to choose."

"Are you saying you think of me as not straight?"

For a second I am confused. "No. I was making a false distinction. I'm sorry."

He sighs. "Sometimes I think I'm queer but not gay. As in, flexible. Or malleable. I don't fit into the gay male ecosystem."

I realize what has changed about him. He has actually grown while he has been away these three weeks. His limbs are longer. The angles of his face have hardened.

"Did you think of me, really?" he says finally. "While you were in Kenya?"

The air is suddenly squeezed out of me. I look up at the ceiling, as if Joanna is suspended there like one of the entities in *Poltergeist.* "Can you lower your voice? Yes, of course I thought of you. I missed you," I wheeze. "When I don't see you it feels like I've lost my right arm, and also a friend, and also a colleague, and something else."

His eyes are suddenly urgent. "What else?"

The grandfather clock Joanna inherited from her father strikes one, startling us out of our dense commitment to what we are about to say, or what I am about not to say, what I have said and cannot say.

"I hope you and I will make a truly exceptional film together. I think we have the chemistry to do it. I hope we'll have a long career together. I don't see it as one film." I think I am finished, then I say, "You are with me, always. I want you in my life."

"But not like this."

"Like what? It wouldn't last, we would resent each other. I wouldn't even know what to do. I could be accused of abuse. You're too young. I'm too old."

"You're afraid."

"Yes, I'm afraid."

Without knowing what I am about to do I rise and sit next to him on the sofa, the sofa Joanna and I bought from the Habitat fifteen years ago when Elliott was seven years old and in primary school in the 16th arrondisement. We sit, our thighs aligned but otherwise not touching, clutching our hot water bottles to our stomachs. The hum of his existence is my hum. I feel enveloped in a golden membrane that expands and contracts around us, like the breathing of a much more powerful being. A guardian spirit, if you are open to that.

The memory ignites into an image, sparked by the night, by Elliott's hands, which lie on the sofa like discarded sea anemones beside me. I am teaching Nathan to swim in the London Fields Lido, holding his eight-year-old body, wet and bony as a fish. He did not learn to swim in the Indian Ocean as I did. A note in the hum between Elliott and me has the same currency as my son's existence, perhaps even threatens to replace it. I can feel Nathan fighting to retain me. But there is the wine glass of Elliott's throat, the cardinal clarity between us, the air of optimism he injects inside me. *For night is the mechanism by which mere mind is converted into mere sexuality, mere sexuality into mere mind, and where these two abstractions hostile to life find rest is in recognizing each other.*

I quote Benjamin's line to Elliott. "That's about Karl Kraus. He advocated a continuous curbing and checking of the mind — that's Benjamin's words, not mine. Kraus kept a logbook of his attempt at controlling himself. He gave it the title *By Night*. He was afraid of the night, he had a *Threepenny Opera* concept of it, all whores and thieves and sex. So far, so bourgeois —"

Elliott cut in. "Do you think that kind of control is possible?"

"All writing is a form of control. Living — that's another matter."

"Writing *is* living, don't you think?"

It is three in the morning when I put four blankets over Elliott. The next morning Nathan knocks on our door. "Dad, there's a guy on the sofa." Beside me, Joanna does not open her eyes, but I can tell she is awake.

"That's Elliott," I mumble.

"Oh, okay. Shall I make him a coffee?"

"Only if he wants it."

Joanna stirs. "Doesn't he have a home to go to?"

"He does, but he's twenty-three and thinks nothing of spending the night on someone else's sofa."

The window leaks light. Sunrise is at 6:44, the World Clock says. We are in Aries. In three weeks it will be my birthday. I am on the cusp — of Aries and Taurus, but also of another invisible perimeter. "Aries isn't really a filmmaker's sign." Rachel's voice still ricochets in my head. "Too fiery and obdurate. Although it's the first sign in the Zodiac and it has an energy of beginnings and renewal." Then she looked at me with those swimming-pool eyes of hers and said the best thing anyone has ever said to me. "You have a rare ability to turn people's lives around."

I don't think of Rachel as much as I should, but she is here, suddenly, with me now. I feel her presence in the room. She died at fifty-six. We had been at university together, her mother and my mother were cousins. Lucy is named after her, taking her second name.

After university Rachel spent years in India learning Vedic astrology. With her death I lost my access to myself, to the future, which she had become good at predicting. I would consult her on finance, if production and distribution deals would come together (to this day Joanna knows nothing of this). I had a rule that I would never ask her about emotional issues, or my marriage. *Okay, this is business only*, Rachel put it, in her tart voice. She advised many studio heads, stockbrokers, A-list actors. Even though I was her friend she kept their confidences; I still don't know their names. It is reassuring to know there are others in the business as superstitious, as wary of fate, as I am, at least enough to check on its intentions from time to time.

Yes, the sun keeps rising and the day is 10.57 hours long. In three weeks' time it will be my birthday, the clocks will leap forward, and the worst will be over.

X

March brings another Arctic blast, which the media hyperbolizes as the "Beast from the East." Joanna has on BBC Radio 3. Large parts of Scotland at a standstill, people trapped on the M80 overnight. *Storm Emma brings blizzard conditions to southeast England.* Can't we just have cold weather? I ask Joanna. I miss the historical British restraint: *We're in for a spell of rather chilly weather.* Nathan informs me the hysteria has something to do with hashtags.

I put my hand on the wall to steady myself. The problem isn't physical, but that I feel I am trapped in a sinister conspiracy of forever winter and Brexit, which are the same creature in different forms. Joanna, who is in the kitchen doing something with puff pastry, snaps to attention. "I've made you an appointment, Tuesday, 3 p.m. Harley Street. Forget the NHS. Netflix is paying."

"I hate Tuesdays and I hate 3 p.m.," I say. "It's a dramatic dead zone."

"Good," she says, "because the last thing I want in the doctor's office is a drama."

"Do you really care, or are you only worried what you would say to the children, 'Sorry, kids, your dad's dead. He might have been saved but he had to wait six hours in the A&E at the Homerton.'"

She recoils. "Don't joke, Richard."

I am thinking, *If only I could sit with Elliott, if only I could bask in his confidence again, be snow-blinded by his pristine luck.*

The air in my lungs is burning. I walk back out the door, without my coat on. The door clicks shut before I realize I don't have my keys. I inhale the white air. *This is what I'm looking for*, I think, *an experience more real, denser, than actual life.*

Joanna opens the door, my keys in her hand. She is wearing her padded Barbour gilet. Her face looks . . . drawn, somehow. For the first time, since Lucy had whooping cough as a baby, maybe, I see real worry on her face. "Richard, it's freezing. Why are you going out in this terrible weather?"

"To avoid being derivative."

"Okay fine, but where are you going?"

"I don't know, I'll see if Elliott is up for a drink."

"What, now? With no notice?"

"I need to talk through scene 76."

"Why? Every other script you've written on your own. You never consulted me on a scene."

"Because he's my *lead actor*, he might have some insight." I am ashamed at the sarcastic list in my voice. I am ashamed of myself more generally.

"Well, text him before you leave the house, not after, otherwise your fingers will freeze." She hands me my set of keys. Before she shuts the door I cast her a look that she returns, carefully packaged in a knowledge I can't quite decode.

On the step I take out my phone and start to text but lose patience.

"Richard?" In his voice is a note of pleasure. It is unmistakable. You can tell a lot from the way a person answers the phone. Perhaps that's why no one wants to speak anymore. They don't want to give themselves away.

"I'm coming over."

"Okay." There is the slightest pause.

"Are you alone?"

"Yes, Mum's in Manchester with the show."

"Stay there."

"There's nowhere to go. Have you seen the news? There's snow in Milan, the Danube is iced over. It's colder than —"

"Than the Arctic. Yes, I know." I breathe into the phone before I know I will say it. "Elliott, please don't go away."

"I'll see you in a bit," he says. "I'll get us kebabs."

I have never felt cold like this before in London. Berlin cold, Prague cold, when the air stiffens as it passes through your nostrils. The minicab firm is booked out. I don't have Uber out of principle so I take the 106, which is still running, fleet red juggernauts gliding through streets of hushed, solemn snow, then from Finsbury Park the 29 toward Camden. I don't know what I will do when I arrive at Elliott's. Winter is not a season for romance, if romance is what you can call this hollow, urgent yearning.

The city is silent, as if someone has pressed a giant mute button. Even the sky is serene. I worry about the birds — how will the parrots and the two Egyptian geese who nose across the park near the house and who may or may not be stranded on their migratory route survive the night?

Joanna falls away behind me, as if I never met her in the cafeteria of the film school where we ate mashed potatoes and glutinous beef until Delia Smith and espresso impressed itself on the country's consciousness, as if I never saw our two children plucked from the portal between her thighs. I realize I could leave my whole life behind, watch it depart like a train sucked into the steppes, into high frozen plains where women in furs command golden eagles on their arms. I will not think, only pray. Pray I will survive the exile that is coming, from myself most of all.

◢

"Come in. I've got us a treat."

"I can't —" I close my eyes. There are tears on my eyelashes. They seem to have frozen.

He tugs me in and dusts the snow off my shoulders. "Man, you're shivering. Come on." He puts his arms around me and I remember how slight he is. He feels like a twig you could snap in two by mistake. "You're melting on me." He tugs my coat off. "I managed to download *À Nos Amours*. It's a pretty ropey copy but watchable."

A coal fire slumbers in the fireplace. Our kebabs, wrapped in their paper, sit like relay batons on the coffee table. He pulls me down beside him on the sofa. From behind me a squeak comes, then a burrowing nest of limbs. Mortimer, buried in the cushions again.

This is the scene: a coal fire, lava glow. Elliott and I, our faces periscopes above the sea of the sofa, looking at each other, thrilled and terrified and at home, the dog wedged between us at our bodies' most proximate edge, like a Victorian chaperone. Elliott's eyes morph from olive, to green, to blue. I find it impossible not to stare into them. Each time I find something new. Around his irises is a slender fuchsia ring.

On his laptop the film emerges from its thirty-four year-long slumber. It is 1984 or 1983, depending on what year Pialat filmed, and Sandrine Bonnaire is wrapped against the prow of a boat, a siren in white Mediterranean light as Klaus Nomi blasts through the speakers, only two years before he would disintegrate from AIDS. This Sandrine (as Suzanne) is sixteen, and not forty-seven, living in northern Paris, as she was the last time I saw her at the Césars. Cyril Collard, who also died of AIDS, is one of her boyfriends in the film, I'd forgotten that.

Elliott watches the opening sequence fixedly, awestruck at the grainy CinemaScope rapture of it.

"A whole generation had been handed a death sentence while this was being filmed, did you know that?"

"Richard, we can have the history lecture later."

"The most powerful scenes in this film are improvised, but also they're petrified of him. Pialat was a terror on set. Do you know why everyone looks so shocked in the dinner scene? Because Pialat altered the script. His character was supposed to have died at that point, all the actors were gathered around the table ready to emote with grief, and he shows up, the camera running. The shock is visible on their faces. He's really done a number on them, and they are furious. That's why his first line is —"

"Richard." Under the duvet he grips my hand.

Bonnaire's beautifully blunt face absorbs the camera, as if digesting it. Her coiled, taciturn silences convey more than most actors could do with the sharpest dialogue. There is no shadow of pretence between her and her character. We watch the scene where Pialat tells Suzanne he's leaving the marriage. She will lose him, she realizes that, and he is losing her, to sex, to adulthood. They are deeply sad but also curious about this loss, what effect it will have on them. But also you can see the bond between them, actor-director Pialat and his lead actress. Bonnaire is equal to him, somehow, despite the difference in their ages and experience. She pits her vitality against his experience and triumphs.

"This is the first film I saw that didn't look like a film at all, but real life," I say. "It was frightening."

Elliott leans forward and presses the pause button. He slides away from me, ever so slightly, and turns to regard me. His eyes are fully green now, the colour of old woollen blankets.

"Why was it frightening?"

"Because it shows what film can be — more supple, more honest than life. It made me want to be a director. But I didn't think I had the necessary ruthlessness to elicit that kind of performance from actors. I didn't have the vision, the conviction, the density. And because I understood this lack within myself, I refused to be a dilettante, but I also suspected I didn't possess the moral courage to imagine such total honesty into being. Most films escape you. You end up with a sort of infuriating simulacra of the movie you wanted to make, like a good twin being replaced by an evil one."

Elliott sits back and tilts his head to the ceiling. He exhales, sharp. "I'm not sure I like it. I'm sorry. It's too — intimate. I'm not ready for it. Is this really the kind of film you want to make, with *Benjamin*?"

For the first time, the difference in our ages is solidly apparent. He finds the emotional intensity and intimacy of the film squelchy, off-putting. I know why — there is no irony, no mobile phones, no mediation in this story of budding sexuality and family breakdown. It is like watching a pride of lions take down an elephant. You either look at the cruelty of life full-face, or you look away. Neither is right or wrong, but whichever you choose is a moral position.

I have a belated realization: Elliott is challenging me to look away — from myself.

"I've never felt I was totally convincing, as a man," I say. "My mother once said I was effeminate."

"Usually it's the father who says things like that."

"You haven't met my mother."

"What's she like?"

"Monica? She was very much in favour of boarding schools, put it that way. When I was twelve she sent me to the bush to stay with a Pokot family for a month, to toughen me up."

"What did that mean?"

"Well, for starters, Somali cattle rustlers run away when they see a Pokot coming. We bled the cattle before breakfast and then did target practice with bow and arrow before going out to hunt buffalo, then we slept on the ground at night — no blanket or pillow, let alone a tent. We used to say a prayer of sorts before going to sleep that translates as 'if the lion eats us tonight let us not lament but poison his guts.' Thank God I didn't stick around long enough to have to go through the initiation ceremony that turns boys into morani — that's warriors by the way."

Two fingers find the outer edge of my ear, where there is only cartilage. He pulses it between them, a sensation so pleasing I think I might explode. "You are a kind of warrior," he says. "You've fought to be where you are. You've made it through." He extracts his hand to pour us two shot glasses. "Whisky," he says. "With a *y*. For courage."

"Yes, courage."

Elliott has drawn the shutters across the windows of his mother's living room. Above them, the street lamps look ancient, like gaslight. Yellow snow falls across them.

I know I will soon be in his arms, bony and slight as they are, they will hold me as well as Joanna's have, and I will miss her for a moment, and I am so sorry — she is a better person than either of us, she is astute and resilient, a magus among men. I see her as the final shot before the credits roll, framed against a turbid Panavision landscape, some seedy river or wet shire, the landscape of this country I have tried and failed to make my own; she is of this place and she will go on and on, relentless, the drone shot of her lost to the troposphere, forever.

Elliott stands and holds out his hand. The time has come.

"What about the kebabs?"

"Are you hungry?"

"No."

"So, I'll put them in the fridge, or Mortimer will eat them." He carries them on their plate, opens the door, shoves them in. "Are you going to tell Joanna?"

"I'll send her a text. I'll say I can't get home. There's no buses now, too much snow."

"Snow in March, I wonder if that's good luck."

I say, "Anything can be good luck."

He comes closer and closer, eating up my field of vision. The house is freezing now, so there is no slow seduction or undressing arousal. We get into bed with our shirts and underwear on. At the last moment I remember to take off my socks.

"I don't know what I am doing," I say. "Which is not the same as what to do."

"But you do know."

A light spreads inside me. I have seen it before, in some of my shots, in the summer we filmed *Torch Song* in Berlin. It was thirty degrees every day and we lived on wurst and Alsatian wine. I have seen it in London, brick neon nights when I've stood in a high-vis on the side of a motorway with my crew, arranging a fantasy until blue soaked the sky and the buses returned to the streets, like migrating wildebeest coaxed home by thoughts of pasture. Or *The Grass Is Singing* shoot, the late Limpopo spring plated with the brass light of my childhood, fever trees on fire. Hale, beery light, the camera shoved to face the sun, a leering overdose, until we were drunk on it, all of us.

Elliott curves over me like a question mark. He is a bridge, taking me out of myself. We are striking out on a road black as liquorice, lit only by the moon.

Richard. My name in my own ears, in his voice.

"Could I ask you to do something?" I say.

"Sure."

"Could you just lie on top of me, for a while. I mean, just lie there."

He stretches out on top of me. He is light and heavy at once. I feel the air pressed out of me. I am being taken back to myself, more a plume of a spirit in the shape of an animal. An image-memory comes and goes, so quickly I can't quite see.

A mind-photograph of my father buried underneath an amber body, the lion's giant clamshell paws on either side of his neck. They would lie like that, when Siwezi was still young and not too heavy.

Elliott lays his face down on mine, cheek to cheek. His mouth is hot in my ear. "Like this?"

I say, "Like this."

Where there is character there will, with certainty, not be fate, and in the area of fate character will not be found.

He falls asleep. Gently I slide him off. He curls next to me on the bed. His hair on the pillow is alive, a separate animal that may get up and walk away. His scapulae jut out from his shoulders at right angles, like the legs of 1950s chairs. Who said it? *The greatest intimacy is not sex, but to watch someone sleeping.*

I reach for my phone, still in the pocket of my trousers, slide it under the cover, then up above him, searching for the angle, propped up on my elbow, the camera a miniature drone hovering over his face. In sleep his face has relaxed into another person's, his eyelashes lengthened until they seem to touch the tip of his nose. *Very few people know who they are, sexually.* Another unanchored line I have read, somewhere — an interview with a novelist, I think. I am always reading interviews with them, authors, those people who fashion an entire world all on their own. I too am looking for direction. The phone camera makes a shutter sound as I click. Some part of Elliott's brain registers it and alerts his eyelashes, which spasm briefly, then are still.

XI

Finally the day is here. Friends and colleagues are assembled like extras. The scene: INT. A birthday party — Richard's house.

Outside, London plane trees are thinking about blossoming, the cars belonging to our friends are parked far and wide, amongst them too high a BMW head count to suggest these are my friends only. Indeed, they belong to Joanna's line producers, financers, the sharp-suited men she meets in Soho private members clubs to seal the deal.

The background artists (American-speak for extras) are assembled in the living room, which looks somehow shabby next to these people. Our house is grumpy. It doesn't want to host the event. I wonder if it is sour grapes, if all its Victorian ghosts are not impressed that we regularly make it to fifty these days.

At midnight I became officially too old to die young. I have now outlived Benjamin by two years. How young he was, when he chose to take the pill that ended his life. The stresses of life in exile, in internment, life on the run, had taken their toll. Those gangsters called Nazis had taken away his peace of mind almost a decade before.

I go downstairs. I have been away from the party only five minutes, to get my breath and bearings and try to confront the feeling of solid loss that has overtaken me. I feel I am being crushed, but by what?

The first person I see is Elliott, billowing in and out of the crowd. From the vantage point of the stairs he appears to be floating, floating, a jellyfish. He perches on an armchair, talking to Nathan, who is outwardly friendly but also wary. I can tell only by the frequency emanating from my son, an invisible current which is also mine. *He knows*, I think, in some elusive emotional chamber. As for Elliott, he has thrown the "on" switch, and beams, lunging toward people, shaking their hands. You would never know how contemplative he is, how uncertain.

My eye seeks Elliott out again and again. As long as he is in the room I feel calm, but if he leaves my viewfinder a sharp abstract panic grips my lungs and I forget to breathe.

Joanna swirls by. She is wearing something by Whistles. The diamond she bought herself with Sky money to replace the modest wedding ring I was able to buy for her twenty-one years ago grips her fourth finger.

I can't commit to this scene, I realize. It has a wounded realism I don't like, it is too self-regarding. The air feels displaced, as if it were destined for somewhere else and has been re-routed here.

Nathan and Lucy idle by the breakfast bar, restlessly alighting between clumps of guests like discontented hummingbirds. Lucy looks the women and men up and down and, following her forensic gaze, I see the imperfections she has diagnosed: the creamy layer at the top of thighs visible through optimistically thin spring dresses, the unusual quantity of men who have the cultivated unkempt professor/blocked writer look of Michael Douglas in *Wonder Boys*.

Benjamin is here too, although he does not like parties. He is a one-person-at-a-time guy, a studious, intense conversationalist. Talking to more than one person at a time prods us into being performers, he thinks.

He approaches me with something that looks like a hot water flask in his hands. His fingers are white and cold. He wears no hat this time. A moss green tie drapes his neck, too tight, a noose.

"I'm going to tell you something." There is a note of finality in his voice.

"Oh yes?"

"I have a message, from Kraus. He did politics better than me. It is from his 1939 speech, written two months after the outbreak of war, 'In This Great Age.' 'In these times, when precisely what is happening could not be imagined, and when what must happen can no longer be imagined, and if it could it could not happen . . . in these unspeakable times, you can expect no word of my own from me.'"

"Thank you," I say. "I guess that's my birthday present?"

"Where are the canapés? I haven't eaten since 1940."

I watch him dissolve into the crowd.

I find Elliott in the kitchen, talking to Neil. His eyes have locked onto Elliott's in a way I don't like. I consider taking one of our Messermeister Meridian Elite Chef's knives from the drawer to hold it against the tattooed nape of his neck. *Hands off. He's mine.*

I prise Elliott away from Neil and open the door to the garden and its patio that has been a dark wedge all these winter months. We close the door and stand there alone in the night. There we watch the assembled guests through door and window to the kitchen and living room. They are fish, floating through aquaria, nibbling the meniscus of the moment, searching for substance. I expect all heads to turn toward us, an accusatory Greek chorus, but they go on talking to each other, chewing on canapés.

I tell Elliott the news I have been withholding from him for a week now: Neil and Joanna have failed to get the reinsurance in time. We will have to film next summer. We found out only yesterday. "I don't know if you'll be available," I say.

"I'll make myself available."

"Elliott." My use of his name startles him. I haven't used it often. We haven't needed names. "It's not that easy. You don't know what can happen in your life in a year."

"Why do you always say that to me? It's like you expect me to nominated for an Oscar or something. Not that much changes, Richard. I know you feel you're completely stuck, that your life is somehow over, but it's just not true. Your life is just beginning."

He looks into the garden at an oblique angle, toward everything and nothing, a triangulated, wilful sightline. He always does this when he needs to consider a difficult question. "I want to go through this experience, with you."

I breathe in, out, trying to control the clutch at my heart.

"I believe in this film," he says. "I know he is there. He is here."

Suddenly I am floating free of my life. I see my family in the room beyond me, still doggedly tethered to the earth. I feel a tenderness for them, a concern, but I can't get myself to descend back to their level.

I have what might be called an out-of-body experience. This me-Richard has a vision, a glowing orb, like the sun installation at the Tate by that Icelandic artist whose name he can never pronounce. He can see it coming, a superheated summer followed by a sinister, warm autumn. Time is broadcasting itself back to Richard, as if it knows he will no longer be in it.

And Richard, ever intuitive, has picked up this frequency and recognizes that the future is vacated of him. He starts hoarding moments and taking risks. Elliott is one of them. He represents Richard's increasingly fugitive present, the hungry nostalgia that has installed itself inside him.

He thinks, *I am trying to rectify my life.* It has been a life lived in-between: between black and white, Africa and Europe, cinema and literature, art and commerce and possibly — of late anyway — male and female. *The real life is the life you are living.* But is it true? He has invented his life. It is not a given, pre-defined realm. Desire has shaped the whole trajectory of it, but that was the desire to make films. Now he finds himself inhabiting a different, contrary, form of innocence. *I am not going deep enough*, he thinks. Then, *I may never get to the bottom.*

Elliott's eye falls upon me, again that disturbing gaze — young, old, open, shuttered, judicious. "It's your birthday, you shouldn't look so sad." He tries a smile.

"I feel I am drifting away. Or that my life is leaving me."

"Are you scared?"

"Terrified. But also free."

Elliott angles his body very slightly toward me. I feel his fingers grip mine, behind our backs. We are turned away from our darkling garden, which is coy tonight, as if it is witnessing a secret. We swing around to view the lit living room, a silhouette theatre in the deepening twilight, to see people moving back and forth, carrying champagne glasses like trophies, their heron necks.

"I like your friends."

"They're not too bad."

"Maybe we should go inside."

"I'm quite happy out here with you."

"You're turning into a curmudgeon."

"And you're patronizing me."

He smiles: hesitant, with a hint of secret in it. "I knew you'd say that."

Inside, beyond the calla lilies and the peonies Joanna has bought, her gaze falls on me. She sees our silhouettes, backlit by the garden light, Elliott's head at my shoulder. She sees the energy which encircles us. There is rain in her eyes. A cascading knowledge.

I have a vision of what I know to be a proximate future. It is June 2018. At 20:48 the skies are salmon pink. Half a dozen British Airways and one El Al jets arc over our house, threading the waypoints to the Heathrow runway. A black-and-yellow police helicopter circles above. A group of birds, white wings, black bodies, flies in an ellipse among the mobile mast towers that crown the Council estates around the park. Now a silver sky, mostly high cloud, moving fast from the southwest. The cathedral of London plane trees waves their balustrades in the wind.

Elliott and I float across the deck in the darkness, our arms brushing against each other, he opens the door and a thick heat overtakes me, a throng of lucid voices and the heady, iron smell of red wine. I have never been happier, because Elliott is beside me and my wife and children are in the kitchen, Benjamin is here too, sitting in my father's armchair in the corner, reading the *Frankfurter Zeitung*. Suddenly I can hear everyone's heartbeat as if they are separate instruments tuning up in an orchestra, beating in synchrony, all the moments when we first met each other intact in our memories, we know our points of origin. These friends' faces turn toward me and for a fraction of a second I register the look on their faces, which runs exactly, uncannily, like the cobalt rivers that coursed through my father's land, the Sosiani River sluicing down the plateau of Uasin Gishu, but no they are aghast, abrupt gargoyles, their mouths dripping like an Edvard Munch painting, and I feel it claim me all at once, the feral red oblivion.

PART II

DAY

I

"Cut. That's the scene. Thank you, everyone."

The actors fall out of pose and scatter into shade, gulping water. It is as if a tableau has been shattered; its pieces knock against her ankles.

She draws her sunglasses over her eyes. The grip has erected an umbrella the size of a small marquee for them. She joins Molly, the third AD, and Wedge and Anton underneath its shade, but still the sun bores through it. This year summer has come early to southern Italy: it is only late May and thirty degrees in the shade.

The fixer, Giulio, was right: Capri is overrun, even this early in the season. The tourists — mostly cruise ship groups and coach tours as far as she can tell — clump by the gelatería, requiring Molly to shoo them out of shot, but they keep coming back and congealing in the strict brew of heat, like flour added to soup.

"Joanna, how long do you want this track here?"; "Joanna, that line came out too downbeat, can we possibly go back in?"; "Joanna, it's Tony on the phone from LA, I think. Or maybe New Zealand. Wherever he is, it's 3 a.m."

She has never heard her own name spoken so often in her life. She has become a military strategist, ruthlessly making lists in her head before she has even formulated a thought. *Yes, no, yes.* She knew it would be like this. She'd been on set enough and seen directors doing more or less what she is doing now, but they'd made it look easy, especially Richard. Or easier.

Her head swims with heat, with hesitancies. They feel the same. She retreats to the shaded side of the street and lays her head against a peach-coloured wall. Its coolness sinks into her scalp.

Her gaze alights on Elliott in shirt and tie. Even in the phenomenal temperatures he never complains or flags. He seems to run not on ordinary kinesis but some kind of inner halogen. On the live monitor he literally glows. She wonders if this is what is called star quality, or if it is something more metaphysical.

Her crew flash up and down the narrow streets, doing her bidding. For a moment they have forgotten her. She looks up at the vertical cliffs that separate Capri from Anacapri, which sits a hundred and fifty metres higher up the island. Not even a goat could scale them. She absorbs the island's Bond villain appeal: the stark arroyos, the shattered, terraced land, a layer cake poised to crumble into the sea. The lair of Dr. No indeed. She'd read somewhere that the Emperor Tiberius brought his enemies here and hurled them into the sea off its six-hundred-metre-high cliffs.

The crew bus shuttles them between the two towns, twinned by their names, like the Arctic and Antarctica. It journeys along a hairpin road that genius or insane engineers built bolted on the side of the cliff face with concrete stanchions. After the first run she learns not to sit on the sea-view side of the bus. The leering drops into the ocean below make her sick to her stomach.

By late morning heat has claimed them all; so far she has been able to shoot only until 9 a.m., when the hordes arrive off the constant ferries from Naples. *Fifteen thousand people*, Anton shouts at her as the boom operator dismantles his stick, *every day!* They're mostly gone by 5 p.m., thank God. There are two Capris, she has learned: the dusk till 9 a.m. version, when something resembling ordinary life takes place, and the dayshift, nine till five, Decline and Fall of the Roman Empire version, featuring clots of Brazilians and Malaysians zombie-ing behind a green umbrella held aloft by their tour guide, slurping melting gelato.

After they finish the early morning shoot she trudges back up — there appears to be no horizontal ground on the island — to the villa they have rented for the cast and crew. Elliott materializes and falls into step beside her.

"You're fit."

She gives him a sideways look. "How can you tell?"

"We're walking up a seventy-degree slope and you're hardly puffing."

"Well, I run for an hour every day."

"Where?"

"Around London Fields. Although it's flat as a pancake so that hardly helps here."

He smiles. "Flat as a pancake. That's not English."

"I grew up in New Hampshire."

"You don't have an accent."

"I came back to Britain when I was twelve. I lost the accent quickly. Survival strategy."

They enter a narrow lane which switchbacks up the mountain. Now even she is puffing, although lightly.

"Is your family American?" he asks.

"No, but my father taught at a university there when we were little. Then he got a job at Durham and we came back."

They arrive at the villa. The cool hallway yawns; the house is too bored with the heat and the eternal crowds to welcome them. The whole island projects this same ennui, from the ice cream sellers who try to gouge her by giving her ten euros less change than she is owed to the Rolex watch shop assistants, close-shaven men who wear aviator sunglasses and smoke incessantly in the doorways of their customerless shops.

Without a word Elliott half floats, half galumphs, down the corridor. She feels a reluctant stab of guilt. He is a little afraid of her. She has done nothing to discourage this.

Giulio had found the villa. She likes the cool mesa of its patio, from which she can see the lower plateau of the island and beyond the Amalfi Coast. It is too hazy to see it, but she knows Vesuvius is there, muffled in the gauzy air. She will grab a couple of hours' sleep now, in the apex of the heat. She creeps into the centre of her bed, where she takes refuge from the island's verticality. The last couple of nights she has had dreams of falling, plummeting down cliff faces. She is worried she will throw herself out of bed during one of these nightmares.

As she falls asleep the known facts of her life dissolve. She tries to catch them before they disappear. She knows the date today is May 29, and that she had managed to solve the re-insurance issue and crew up in the five weeks since Richard's birthday. So many people had offered: *It's all we can do, Joanna.* Obstacles dismantled themselves, previous foes morphed into aghast helpers. She does not remember taking a specific deci-sion to go through with the film. Elliott was available; she secured Chloe Martin, the actress Richard had first on his list to play Asja, which was widely considered a miracle, as Chloe was riding a wave. She signed papers, inserted electronic sig-natures, she scanned documents and sent them to a herd of lawyers. It was as if someone had pressed a go button in the halls of fate.

Her phone buzzed. Nathan's face bloomed briefly on the screen, then receded. She'd call him later; she couldn't face it now, she needed rest. The children were in the stolid care of her mother, who made them latkes with caviar and vegan sandwiches of avocado and braised pumpkin. She was sure Nathan and Lucy were relieved to be in the twilight zone of Chiswick, away from Draft Manor, which had become a mausoleum, uninhabitable to all of them. New energies moved through the structure she once thought of as her home, unstable bursts of air under door-ways that ruffled her ankles, doors swinging wildly in invisible breezes. She'd twice had to get up in the night to check someone hadn't broken into the house.

In the dream she is falling into a lair of light. On her back she still feels the impress of the hand that has pushed her. She longs to return to the warmth of its touch. She tries to brace against the impact but is paralyzed. Green flutes, the sun's emerald corona before sunrise, surround her. Fear loosens her from her body. Above her the island recedes, its steep indigo cliffs, the seagulls who patrol them and whose calls will colonize most of her scenes so that she will need to have them digitally snuffed.

Richard would be there, at the vortex of the entity she was falling through. She was more sure of Richard's presence now. His voice directed her every moment. *Joanna, remember you'll have to do pickups, no matter how thorough you are. Joanna, send the dailies to Ellen by WeTransfer so she can see if you've got continuity issues; Joanna, on set the actor's needs trump your own. I warned you, Joanna,* he finishes in his agitated baritone, *a shoot is a state of rapture and terror. You have to make the right choice every second. In that way, making a film is exactly like falling in love.*

◪

"Action!"

She pulls her face from the throat of the live monitor. She has one chance to get the shot where Benjamin and Lacis walk through the ruins at the Villa Joris and are engulfed by a sudden cloud of spring butterflies. The butterflies had been sent from Sardinia in a box. "A one-shot shot," as Anton says.

"Elliott and Chloe, three steps to the right, you're off-centre."

Her voice sounds strange — hoarse, as if she was coming down with —

Joanna.

Joanna.

Joanna.

"Whoa —" Anton's balding, flushed face coheres from raw air. "Okay, everybody, we're taking a break."

Suddenly Molly is herding the actors and crew into a rectangle of shade and her hands are wrapped around a cold glass of soda water, how much later? A rupture has opened in time. An hour might have passed, or a minute.

Beside her, Anton's sunglasses fail to deflect the flare of Mediterranean sun. She sees herself in the reflection: middle-aged woman, skin crisped around the edges, a little long-faced, as Englishwomen of her background tend to be, under a white straw hat.

She swats Anton away. "I'm fine. It's just the heat."

"C'mon, Joanna. We need to get you checked out. You of all people know this."

"I'm not a producer here. Okay, not only."

Anton guides her, subtly, to a chair in a wicker forest of café patios. "I realize that. You're double-boss. But you also nearly passed out." The café owner had been unhappy with the shoot the previous day. He'd complained to Giulio about lost business. Now he sits beside her, fanning her face, saying, *Signora, signora, che cosa?*

"You haven't given yourself a chance to grieve."

"Oh spare me the Five Steps. I'm *working*. We're going to lay more track and do the piazzetta shots from an elevated angle," she says. "I want it to look as if someone is peering down."

"Are you sure?"

The truth is, she doesn't know. As she was filming, a strange thing was happening: scenes that looked utterly convincing when watched with the naked eye failed to translate themselves to the camera. When she viewed the rushes, they were dead as doornails. On the other hand, moments which appeared trite or overegged acquired a gutsy actuality in the live monitor. *You have to go with the camera's eye, not your own.* Richard had said this, in lectures and Q&As. She hadn't really understood what he meant until now. Why should the camera be a superior judge of authenticity? As if the camera, and not life, was in charge.

"Okay, we'll go again in twenty minutes." She stands. Anton reaches out, as if to take her elbow, but at the last moment snatches his hand back.

She walks across the square, conscious to keep a steady line, like a drunk driver doing the breathalyzer test on a highway. When she was a producer, no one questioned her right to raise money for a film. Now that she is behind the camera, her every decision is, if not questioned, then monitored.

Richard was right: filming is hell. Everything has to happen *now*. In replaying moments in her search for the perfect take, she has come to realize how mutable reality — if that is what you can call it — is, how easily it can be disrupted and channelled into different rivers. She has a newfound respect for the moment-to-moment ambush of actuality. She turns around, head inclined, to share this revelation with Richard.

Her feet drag underneath her, reluctant to leave the ground. She walks nonetheless, eyes behind outsize Sophia Loren sunglasses, a last-minute purchase in the Naples airport. *Get the actors to find their rhythm with the filler scenes first. Build up to the most emotionally demanding at the end. Don't leave your actors spent — they will never say so, but they will resent you for it. Don't put them through the wringer unless you have to.*

The walk to the piazzetta is short. The island is tiny, so much so that what look as if they should be kilometres on the map turn out to be only ten minutes away. She is constantly coming up against the island's edges and resenting them.

She and Elliott fall into step.

"How are you feeling?" he asks.

"Fine, just the heat and dehydration." She reconsiders. "Actually it's the crowds. I don't like having an audience."

"You just have to block them out."

They come to stand in front of a bookshop window. A sign, in English, is pasted to the window: *air conditioning*. From the window display a large coffee-table book stares out at them. It has a black-and-white cover and a purple border.

"*Amori et Dolori Sacrum: Capri — Un'Infinita Varietà*. A shrine to love and sorrow," Elliott translates.

"I don't see any sign of sorrow," she says. On its cover four bare-buttocked young men lounge on a terrace, beachball backsides, a leopard skin rug, taut hamstrings, as if they have just leapt off Greek amphorae. This was an island of sybarites."

"I love that word."

His voice floats toward and away from her. She puts her hand on the shelf. "I need to sit down."

He frowns. "You're not eating, are you?"

"I haven't been able to —"

"I know. I can't either. I've lost a stone since —"

"Okay," she barks. "Let's get back to work."

Elliott and Chloe take their places. They play the scene, their heads listing toward each other, Elliott-as-Benjamin repelled only by the perimeter of Chloe-as-Asja's straw boater hat.

Something is wrong, or at least not right. She can see they get on, Elliott and Chloe, but a vital spark, a latent ferocity, a subtext, is absent. Something is not ringing true. It registers as a note, thin, tinny, ringing in her ears.

"Elliott? Can I speak to you for a moment?" She takes him by the shoulder and steers them to a wedge of shade. "Consider the fact that Benjamin is married at this point. He is infatuated but also wary of this woman. He already knows she can change his life."

He nods, his face rapt and serious. "His infatuation is intellectual. Or political."

"Yes, exactly."

They did the scene again, and again. Two hours later, the crew wilting in the heat, she called it a day.

She returned to the villa to shower. In the late afternoon there was a knock on her door. She opened it to find Elliott there, perched on the edge of the hallway, as if he was about to do a runner.

"Would you like to have a drink?"

"Sure." Again she saw the dark note of fear in his gaze.

There were only two bars in Anacapri town. One had walls of plexiglass, like a giant cube, overlit and dominated by a flatscreen showing football. That night everyone was watching a man she knew to be the new prime minister. He reminded her of Emmanuel Macron, although this man's politics were very different.

They settled on the bar across the street, a marine-themed restaurant. Their table was a barrel. A lobster sculpture held their menu in its claws.

A harried waiter appeared. "A drink, signora?"

"Yes, sure." She was trying, and failing, not to drink on set.

"I don't know what I'm doing wrong," Elliott said. "No

matter how I try to wrap myself around the lines I can't find the right tone."

She told him what she knew of Richard's intentions: that Richard had wanted this whole section of the film to have the feel of halcyon days, a gilded period of suspension. And on the surface, it was: on this island Benjamin met the woman who was by all accounts the love of his life.

Infatuation is the worst possible thing that can happen to any human being, after lust. Richard spoke to her now from somewhere in her stomach. His script was full of the scald of infatuation: Benjamin's for Asja, Asja's for communism and, later, Benjamin's for the chance of escape and survival.

"He said something similar to me." Elliott flicked his eyes up to hers. There was an obscure challenge in them.

She did not know Elliott well, yet, but she had the profoundly disturbing sense of being bested by him, despite the fact he was half her age. She suspected Elliott had a much firmer grip on truth than she did. The resentment she felt at this was beyond any jealousy she had ever experienced. She was afraid he would perceive it and fear her more, or worse, pity her.

Elliott opened his mouth, closed it. She somehow knew he was about to speak about Richard. She'd noticed they were both reluctant to voice his name, like a taboo.

"Richard," he began, "wasn't sure how I could communicate Benjamin's sense of predestination, of doom even, apart from a permanent wistfulness of expression. Which neither of us wanted. So I've adopted a belligerent note, as if he is committed to outwitting his fate."

"I agree. Benjamin was hopeless at dealing with so-called real life — that's what everyone says, he himself admitted it — but if you look at how he manoeuvred himself around Europe those years, he was quite canny, staying with friends, never spending any money, always on the move, always looking for inspiration and finding it."

They fell into silence. They watched people pass, their eyes falling, she noticed, on the same places: the legs of girls tanned and thin, several of whom were speaking Russian; she caught fragments as they walked, or sauntered, savouring their own reflections in the glass-box bar opposite. Men passed, dragging their eyes like fishing nets over the bodies of the women. She had noted that the men of the island often had green or dark blue eyes. It seemed a local trait. They did not look entirely Latin.

She didn't know why she proffered what she said next. "I'm going to stay in Italy for a week after we wrap here."

She hadn't even told Neil this. Why was she confiding in Elliott? She wasn't quite convinced by his old-soul-in-new-clothes persona. A grain of distrust lay between them. They both knew it. But since Richard's death, a dizzying instinct to kamikaze her way through her future had gripped her. What did it matter now what she did or didn't do?

"Oh," Elliott said.

"There's a break before we go to Norwich and I've been asked to speak at a special screening of Richard's work. Two, actually, in Rome and in Milan."

"Which films are they showing?"

"*The Grass Is Singing* and *Torch Song*. They were part funded by Cine Italia. They heard I was in Italy and invited me. I thought, *Why not?*"

"Can I come?"

"What? No."

"I want to come. I'd like to say something, to do something. For Richard."

An energy moved between them. She didn't know what to call it. A thickening. "I don't know, Elliott. It's all been booked."

He did not protest or try to convince her.

"Richard's mother lives in Siena. I'm also going to see her." She didn't say *for the first time in a decade.*

"Richard sounded as if he wasn't close to his mother."

"Did he?" She did not quite say, *Why would he tell you that?* But she conveyed, with what remained of her wifely proprietorial gaze, something of the sentiment to Elliott.

"Yes." A pained note strained through his voice.

She felt a stab of shame. *Why are you being so mean to him? He's only a few years older than Nathan*, she told herself.

"Well, Monica is the last one standing in the family. Which is exactly how she likes it. So I'd better go and give her my condolences." She rose. "Shall we get some gelato?"

The gelatería was a few doors down. She watched as Elliott ordered, pistachio, no, cioccolata. He changed his mind three times, swaying between the banks of ice cream. The woman serving him indulged his indecision. He cast her a pained look. It occurred to her he might be experiencing a visitation, perhaps of grief, in these ice cream flavours. She has these too, in the most unexpected moments.

That night in her villa bedroom she tips into a precipitous darkness, more ravine than sleep. She shoots awake from a tiresome, over-obvious dream about trying to call Richard on her mobile phone and her fingers sliding off the screen, or not having enough credit.

She props herself up, arms rigid in front of her, her calf muscles cramping. She gets up and hobbles around the room to stretch them out. She has neglected to call her children. What kind of mother is she? The truth is, they are far from her thoughts, and safer and happier with her own mother than she had been. Since Richard had disappeared (this was how she thought of it), she had felt her claim on her children weaken. Yes, she has abandoned her children, and it served them right, because their father had abandoned her.

Her window looks out onto the Marina Piccola, the small harbour on the south side of the island. Speedboats gleam under a waxing moon; from afar they are small flint arrowheads poised to be flung across the Tyrrhenian Sea. The scene is bleached, unreal. Her life has taken on the same feeling, these past few weeks.

Only seven days after Richard's death she'd phoned Neil and said, "I'm taking over."

She can still hear Neil's intake of breath, the note of raspy horror in it. "But that's absolutely barmy, Joanna. Richard hasn't been in his urn for two days."

"Strike while the ashes are hot, isn't that what we do in this business?'

Another sigh, or sucking in. "I didn't think you had it in you."

Yes, she thinks, *just watch me. I am Medea*, snakes on the head — no, that was Medusa — someone tearing her hair out in a Greek play in any case, woman clothed in red robes, hectored by the cruelty of life. In any case, she is the deranged woman, standard issue unhinging-by-grief. Richard would be impressed. He'd refused to cast her in this role all the years they were together, thinking her the ultimate rationalist, and finally she became his creation. If she can keep up the performance, he will never be truly dead.

◢

The swimming pool at the Faro was hidden from view, below the lighthouse that gave it its name. They all arrived in the rental van Giulio had procured. Like most of the cars on the island, its paintwork had been scraped off in patches by encounters with the guard rail on the road that snaked down the sheer cliff.

They walked into an open-air bar. A woman wearing gold trainers welcomed them.

"Would you like a group discount?" Joanna looked behind her. She realized she had acquired an entourage, and that she was in charge of everything now, even leisure. Richard had warned her as much: *Everybody follows you around asking an endless stream of permissions to exist.*

She eyed the day price: twenty-five euros. "The thing is we are making a film on the island and we have a break." She gave an apologetic shrug, as if it were her fault, which of course it was.

The crew jostled behind her, excited as children to be going to the seaside. She slid her sunglasses over her eyes against the blare.

"Certamente, signora." The woman let them all in for ten euros each. They bustled past her, shedding clothes as they went. Within a second they were squabbling over the sun loungers.

A crash, like a piano falling inside her. This happened often now. She would be sailing along fine, oblivious on a sea of busyness, then suddenly this terrible descent.

Elliott took her elbow gingerly. Ahead of them, children leapt from rocks into the sea.

"Let's sit down." Elliott led her to a sun lounger.

Immediately, a waiter appeared with a menu. She forced her eyes to focus. *Zucchini flowers and buffalo mozzarella cheese salad, 26 euros. Local seared tuna, zucchini "scazece" with fresh mint, 28 euros.* "Jesus" — she handed the menu to Elliott — "there goes the catering budget."

"Per lei, signora? Y suo figlio?"

"He's not my son."

Elliott smiled at the waiter. "I'll just have an order of chips."

They turned as one to look out to sea. The crew were already in the sea, laughing, paddling, swimming. It had been the right call, to wrap for the day. They were all exhausted beyond the usual mania of a shoot, by the heat, the crowds, the island's *Prisoner of Zenda* energy.

There was no beach on the island, only a sloping concrete wharf with scores in its surface. Children patted up and down this, barefoot and dripping. The sea was an unusual colour and consistency, like dark green marble. Huge brutalist rocks rose directly from it. In the distance was — what? She challenged her poor southern Mediterranean geography: Sicily, Lampedusa, Tunisia. Or even Ibiza, where Benjamin also took refuge.

After Richard's death she returned to the biography of Benjamin she'd started reading, out of duty, when she was merely the producer. It was clear Benjamin had been unusually — for an effete urban intellectual — drawn to the wild landscapes of southern Europe. He'd spent years, all told, in Italy, southern France and on Ibiza. The late 1920s, years after the scenes they were filming now on the island, had outwardly been a time of difficultly for Benjamin, of economic strain, his hasty and costly divorce from his wife, Dora. Travel was his medicine, his biographers suggested, and there was something in the rugged vitality of the hot southern edge-lands which attracted him. She felt it too, being here, even from inside the inferno of a film shoot: a release into the gravity of reality, an odd sense of plummeting and flying at once.

A shout from the water hooked their attention — Chloe was being hurled into the water from the sturdy shoulders of Sean the grip.

"I don't think we're insured for that," she said. "Are you going in? The rest of them seem to be enjoying it."

"I think I'll just look for a while," Elliott said. "But you go."

She went to the change rooms, which were hewn out of sheer rock, as much of the island seemed to be. Into a locker she deposited her watch, her mobile. She'd only brought one swimsuit. A green bikini sat awkwardly on her pale hips. She'd lost weight, her hip bones and ribs were visible. She'd gone into Samantha's office two days before coming on the shoot and one of the junior casting directors had seen her coming out of the lift. *Joanna, you look fantastic!* Almost instantly she had covered her mouth and the colour had drained from her face. *I'm so sorry! I didn't mean — I'm so.* Joanna had said, *It's fine, it's fine,* absolving everyone of the discomfort of their pity.

She dropped the towel and made determined steps toward a ladder nestled among the dark basalt rocks. Elliott saw her hesitate. He cupped his hand against his mouth. "Go on, Joanna."

They exchanged a smile, sweet in its hesitancy, its tenderness. Her body recoiled in delight and shock from the sea, which was colder than she'd expected. She swam. Her hair unfurled itself from the braid she habitually wore on set. It Medusaed around her, a dark corona. Her breath underwater was suddenly loud, the breathing of giant sea creatures which may or may not circulate beneath her. The water was the granite colour of the island's rock and this harmony created the strange feeling that she was swimming through not liquid, but stone.

As she bobbed between the surface and underwater, her eye fastened on Elliott's pale figure, sitting bolt upright on the sun lounger. He held his hand over his forehead against the glare. She saw his eyes searching for her, tense, even anxious. She brought her hand up and waved at him, still uncertain if she was the object of his gaze. He waved back. The smile he gave her was familiar, not unlike Richard's. She really hadn't thought of it before, how alike they looked, both rangy, thin, their exaggerated eagle features.

She emerged from the water. Elliott held out her towel and put it round her shoulders.

"It was colder than I thought," she said. "You should go in."

"Okay." He stood, his chest so pale it looked like marble. He hesitated at the ladder. "You'll still be here when I get out?"

She blinked. "Yes, Elliott. I'll wait for you."

He swam away, splitting the water in swift strokes like knives.

◢

They shot for the rest of that week on the island. She could hardly keep up with the rushes and working out the adjustments to the shot list for the next day. She really needed a producer who wasn't herself to boss her around. She wished she'd asked

Neil to come on set and fuss in the background with his round architect's glasses, looking like a permanently disgruntled owl.

Yet she clipped through the scenes. They shot in the mornings, pre-cruise ship invasion, they rested in the afternoons, then resumed shooting from 5 to 8 p.m. Then they all peeled off to the lobster-themed bar, whose Argentine owner was accommodating, for dinner, sitting in a voluble table of fifteen. She was beginning to enjoy the island, she realized, just in time to leave it. This belatedness happened often in her life; she had the impression she was always arriving at understanding just slightly too late. It was as if time itself was reluctant to accommodate her.

On their last night on Capri they ate as a group above the town, on a terrace high against the mountain. Geese kept by the restaurant owners squawked in the moonlight. In the distance was the sea and, beyond it, the dark shadow of Ischia.

She stood. The table quietened. All eyes slid toward her.

"I want to thank everyone for your hard work pulling this off," she began. "I also want to thank you for bearing with me. I don't know that I am doing the job Richard would have done. But at least we are here, we are making this film."

She paused, to gather herself for what she was about to say.

"Richard used to say that shoots are violent experiences, when you are in charge of them, because suddenly there is no time, and what time there is is money, and you have no opportunity to really think and consider what you are doing, you just have to rely on everyone's professionalism and do it. He used to get two hours' sleep a night on set, he said, and even that was taken up with dreams about things going wrong. I used to think he was exaggerating, but now I understand. I want to thank you all for being here, for giving it your all. I ought to say we are doing this for Richard, but that would be sentimental. We are making this film for all time and for ourselves."

Fifteen faces looked up at her, all with the same expression, as if they had been cast as extras in the film they were shooting. She saw concern, and a shadow of something else she could not identify and which moved across their visages fleetly, on its way to another destination.

She sat down in silence, apart from the delicate honking of the geese in the wind.

Her eyes sought out Elliott, but he was not looking at her, or anyone. He raised his glass in a sidelong, offhand way. The unidentifiable shadow had left his features, but she finally located it in its trace — sorrow.

Sean, the grip, a sandy-haired man from Bristol with the lilt to prove it, raised a glass. "To Richard," he said. "To Joanna." It was the first time she'd heard their names leaning into each other since his death. "Hear, hear," a chorus of voices said, but Elliott's was not among them. He was looking off into the Mediterranean. She followed his eyes to where three cruise ships — lozenges aflame with light — tracked their way across the blackened sea.

II

rue to its name, the Frecciarossa train was a red arrow pointed toward Florence, hurtling so fast she was glad she was sitting forward. An Italian football team circulated around them, gigantic young men with bread-loaf quadriceps the same circumference as her waist. They were restless, orbiting the carriage constantly, spilling bottles of water, bumping her shoulder and then apologizing profusely, calf muscles flexing in the aisles.

The train streamed over cobalt rivers. As they moved northward the country became greener, less stoic. She looked out the window just in time to see a hill town materialize above the valley. A chocolate-coloured cathedral perched on a miniature mesa, houses huddled around it. She took out her phone and pressed Google Maps. The blue dot struggled to keep up with the airliner velocity of the train. Her instinct was right: Orvieto. The name rolled around in her mind, a brass bell ringing darkly.

She and Richard had had their first real argument there, one night in a thin pensione. It must have been in the year or two between film school and when they were married. *Getting married doesn't change anything.* This was the ethos amongst her friends, who had forgotten to get married or had done so only for tax and children and inheritance. But it had, for her. Being married had made her feel more welded to the world, a substantial individual, a grown-up.

The train slowed. They were in Florence already. Trains used to take forever. She remembered epic journeys she and Richard had done — when would they have been, when did they end? — when it had taken ages to get from Paris to Nice for Cannes, and London to Berlin had been a two-day journey.

A sign slid into view: *Santa Maria Novella.* She leapt up, tugging Elliott with her. "What's going on?" Elliott slid one headphone off his ear.

"We're here," she said.

They alighted, plunged into a throng of football players, who jumped up and down shouting unintelligible slogans. Elliott shot her a worried look. A riot, or what looked like a riot, was in progress on the platform.

"Maybe they've cancelled lots of trains," she said.

On the concourse were hundreds — maybe even a thousand — people. She'd been through the station more than once with Richard, en route to visit his mother. She couldn't remember ever seeing so many people. They craned their necks up to the departure board. No cancellations. People coagulated around them. She couldn't see an exit.

"Come on." She looked down to find that Elliott held her elbow between his thumb and fourth fingers, a delicate clutch, as if she were a piece of glass.

He pulled her through the knots of people. They passed under huge historical images of the train station, a Mussolini-era bunker, and past the giant poster for *Le Fiabe Incantate*, Disney on Ice, left over from Christmas. They emerged scowling against the sun, into a vast station forecourt. Three police cars and dozens of African men occupied the plaza. The contrast between the hordes in the station and the empty surrounds disoriented her. She felt her step falter.

"Joanna?" Once again, in Elliott's mouth the word sounded vaguely mistaken, as if she'd been given the wrong name at birth. "Are you okay?"

"Yes, just — there's so many people. I realize global population has doubled in my lifetime, I just didn't expect them all to be in the Florence train station."

Elliott shrugged. "I'm a millennial. Overcrowded European transport hubs are all I've ever known."

Yes, she thought, this was how it was now — ordinary human activity had the aspect of a furious demonstration, a political protest, but one conducted while licking ice cream and tending one's wheelie cases like flocks of recalcitrant sheep. *Get with the twenty-first century, Joanna*, she heard Richard's voice say from somewhere inside her.

A text arrived. Richard's mother had sent a driver, a neat, impatient man. He hustled them into the car, then drove through streets which were an outdoor version of the train station. Vast queues of people wearing sports shirts spaghettied around the city.

They sat, side by side, on a back seat that had the creamy feel of leather. She looked out the tinted window. "The sky in the north is so different." She hadn't meant to say it out loud.

Elliott pushed his headphones away. "Say again?"

"Richard used to say there was a knowing note in the Tuscan sky, as if it was perfectly aware it had been painted by a thousand masters. Smug sky, he called it."

"That sounds like Richard. He had a knack for projecting emotional states on to inanimate objects."

"He didn't think they were inanimate. Richard believed everything was sentient. We just haven't evolved sufficiently to see it."

They came off the autostrada onto a narrow road lined with rust-coloured buildings — the outskirts of Siena, already. But they'd been in the car only minutes, she was certain, rather than the hour it took from Florence. She was no judge of time anymore, apart from cinematic time. She had learned quickly to calculate the duration of the scenes she shot; she found she was elongating them, departing from Richard's script to frame wistful moments her actors were only half-aware of inhabiting: temps mort, dead time, a term she had always loved, invented by the French nouvelle vague masters, who kept the camera rolling when their actors thought they'd finished acting.

"I'd better give you a primer on Richard's mother."

She relayed to Elliott the digested version of Monica's life. She was Italian, quasi-aristocracy. She migrated to Kenya with her parents, kicking and screaming at being ejected from their villa in Bergamo, at age six. The parents bought a ranch. They parents sold a ranch. In between the parents made a fortune exporting the meat of their mixed-herd cattle and Monica had become an Italian/Kenyan hybrid, and also beautiful. She absorbed something of the fierce loyalties and enmities of the people she grew up amongst, the Borana and the Pokot, or perhaps these metallic extremes had always been part of her basic character. She was both aristocratic and wild, a combination that never failed to ensnare men. After her marriage to Richard's father foundered nearly three decades ago, she returned to Italy and bought an urban palazzo with her inheritance.

Joanna had met Monica only six or seven times in the course of her twenty-two-year marriage to Richard. Monica had come to London only once. She'd stayed at the Savoy and worn sunglasses indoors. She considered filmmakers sordid. She used that word, exactly.

"So why are we visiting her?" Elliott asked, when she had finished.

"I don't know. Something primal. I have to honour Richard." She shot a glance across the back seat at him. *Help me out here.*

The car wound up hairpin turns. Clumps of students carrying the yellow backpacks of a foreign language school came into view. They paused at the door to the palazzo. She put down her bag and sighed. Elliott's eyes followed her, a flicker of anxiety in them. He was wearing a T-shirt and a random sweatshirt Chloe had given him on set, *Texas A&M University*. His earphones/mufflers rested around his neck. His bag — Gucci, a gift from his mother — was the only clue that he might not be an ordinary mortal. She was tall, for a woman, but he matched her. Elliott might even be superseding her, she considered, still growing at a supernatural rate as they stood in the street, like bamboo.

"Pronto?" Monica's voice fuzzed through the intercom, imperious in a single syllable.

They entered the cavern that led from the front door to a courtyard. A moped was parked there. A slim ginger cat appeared from nowhere and eyed them. Ahead, at the end of the staircase, a thin woman stood. She wore suede loafers, a navy blazer, a shirt made professionally white by acres of dry-cleaners. Her hair was blond and cut close to her face. Joanna had not seen Richard's mother in enough years that she was recognizable but also off-centre. She was beginning to look like someone else.

Monica turned, rigid as a lighthouse, to regard Elliott.

He thrust his hand out. "I am — I was — a friend of Richard's."

Joanna watched Monica's eyes absorb this information. The moment possessed the density of film. She could have filmed the scene herself: Monica, you both accept and reject his explanation. Convey that you are not taking this young man at face value, that you have an almost animal instinct for the truth and the lie, soldered together, in his statement. You know in the pit of your stomach that what this young man tells you is not the whole story. Yet you must accept him, because your son is dead, and this young man was your son's friend. You must succumb to an old, genetic loyalty.

Then she would say: Elliott, you had intended to seduce this woman with your most available advantages — youth and beauty. At the last instant you abandon this strategy. You are captured by a column of sorrow within her. Confronted with the person who made his bones, you realize for the first time that Richard really is dead.

"And your name?" Monica's tones are mellifluous, her perfect English accent, colonial version, intact.

"Elliott." His voice was full of deference, but also a note of mild warning.

They mounted a short flight of stairs. Monica turned a set of keys, jailor-thick, attached to a long green ribbon which trailed on the floor. She beckoned them into a room where a green lamp was lit, even though it was afternoon. There a mustard-covered divan was strewn with unopened post.

Monica shocked them both by turning around and giving Joanna a surprisingly tight hug. "I'm so glad you've come."

"It's just a short visit. We were in Rome yesterday and we have to be in Milan in —"

"Yes, I know, I read the email. Let me show you to your rooms. Joanna, you're alright to stay in Richard's room?"

Her blood froze — the blood actually halted in her veins.

"Of course."

They followed Monica down a narrow staircase. She and Elliott poked their heads around the door in unison. A cricket bat hung on the wall. On the bookshelf was a raft of books on Italian cinema, in Italian. A giant antique wardrobe would, if opened, yield up Richard's shirts, unworn since early 1980s.

"Elliott, I'll give you the study. It is dark but has a comfortable bed."

"Thank you," he said.

Monica planted one suede loafer on the bottom step. "I'll leave you to it. Come up when you are ready."

Together, they inched into Richard's room. She opened the blue wooden shutters. The window looked onto the back garden of the palazzo. Lime, lemon and peach trees stared back at them.

Elliott cast a look over his shoulder, rose and closed the door.

"She doesn't seem like Richard's mother," he whispered. "I can't see him in her."

"Richard was a photocopy of his father," she replied. "The genes followed the male line, Richard always said. Nathan looks exactly like his paternal grandfather."

Elliott stood, lost, in the centre of the room. How thin he was. Like her, he had lost weight on the shoot. Everyone had, shooting for hours in the sun, walking the ski-slope inclines of Capri, until they all looked like sticks of kindling.

"I have this feeling we're in a game, a sort of simulation," he said.

"We are." Her voice was unhappy. "It's called reality."

Later, they presented themselves in the upstairs kitchen. Monica had changed. She was dressed casually, for her at least, in a bouclé jacket and another intimidatingly perfect blouse.

"Would you like a croissant?"

She pulled away.

"Come on, Joanna, it's not the devil." In Monica's accent the word *devil* flipped back and forth like a fish reeled onto a deck. "I never had to worry about my weight. I always had a perfect figure."

Good for you, Joanna thought.

"I need to see my lawyer now," Monica said. "We could meet for supper. Take the day to explore the city." Monica handed her a set of complicated keys. "Here, so you two can be independent. By the way, how is the film going? You are in production?"

"We've just finished in Capri. We have couple of weeks, then we resume in the UK."

Monica's eyes raked over her body. "I must say the director's life seems to suit you Joanna. You look better than you have in years."

"Thanks."

"It is Richard's film, is it?"

"It *was* Richard's film."

His mother turned and, without another word, left. Joanna couldn't quite believe it, but she heard the sound that confirmed the door to the palazzo closing, then the bang of the gate at the bottom of the stairs.

Stranded at the table, they both exhaled.

"Okay, so that was par for the course with Monica. I say something wrong, she gives me the silent treatment. She then issues a seeming non-sequitur which functions as a piercing metaphor. You've been clenching your jaw."

"Yeah." He blew out a breath.

"Come on, I'll show you Richard's favourite places in town."

Elliott stopped in front of a photograph hung in the museum room, above the mustard divan. In it, a dark-skinned young man with Richard's eyes stared out. Elliott moved closer to the photograph, squinting.

"That's Nico."

The name exited Joanna's mouth rustily, through lack of use. It had become the name of a stranger. She'd never met Richard's brother, he had been dead for three years by the time Richard moved to the UK.

"What happened to him?"

"He was stung by an Africanized bee when he was young. They didn't know he was allergic."

Elliott drew back. "He never mentioned a brother."

"No? Well he's been dead a long time."

The photograph stared back at her, at them. *What would Richard have become had I lived?* This was its question, and the reason both she and Richard had always avoided looking at it, even if Monica had placed it like a sentry to the door of the house.

"Where are the pictures of Richard?" Elliott asked.

"There aren't any."

As they walked down the stairs, past the interior courtyard and the watchful ginger cat, she felt haunted by the unfamiliar phantom of Nico. There had always been a spectral dimension to her husband. It was one of the many reasons he made films, perhaps, to feed the ghost of his brother.

Outside, they joined a flow of people walking down the Via Camollia. The narrow streets of the city funnelled people into processions. Richard had always thought the city design claustrophobic and manipulative.

She took Elliott to see the view from the fortezza, the walled gardens overlooking the city. They leaned over russet ramparts. Raised islets rose out of a dull mist. The branches of a lemon tree draped over them. Small, hard lemons brushed their shoulders.

"Tuscany looks like the ocean," he said.

She had thought this too, but had never found the words to describe it.

"There was a scene just like this now, in *Voyagers*," she said. "He filmed part of it here —" She gestured down a long, thin avenue of trees. "It's his story, really: a boy grows up in Africa, hears the siren call of culture, has to leave Africa to find it, realizes he can leave Africa but Africa is inside him, he will never dislodge it. He comes to Europe and meets a family he never knew he had. But he will never be European, Europe will always be an enigma to him, no matter if his mother is Italian and he makes films about people trying to find themselves in an ocean of others."

Elliott's gaze was fixed far beyond the exclamation points of Tuscan pines, the smoky palazzos studding the hills. There was an ephemeral vein to Elliott, she realized. Richard had said as much. He was the sort of person of whom people said or thought, *He is not quite of this world.*

They carried on through ochre alleyways. A painting of a goose in a shop window caught their attention. It was draped in a green-and-red flag. The goose was papal, regal in its gooseness. They stood in the window and regarded it, their reflections judging them. She was as Monica said: tanned, thinner than usual. Elliott looked like any other young man in Siena, dressed in a baseball cap, jeans and trainers. He had the ability to disappear into others, as all actors do, she observed, but also something of an uncanny ability to blend into humanity in the abstract. If you passed him on the street, you would not think he was anything special.

When they emerged onto the piazza of the cathedral Elliott came to a halt. "Wow."

"Yes," she agreed. "Wow."

Even Richard, who hated churches, was in awe of the cathedral's rose-and-onyx striations. She had to hand it to the cathedral, it had charisma.

She bought them tickets. Once inside, the obligatory tourist throng that was everywhere in Italy dispersed in the gigantic interior. A man in a striped shirt, its horizontal pattern matching the marbled columns of the cathedral so perfectly he almost disappeared, took pictures of himself against them, tiled in marble of alternating white and verdigris.

She and Elliott separated. She stood beside what she thought might be called the baptismal font (her church vocabulary was terrible). There was something modern, almost art nouveau, in its design. It was an immersion chamber, somewhere for divers to decompress or astronauts to learn how to deal with zero gravity.

She manoeuvred around people wearing shorts and sat in a pew. From there she watched Elliott perambulate, head clutched between headphones. They came together again under the cupola, lit by a pentagram of spotlights. In the centre an eye of light, platinum-bright, shone through.

"I never liked churches much," she said.

"And now?"

"Now I imagine I might see Richard in them, that they're some kind of zone of encounter between the living and the dead."

Elliott's eyes assumed the dark green marble of the cathedral. Swirls of people gathered and dispersed around them. "Did you love Richard always?"

"No," she said, straight away, relieved that someone had finally asked the right question. "Not always. But I do now."

◢

"This is not normal."

"What is not normal?" Joanna asked.

Monica looked at her as if she were a simpleton. "It's been so cold. It's May. This is Tuscany."

Joanna and Elliott sat in garden chairs, Elliott's face hidden behind a copy of *The Divine Comedy* he'd found on Richard's childhood bookshelves. Joanna watched as Monica stalked the garden, a cup of herbal tea in her hands. She knew it was herbal because she could see the tag peeping over the rim: valerian. Monica had never slept well. She remembered Richard telling her his mother dated her insomnia to her years in Kenya, up all night every night waiting for cattle rustlers to burst through the door.

Monica's arrow eye found her. "I didn't come to the funeral because you didn't have one, in case you are wondering."

"Richard wanted to be cremated."

"I will never have a resting place where I can visit my son."

A sudden wind breached the garden walls and cut through Joanna's thin leather jacket. Her thoughts were suddenly abrupt and confused. *It is her right to say that, as a mother to Richard's mother is one of those people with no internal rear-view mirror. She has no actual conception of herself as part of a suite of beings. She is the only person in the world.* Yet she had a horrifying animal magnetism, Joanna thought, a bit like Donald Trump. She watched now as the sun latched onto Monica's face in a deliberate way, as if determined that Joanna should know how papery her skin is, how mottled by moth-shaped sunspots. Monica's green eyes found her. They were slightly iridescent, like the insides of mussel shells.

"Why have you come here?"

The question was meant for her. Even so, beside her, behind Richard's Dante, she felt Elliott stiffen. He lay the book on his knees and unfurled his shoulders, sitting straight in his chair. He turned his gaze toward Monica. His eyes deepened, not in colour but density. He looked instantly ten years older.

"Because I was filming in Italy and you said you wanted to see me."

"Where are Nathan and Lucy? Why have you brought him and not them?" Monica's beacon face, those proud eyes, the eyes of a wounded aristocrat, bore into Elliott's face with the density and precision of envy.

"Monica, Elliott is here out of respect for Richard."

She was tugged back to the moment, when would it have been? Sometime in late January, when Elliott met Nathan and Lucy for the first time. He had come to the house to run through the script with Richard. He hadn't yet been signed to the film. It was also the first time she'd met him. She'd noticed immediately a wariness on Nathan's part, a charged instinctive dispute between her son and Elliott. Lucy gave Elliott quick, astonished looks out of the corners of her eyes and followed her brother's lead. Elliott had dealt with it well at the time, she thought, the three of them peering at him like a Greek chorus from the darkened wings of the kitchen, waiting for him to reveal his tragic flaw.

"Nathan is doing A levels," she explained. "My mother is taking care of them."

Monica gave her a steady look. "Will he pass his exams? Given that his father has just died?"

What's it to you? This is the most interest you've ever taken in your grandson, she said, but not aloud.

"It was his decision. He thought it would help him, to have to concentrate on his future." Joanna followed this with an impromptu confession: "I'm proud of him."

Monica did not want to eat, she informed them, so Joanna took Elliott to the osteria opposite the house. They sat on the pavement. She ordered them both large glasses of Sangiovese.

"Sorry, you're drinking whether you like it or not," she said. "Could you take off your sunglasses please? I find it hard to talk to people if I can't see their eyes."

She watched his face flinch, absorbing her rebuke. His hand swept the glasses from his eyes. She could watch his face all day, she realized, it was like a lion on the savannah, circling its prey, although in a detached, intellectual manner that had nothing to do with devoural.

In a second her annoyance vanished and was replaced by trepidation, for her but mostly for Elliott, that throughout his life people would fall into the same fascination, and in their rapture they would hurt him.

"I thought it was going to be alright," he said.

"Yes, me too. But Monica's treacherous. A snake. That's Richard by the way, on his own mother, so don't think I'm anything more of a cow than I've already been to you."

"She's not happy, is she?"

"I can see why not — a divorce, a son killed in a freak accident, another son newly . . . dead." She let the word wheeze out of her. "But she doesn't do herself any favours. She just doesn't like people very much."

The wine coursed through her body. She felt marginally better.

"I'm enjoying being here," he said. "I mean in Italy, with you. Despite everything. I can't explain why."

"I'll take that as a compliment."

She did something she didn't realize she was about to do. Her hand found his across the table. She gripped his fingers, lightly. They were cool and pulsated very slightly with a nameless energy. "Thank you for coming. Now that you're here I'm so — grateful. I don't know what I was thinking, planning to do this on my own."

He did not pull his hand away. "For me it's a continuum

of the shoot. I don't want it ever to stop. I mean, it's not easy, what we're doing. But it's the only thing that feels real, to me. I can only locate myself when I'm on camera. But I need to start living, soon, I'm aware of that, to really live, off-screen. I can't play at living for my entire life."

"'The only real life is the one we are living.'" She released his hand. "Richard, again. He struggled to live outside his work. When he was filming I lived with a ghost, he was never home. When he wasn't filming he only lived to get back on set. I tried to bring him back to the now, to say, 'Nathan needs new Reeboks for school'; 'We haven't been on holiday in three years and don't count the time we flew them to Australia when you were AD on *Red Sand Sea*, the children don't like visiting you on set because you're there but you're never there.'"

She stopped. She missed Richard, she mourned him. But she was also soaked in regret for what and who she had been. Now that Richard was dead, she was fully exposed to herself. There was no buffer anymore between her and her ambitions. She had gone into film school wanting to be a director and come out a producer, in part because Richard was the more convincing creator — in touch with his emotions, scattershot, wayward, instinctive. He relied on his feelings, if that is what you could call the weather that passes through us, she considered, whereas she interrogated this realm mercilessly: *What are you doing inside me, why should I follow your lead? Will you leave me alone, please?*

She discovered she was a good organizer, she had a knack for the business of filmmaking, she enjoyed working behind the scenes. She didn't have the talent or charisma to be in the thick of other people's emotional fields, to galvanize them into constructing a different life. It was not necessarily a gender issue, but men had had millennia, thousands and thousands of unseen and unrecorded years, to perfect their assault on reality. She would only ever be playing catch-up.

Her Italian was good enough to overhear a comment made at the neighbouring table. There, a woman not unlike Monica — older, regal, well dressed — said to her companion, another woman: "She used to be very beautiful, but now as you could see she is ruined. Her body, though, is perfect."

It was harsh, such talk of ruin among women. She can see it coming, for the first time in her life; someday someone will say the same of her.

She found Elliott's gaze on her. Again, she had the disturbing sense of being looked at by an intelligence far older than the body it inhabited. How can she explain to Elliott that death was never in the picture before. It was never part of her life. It had been a fog bank viewed out to sea. It might never make landfall.

They finish their wine, watching people in duffel coats stream by them down Via Camollia, a stream of images and shadows. It is the first time she has been in Tuscany when it is gloomy and cold. The planet itself is punishing them, this is what she thinks, for their addiction to profit. She can't really blame it. But nor can she fully accept the fact that she has to confront the task of imagining the end of the world in order to have a chance of saving it. She has to believe life will continue, the planet and civilization both; she has to find a way to look forward to being in the world.

An epic gust of loneliness rattles through her. She is not at home here, amongst the Tuscan aristocrats, but she doesn't want to return to Britain. She doesn't know where home is suddenly. She fears a catastrophe for her country. For the first time in her life she finds herself praying not for herself, but for her people, collectively, to be saved from the horrendous historical error of Brexit. These cold nights she lies rigid in Richard's childhood bed, as if sitting vigil, Captain Scott of the Antarctic's entreaty booming through her mind: *for God's sake look after our people.*

III

"What a period piece." She threw her coat on. "Why have they staged it as if it were the 1940s?"

"Joanna, in Yorkshire the 1980s *were* the 1940s."

It was mid-March. They had gone to see *The York Realist* at the Donmar. Richard knew the director, who had given them house seats.

"The story architecture doesn't really stack up," Richard muttered as they descended the stairs and spilled onto the Covent Garden pavement dusted with snow. "Christ, it's mid-March. Not to be confused with *Middlemarch*," he grimaced in her direction, "but will it ever stop snowing?" He tugged on his flat-cap hat that she always begged him not to wear. It made him look like a racehorse trainer, or Tony Benn.

"I don't understand what's keeping them apart," he went on. "Yes, commitment to place, yes, the weird thrall of convention. But it's the AIDS era. It's not mentioned at all. Why didn't they stage the Mystery play? That would have made the moral equivalence more apparent."

She didn't comment. She was used to his barrage of criticism, post-play, post-film, post-anything. Richard had turned on his phone the moment the play was over. She remembered that now.

"Are you expecting a call?"

"They could have shown more physical intimacy," he said.

She had ignored the fact that he ignored her. Still, a little bell of alarm had sounded, somewhere in her stomach.

They crossed the road to Belgo. Earlham Street was hemmed in white, as if someone had drawn the street in chalk. They descended into the cave-like restaurant. Richard asked for them to be moved away from the hordes of twentysomethings drinking raspberry beer. Even so it was pandemonium. Every single person around them was talking, no, shouting, into their mobile phones. Others laugh-shouted, so loud it sounded like gunfire, their mouths open, the strict lilies of their throats held up, as if in sacrifice.

She began to regret their choice. It would be too loud for the intimate talk she needed to have with him. This need — if that was the word, it was more a vague anxiety — had pressed itself on her for days now. She'd been waiting for Richard to stop writing, waiting for the moment.

"So, we haven't had a chance to talk," she began.

Richard was scanning the menu. "What about the Thai mussels, that's what I always get. Wait, March doesn't have an *r* at the end. Do you think I should get chicken?"

"Richard."

He put down the menu and placed his chin in his hands, supported by his elbows on the table, a gesture she had never seen before, in all their years together. "Sorry, what?"

"About Elliott. I asked what you know about him, since we seem to have signed him to the film."

A dutiful expression overtook his features. This meant she was being a chore, but he would humour her. "He told me about his father, finally. He was British. Worked for the UN, then for a private business consultancy in London specializing in technology. He was shot dead in Luanda, when Elliott was fifteen. He has no brothers or sisters. His mother's career has gone from strength to strength. She's never had another relationship, not that Elliott knows about. His father's death detonated a grenade beneath them and they are still picking up the pieces."

"And school? Where was he educated?"

"Paris, initially, then the Lycée Charles de Gaulle here. He started getting roles when he was fourteen or fifteen. He took a year longer than the rest of his class to get his IB. He's good at art, loves collage and ceramics, but bad at math. He liked chemistry. Somehow they forgot to teach him European history but he says he avoided it too. His family is too implicated. He didn't want to know."

"What do you mean, implicated? Were they Nazis?"

"The opposite. One grandfather is Armenian, the other French. The French grandfather was shot during the war. He didn't tell me how, or where."

She had an image of Elliott, lined up in front of a firing squad. "A father and a grandfather shot dead," she said.

"That's the sum of it."

She thought for a moment before asking her question. She was afraid of its answer, truth be told, but she posed it anyway. "Do you trust him?"

"Yes, absolutely. He's young and emotionally volatile but he doesn't have any malice. Of that I'm sure."

"The young are always ruthless," she said.

She could not identify the source of her unease with Elliott, then. She did her usual professional arithmetic: Elliott needs Richard and more than the other way around, at this juncture in their careers. Elliott himself is polite, intelligent, fiercely so. He wears his emotional intensity lightly. He is maybe a little fey. But lately the faintest whiff of evasion has begun to emanate from Richard, a thin flume of smoke. It only appeared around Elliott, or at the mention of his name.

He squinted at her out of the cavern darkness. "I want to do the scout myself in Capri. Just after my birthday. The light will be too severe any later."

"We need the escrow first, Richard."

"I'm working on it."

"His agent wants more money, Neil said."

"Yes, everyone knows Elliott's on the up. The next Tom Hiddleston, etcetera. But he's not motivated by money."

"Why? Does his mother have a secret fortune?"

"Yes, it's called a three-storey house in Kentish Town."

A folding took place inside her. This was what others saw as her determination, a steely, masculine manoeuvre. For her, though, it was self-preservation. "Why is he doing this film?"

"Because he believes in it."

"He's too young to play Benjamin, you know that, Richard. Why have you cast him?"

Finally she'd said it.

"I don't think you're right about that." There was a note of gravel in Richard's voice, like a car skidding. It made her slightly afraid. "He has tremendous gravitas, more than anyone I've met, including people twice his age. And he's less mercenary than you think." She knew he meant *less mercenary than you*.

After dinner they had taken the 26 bus from Aldwych. She looked out the window as the bus wound its way through the city — snow-laced car roofs, smokers huddled outside the Reliance on the corner of Curtain Road, still going strong after how many years? She remembered when it was the only pub in a wasteland of grim warehouses. The transformation of Shoreditch was a constant reminder that her life has not moved on, somehow. She had tried and failed to fight the entropy that makes up ninety-nine percent of existence. There will be no grand narrative to look back on, she realized, only the television she has produced, Richard's films she has produced, the children she has produced. They will all forget her.

"I feel like we're twenty years older than anyone else on this bus," she said.

"That's because we are."

She looked at her husband, really looked at him, for the first time in months. She had a vision of a road, suddenly, a wide, tarmacked ribbon that narrowed and narrowed, until it disappeared in a spit of sand.

She drew a breath. "I'm worried too, Richard, I just don't show it. Russians being killed on our soil. The ongoing cataclysm of Brexit, which is just another goal for Putin's team. For the first time in my life I'm really, really unhappy to be British. For the first time in my life I'm really, really unhappy full stop."

Richard did not meet her pleading gaze. He looked straight ahead as the ex-warehouses and stark white churches of the district melted into the night. "That's why it's important to do this film now," he said. "I need to assuage this feeling of utter doom." He looked at her, his grey-green eyes inflected with a new note, hard, like crushed diamonds. "Truth be told, Joanna, I feel like I'm going to die. But I want to live. I'm trying to live. Please let me."

"Does it ever occur to you that I feel the same? Exactly the same?"

"You do?"

She lowered her voice. You never knew what people would say, or think, or do these days, although their fellow passengers were all plugged into earphones of some description.

"I feel history has turned against me," she whispered. "At least you're still European, you've got an Italian passport."

As she said this, her breaths seemed to stab her in the lungs. She was so angry, so epically furious, she might not be able to take another breath. Something precious had been stolen from her, and it was not only citizenship, about rights and passports, but the end of a way of being, a state of mind.

"King Edward's Road," said the bus, in its digital voice.

They tumbled off the bus, bouncing contently off the edges of each other's bodies. In those days before Richard died, Joanna remembers moments like these, moments of a nondescript harmony. But also a feeling of separateness — as if she were detaching, slowly, from the city, from her history, from herself. Spring was a tangible presence, but her mind and body were still in winter lockdown. She had the sensation of being at an invisible median, like the imaginary line that ran through Greenwich only a few kilometres away. Halfway between winter and summer, between life and death.

London, the sleeping beast. That night on their walk home she and Richard took in the *Waste Land* view of the city, stretched out over bleak hills, a spectral octopus, its many tentacles studded with suburbs and faux-villages under an ermine sky. The loneliness she felt struck her almost as a premonition.

The next morning they were having breakfast, reading the *Guardian* on their separate screens.

"The Skirpals look like they might recover."

"*Skripals*," she corrected.

Still-alive-coffee-drinking-Richard lifted his eyes from his screen and looked at her, the unforgiving note of his father's eyes preserved intact in them. Through the window on the garden they watched iridescent magpies lever themselves into the trees.

It took her a moment to realize tears were coursing down his face in long, thin runs.

"Richard? What's the matter?" Her voice was made of air.

"I don't know."

She went to him and enlaced her arms around his neck, draping them over his bony shoulders. The gesture shocked them both. She hadn't touched him in affection, never mind desire, in longer than either of them had realized.

"Whatever it is, don't worry. We'll be okay."

He swivelled his head and gave her a look she could only describe as pitying.

In a stroke, as if someone else were painting her consciousness into being, came clarity. Richard was struggling with something. A latent ferocity had entered his every gesture, a new density. It was as if all ordinary activities — making coffee, taking the dog out, even writing — were now tediously, ferociously mundane. Unhappiness cascaded from his fingertips, the corners of his mouth. He stayed up unusually late. She was asleep when he came to bed, but he was awake before her. Her impression was of someone who had been electrified. A thousand volts had passed through him and he was still animated by the trauma. It did not occur to her he might be in love.

In love. The phrase has always made her nauseous, with its claustrophobic self-importance. It clangs in her head, now. Apart from the obvious implications — wife wronged, betrayal, rage, the smoky, palled ring to all of it — it is such a pathetic way to describe what the experience entails, its complete ransacking of what was previously an intelligent, focused person.

Yes, she can pinpoint the moment to those weeks after his return from Kenya, and before his birthday, which doubled as his death-day. Richard's last months of life are now translated into a suspension in her memory. They hover above the ground, unnamed by any sense of separation or lastness. They might have been lived in reverse, from his downfall at his birthday, the champagne glasses smudged with lipstick she put away that night, late, after midnight, aided only by Elliott, who was too in shock to return home. The pile of gifts on Richard's desk, the stack of cards. *Richard, Richard, Richard,* the name inscribed on each card in spidery flourish from what now looked to be an identical hand.

Elliott said it, within hours of him being declared dead in the ICU. *We will find a way to make this film.*

Her face, still flush with the four glasses of wine she had consumed before the event as she was preparing an Ottolenghi tapenade for the salmon, and which were still coursing through her veins when Richard's body had stopped convulsing on the hospital bed as the defibrillators were removed.

Elliott was unshattered. It was he who put her in the ambulance and rode with them, while the paramedic pounded her husband's chest. He was calm, he did not hyperventilate or cry or even swear. She remembers now that he darted glances at Richard, buried under oxygen masks and blankets, his mouth strapped to a machine, beseeching, eternal looks. She'd never seen anyone look at Richard that way before. She remembers now that Elliott's hands were clenched so tightly in his lap she feared his knuckles would leap out of his skin.

She did not have the mental focus at that moment to consider whether she could trust Elliott. She knew he was young enough to still be living his life on instinct. He hadn't had time to construct false selves — although they would arrive, especially if the success Richard forecast for him materialized. He might be dangerous, he might have entranced her husband. But even if that were the case he would just be living, he would have done it without malice. The young were like animals that way.

A pact was forged as she and Elliott sat on the sofa at Draft Manor, the children lying upstairs, ramrod straight with shock in their beds. *We will find a way to make this film.* She cradled Elliott's words in her hands as if fingering a delicate artefact in the abyss of the moment, which she understood immediately would only lead to other abysses, to a vast insoluble ocean of minutes that would eventually congeal into forever.

She felt the deepest level of momentary kinship she had ever experienced with Elliott then, deeper possibly than with Richard or her children, a solidarity forged in a frightening vacuity. At the time she had shied away from this knowledge. She did not have enough experience of Elliott to balance such drastic trust. She was afraid of how much she would come to need Elliott as a living memorial to her husband, whose death might prove the key to many unlocked doors in her life.

◢

March 2018 is a cold spring. Farmers who have been growing lettuces in greenhouses cannot plant them out because the soil is too wet and the soil temperature too low. They have to throw the lettuces away. Asparagus season will be delayed.

The papers are full of the suicide note that is Brexit. She watches a documentary on North Korea. All the borders are lined with armed guards — quite a feat in a country bigger than England. There is no getting out. That is what citizenship means to her — not so much the right to stay as the ability to leave.

The sarcophagus of cloud that hangs over London in the two weeks after Richard's death suits her. She can hide under it. She catches herself staring accusingly at cherry blossoms. *What are you doing here?* she interrogates them. The blackbirds and chiffchaffs are around, but they seem to avoid their garden. She even musters enough energy to buy a feeder on Mare Street and hangs it, full of seed, but still the birds do not come.

What troubles her most is that the children seem fine. They cried, of course, but they picked up their lives, disappearing into after-school nebulae with friends, trawling shopping malls, cramming for maths exams, practising the flute (Lucy) and violin (Nathan) for hours on end, unprompted for a change.

The London plane trees that line the street are ready for resurrection. For the first time she really feels how enormous, and old, London is. It is as if she is suddenly in contact with all the people who have died in the city. They beckon her from half-shuttered living rooms as she walks down the street, peep at her from ambulances; she sees them floating in the Thames, face up, still alive, their eyes full of sky. She's not sure she wants to be one of them. Should that now be the focus of her life, answering the question *Where am I going to die?*

Richard had never seriously thought he would die. His will was all about his work. He named her as his executor. Of course he did — she was the efficient one, good with money. As a creative couple they had long ago switched gender roles. She had gone to the casting session to read for the part of wife and ended up being cast as husband. *We're stronger as a team*, Richard had said more than once. The fact they worked together gave them an advantage in a vicious industry. Who will they be now that it is just her? Richard will have to continue inside her: a child waiting, for eternity, to be born.

IV

Monica insisted on walking them to Piazza Garibaldi to get the car back to Florence. She grasped Elliott first, muttering something in Italian neither of them could decipher into his neck. In Joanna's arms Monica felt like a bird. Her thin metacarpals clawed at her shoulder.

Then they were in a car, winding down the hill through Siena's narrow streets, then back in modernity — autostrade, garden centres, IKEAs — then on a train and chugging through the waterlogged fields of Reggio Emilia. The train was ancient, a powder blue contraption from the 1950s. The windows even still opened.

The blue dot on her phone told her they were transitioning from Emilia-Romagna to Lombardy. Rivers more green than blue veined through the countryside. Epic clouds dispatched mauve rain in serial tropical downpours. Umbrella pines and narrow cypresses flashed by, as well as acres of fields dotted with vermillion poppies.

Elliott woke and scowled. "Where are we?"

"On a train to Milan."

The city appeared, thin contrails of buildings first, like tentacles, then condensed around them. Once again the journey was over before it started. The passengers in their carriage arose and collected themselves. Her phone pinged. Fabrizio had sent a car. He would meet them at their hotel.

She wondered if she would even recognize Fabrizio. He and Richard had been friends since childhood, but she had not seen him for at least ten years. He had gone on to become a director of some fame in Italy. The last film she had seen of his had screened at the London Film Festival a few years ago, a quiet drama about Romanian workers in a mountain town in the Alps.

In Milan the air smelled familiar. It was damp, green. Moments like these, when she realized her Englishness, now caused her profound pain. She might not be able to stomach the loss that was coming. To save the idea of herself she might have to leave Britain. For the first time in her life she was seriously considering it. What were the elements of her country that actually amounted to that word *home?* She didn't know, but the smell of Milan, a scent of north and industry and the sog of rain, contained something of it.

She was waiting in the foyer when she saw Fabrizio arrive. She recognized him immediately; he was going bald, but otherwise he was slim-hipped, groomed. On his feet were a pair of those Christmas-coloured mismatched trainers, one red, one green, that it seemed everyone in Italy was wearing.

"Fabrizio."

They hugged, but there was a note of reticence in Fabrizio's body. All of a sudden she remembered that Fabrizio had only ever paid her the slightest of attention. It was Richard he was interested in, possibly in love with. She had forgotten, or blocked, this knowledge, or the shock of Richard's death had obliterated it.

"Joanna, you look amazing. So, you've been shooting Richard's film?"

"Yes," she found herself nodding, too emphatic. "I've taken over."

She saw Fabrizio's eyes snag on something. She turned to see Elliott emerge from the hotel lift. He had changed into a white T-shirt and black trousers. His hair was still akimbo from sleeping on the train. She had spent so much time with Elliott, focused on him as a vehicle for an idea, that she had forgotten how he unseated people.

"And who's this?"

"Elliott. He's playing Benjamin." Mentally she corrected herself: he *is* Benjamin.

Fabrizio's gaze flared. She watched an evaluative note establish itself. She observed Elliott draw down a shutter in response. She could almost hear it clang. "Hey," he stuck out his hand in Fabrizio's direction. His tone was friendly but his eyes were careful.

Fabrizio led them to a restaurant three blocks away, all the time speaking animatedly of Richard. He kept trying to catch Elliott's eye, she noticed. Elliott lobbed a comment in her general direction. Somehow he managed to convey with its direction and tone that he was excluding Fabrizio, or wanted to. "I've never been to Milan before."

Again, he sounded unlike himself. She realized how accustomed she had become to him. And that at some point — in Siena, maybe — he had stopped fearing and started to trust her. They had gotten along quite well, all in all. On the shoot, in Capri, Naples, their brief stop in Rome for her lecture on Richard's work, even from their adjoining rooms in Siena, they would text each other short, monogrammic messages — *ready for espresso?, just showering, give me 5m* — then meet in the corridor like two spies on assignment.

She turned to him now. "Elliott, what would you like to eat?"

"Hmm?" He gave her a vacant look. "I'm actually not that hungry."

Her instinct was correct. He did not like being an object of desire at all, he actively resisted it. He was physically present but psychically absent. Possibly they had been away from their central purpose for too long. It had been a week since he had been in front of a camera. He was beginning to fade at the edges.

Fabrizio seated them in a cream-coloured restaurant with burgundy chairs. She worried he would try to sit next to Elliott, but he placed himself opposite them. Behind him in a mirror she saw their reflections: the back of Fabrizio's near-bald head, her and Elliott startled out of their symbiosis by an unknown element.

Fabrizio ordered for the three of them, his eye swimming in Elliott's direction at the end of every sentence. In her annoyance was a grain of pity. How terrible it must be, to be in such blatant thrall to beauty.

"So, Elliott" — in Fabrizio's mouth his name acquired at least one extra *t*, *Elliottttt* — "tell me about yourself."

"I'm an actor." A small, knowing smile.

"Yes, yes," Fabrizio parried. "But how did you come to this role?"

"His casting director spoke to my agent. Richard and I met in January." He telegraphed her a hasty, almost guilty look. "It all came together very quickly."

"And did you begin shooting before —"

"Before Richard's death," Elliott's voice bit on the word.

"No," she answered. "Richard and Elliott worked very closely on the script, and in rehearsal. I decided —" She faltered. "It was *our* decision" — she cast her glance to Elliott, who for the first time evaded her gesture of solidarity — "to take the film forward."

The waiters brought more food than she had eaten in months. Around them glossy Italians spoke in streams uninterrupted by the strategic pauses and parries of the English. She felt suddenly oppressed. *Why do you always have to be an outsider? Can't you be content, fit in?* The voice in her head belonged to a pre-married Joanna, now a stranger. She was hearing it more these days.

Elliott gripped his phone. "Sorry, I have to take this. It's my mother. I'll just go outside."

For a while she kept him in the corner of her eye as he paced the pavement outside, earphones in, linking him to his phone.

"That boy is *incredible*," Fabrizio said. "You know who he reminds me of? Juliette Binoche, when she was very young. He is almost totally androgynous. He really could be woman or man, or neither. But why is he here? It's very unusual to do this. Is he under contract for this trip? Is he being paid?"

"He and Richard were very close. They'd become very good friends. He wanted to come. It's good for the film. We need to remind audiences of Richard's work."

She looked at her watch. It was 10 p.m. Her eyes went to the street. Elliott was not there. She felt for her phone. No text, no missed call.

"I think he must have gone back to the hotel to speak to his mother," she said. "It's not like him not to excuse himself."

Across from her Fabrizio deflated so quickly she almost felt sorry for him. After they'd eaten, he walked her back to the hotel. The asymmetric piazzas they passed through were full. In them dogs barked at each other, straining at their leashes.

They said goodnight. Fabrizio would collect them the following afternoon and take them to the Cine Mexico, where she would introduce a special screening of *Torch Song*.

On her way to her room she knocked on Elliott's door. No answer. She resisted the urge to text or phone. He might have gone for a walk, or to a club, although he was neither a drinker nor a clubber, as far as she could tell.

She knew he was angry with her because she had failed to warn him about Fabrizio. He might feel she had led him into a trap. How could she explain she had simply forgotten Fabrizio was susceptible? That she'd forgotten everything.

In the morning she received a text. *Coffee?* Two coffee cup emojis followed. She knocked on his door. He appeared a moment later, slow-eyed.

"Where were you last night?"

"I went for a walk. I ended up sitting in the square looking at the Duomo till midnight."

"I'm sorry," she said.

"It's not your fault. I was just angry in general. I've been having these — spikes, I guess you would call them — of rage. I don't want anyone to see them, even you." He beckoned her into his room. He sat down in one of the hotel's elegant but uncomfortable designer chairs. She joined him in its pair, wincing at the solid plank against her back.

"I don't want to be anyone's object," he said.

"Well, you've chosen the wrong profession then."

Elliott would not look at her. This more than anything confirmed to her she had betrayed him. He had needed succour and she had responded professionally, which is to say coldly. She resisted the urge to leap up from her chair.

"Look, I'm sorry, Richard's nickname for me was Realpolitik. It just comes out of me. I'm not unsympathetic to your plight, Elliott, but you've got to be realistic. You're an actor. People are going to project their fantasies on to you."

"I'm just not good at this aspect of it. Especially with men. Women are —" He shook his head. "Anything I say is going to sound wrong."

"The male gaze *is* predatory, no matter where it falls. Actually the word is carnivorous. Men will eat you alive. They want to. It's something you learn as a woman very, very early. Women have time to get used to being its object. The industry is exploitative and sexualized but it just reflects the larger culture."

"My mother always said I was an innocent, that" — he made a fist of his hand and placed it on his solar plexus — "that in my core I'm not quite of this era. I'm not prepared for its essential ruthlessness."

"All eras are ruthless," she said.

He raised his eyes to hers. They were the most expressive feature she had ever seen, on any human being. One instant they were contemplative, then moody, shuffling between lacks, then radically fierce. Elliott's latent anger was apparent to her now. She'd seen it in front of the camera but not in person, so to speak.

For an instant she had an image of a man's body, not Elliott, not anyone she had knowingly seen in her life, as it flinched, hit by an invisible projectile. The man was darker eyed than Elliott. His body tried to absorb the shock but it was too much. He began to shiver, tiny tsunamis of fear crawled all over his body at once, like crabs.

"We should go." She stood. The interiors — so Milanese and soothing in their beige transparency, the Kartell chairs, the chocolate walls — closed in on her. For a second she was not convinced she could keep breathing, one in, one out, for the rest of her allotted time on the planet. It was too long, and too much effort.

At the appointed time Fabrizio collected them. He was accompanied by his assistant, a thin blond man with a cloud-like air. "The microphone is set up," he said. "We will provide simultaneous translation for you, signora. There may be some questions."

Half an hour later she was in front of a smallish audience at the Cine Mexico. The room was dark and too cool. She began with Richard's filmography.

"*Voyagers* is about a brother and sister, separated at birth, who only discover their connection years later, in Italy. *The Grass Is Singing* is probably his best-known work, an adaptation of Doris Lessing's novel to which Richard was to bring what was described in reviews as his 'natural affinity for the African landscape.' *Ryder* was an adaptation of Djuna Barnes's first novel," she said, "but also incorporated scenes from *Nightwood*. *Everyone Is Watching* followed three artists in New York, their work, their affairs. And then *Torch Song*, which is about a British singer in West Berlin in the late 1980s. After the wall comes down, the Berlin she knew changed for the better, but she finds herself politically and personally disoriented."

She stopped to allow the translator to recap. She could hardly see the faces of the audience; only the front row was visible, a line of unanimated, unimpressed masques. When the translator had finished she started again.

"I'm going to speak about *Torch Song*, the film you will see today," she began. "As a director, Richard sought the input of his actors. Many of the scripted scenes were re-devised on the day of shooting. He would do ten takes of each shot, typically, and decide in the cutting room which one he would use."

She showed a clip. Daphne Hendricks, the actress who plays the singer, looks like a young Christopher Isherwood. "Richard always allowed his actors to dress themselves, as much as they wanted to, to bring a pair of shoes or a jacket they owned, to bridge the distance between them and the character. He would say to his actors, 'Leave thought behind and go into the dynamic.'"

In the question session that followed her talk, a very young, very earnest man put up his hand and said, in excellent English, "You keep speaking of technique, but what about politics? What is the message for totalitarianism in the film you're making now? Why make a film about Benjamin at this time?"

Her brain buzzed. Rhetoric was not her strong suit. Also, she had not expected to have to convince anyone, or to talk about the film that wasn't yet made.

"It's a longing," she ventured, "a longing to explore good faith. To make cinema an instrument for political intimacy."

A thin woman in the front row slumped further into her chair, sour-mouthed. "But that's impossible," she said. "Benjamin was killed, annihilated, in his own language. There are thousands of Benjamins in Europe right now, fleeing police states. Look at what's happening in your own country. You have sacrificed the rights of millions of European citizens."

She took a deep breath. "I have not personally done that, nor do I sanction it. We have all been sacrificed. You are correct, we are living through a right-wing takeover. Not only in Britain but in Italy too. What do you call Salvini's rise to power? In Britain the elite see Brexit as an opportunity to dismantle laws, protect tax havens, allow capital to flow even more freely, which is ironic in a country with the tax and domicile laws we already have."

The simultaneous translator threw her a pleading look. He was prepared for cinema, not politics.

"So all the more reason to make this film now," she said. "It is a period film but it is absolutely also a film for our times. The version I am shooting will make that plain in a way even Richard might not have anticipated."

The air above her closed down, like an invisible vise. She sat down in the onstage chair so quickly stars settled in her eyes.

She dared not look for Elliott's face in the velvet darkness of the cinema. She knew what she would see: embarrassment on her behalf. He could not help but register his true feelings on his face. This made him a potentially great actor but a terrible liar. She knew he did not go for a walk the night before, or not only. He had told her what she wanted to believe. Another unbidden tableau forced its way into her mind: Elliott in a dank club, surrounded by shirtless men — or would it be women? — all wanting to brush against his lean, young body. But she found she could not complete the vision.

The cinema's lights went up. There was scattered, half-hearted applause. She walked off the stage in a blur of shame.

She felt Richard's gaze rest on hers, its slight but insistent impress. She had been feeling this since she had set foot on Italian soil. It was his country, after all, or one of them. Travelling with Richard and his three passports had been like taking a trip with James Bond. Yes, if he was still anywhere, in some frustrating parallel dimension separated only by plexiglass, say, he would be so miffed not to be with them here.

In the future, the week she spent travelling with Elliott after the Capri shoot would resonate in her memory, unaccountably vivid, like a film she had made of it. She would realize, belatedly, the reason for its intensity: her memory failed to distinguish between scenes she was shooting and scenes she was living.

In her memory-film Elliott is beside her, muffled between his earphones, eyes closed or trained on the landscape as their train flashes by at sinister speed. He really does grieve for her husband, she understands. Now he too is alone, released into the permanent witness programme Richard's death has created for them.

A moment from their journey to Milan rests inside this film, turning around and around on a dais. Their train tracks over a sudden bridge. Elliott stirs, or seems to. "All the rivers here are green, have you noticed?" he says, but in Richard's voice. She turns to answer but his eyes are closed. He is talking in his sleep.

V

On the upstairs landing she was confronted with the spectre of her son. He looked changed. Had he cut his hair? Had he grown a centimetre? A new note, some perplexity, had appeared in his eyes during the month she'd been in Italy. Finally, she located it: Nathan's eyes were becoming Richard's eyes. He was growing into his father's shadow.

"I'm just going to the edit suite," she said.

"Why don't you do that at home? It's all computerized now, anyway." Nathan's voice harboured a tinny note of complaint. *You're never here. Our dad is dead.* Without another word he dematerialized down the stairs, wearing huge red trainers, their tongues hanging out of their laces. She can't remember having bought them — her mother must be the benefactor.

"See you later. I'll be home for dinner," she called to his silent, retreating back.

Ellen was waiting for her at the studio. In the grinding heat of midsummer shirtless men packed into the Caffè Nero terrace on Old Compton Street while she and Ellen gestated in the studio's cold, air-conditioned womb.

As it turned out, she had made basic errors, such has not giving the actors sufficient headroom. The crowns of Elliott and Chloe's heads were pressed up against the top of the frame in a few shots. "It will add claustrophobia, a sense of persecution," Ellen said generously. "We can make this work." The snap of experience in her voice was reassuring. Richard and Ellen had worked together since the beginning, on *Voyagers*. Next to Ellen she felt it most acutely, even more than when she was on set, the raw fact that she was not her husband.

They watched Elliott blossom on the screen as Walter, all cream linens and a sensible moustache. "His eyes are astonishing," Ellen said. "They're old, much older than he is. He's very beautiful."

"Yes, but his beauty is a decoy."

"That's exactly what Richard used to say." Ellen's mouth collapsed oddly around his name, as if she were avoiding a hole. "'We're too ready to project qualities of intelligence and moral beauty in the presence of physical beauty.' I hate that about us. We are so shallow. The beautiful really are exalted, but we put them there. I hope you're not in love with him, Joanna."

She flinched. "What makes you say that?"

"I don't know."

"Richard's body is in an urn. I have no idea how he got there. And you accuse me of falling for a boy only a few years older than Nathan?"

Ellen's eyes widened. "It's not an accusation."

"Why is everyone so suspicious of everyone suddenly?"

Ellen gave her a blank look. "What do you mean?"

"No one has any faith in anyone anymore. Why would anyone believe I'd share a hotel bed with Elliott when my husband died only two months ago? Who would imagine such a thing? Why would Elliott even consider doing that? It's" — she rummaged for the word to accurately describe the roil in her stomach — "*depraved.*"

Ellen opened her mouth, closed it. The parched look in her eyes was the same as in the terrified ranks of medieval peasants in the Sienese frescoes Richard had taken her to see on their few trips to visit Monica — as if she'd just seen a demon.

They said no more on the subject. They worked in silence, the blast furnace of the summer city baffled away by edit studio–issue walls. Normally it would be a relief, returning from the chaos and throngs of Italy, the scene of her first real location shoot and not a triumph but not a disaster either (Ellen's phrase).

But she has not returned to the cool green island she knows. The country is frayed, overheated. In what will come to be thought of as the long, hot summer of 2018 she begins to have problems sleeping and to stay up very late — 1, 2 a.m, drinking half a bottle (conservative estimate) of New Zealand Sauvignon Blanc every night. She starts to keep a diary, not so much to try to make sense of her feelings — she long ago gave up on that possibility — but to keep track of the weird duet between her inner life and the surreal political sphere of the outside world.

The nights are hot. She sleeps with the window open — always a risk in London. Her mind wanders, unauthorized, to the day before Richard died. She had gone shopping for flowers, just like Clarissa fucking Dalloway. She went to the Kingsland Road, which was slowly levering itself from being a mattress graveyard into a street of restaurants with granite frontage and names like Untitled where Prosecco bottles were slung like guns over the bar.

She was looking for flowers for his birthday party — not lilies, that would be too macabre, not to mention too literal, never mind literary. How could she know death was nibbling at her ankles? It had already taken up residence inside their home, sitting like a lugubrious djinn in the corner of their bedroom, disguised as a pile of clothes.

Then the truncated birthday party, Richard's collapse, all of it as if a tornado had swept into her existence and funnelled her up, high above what she thought had been her life but which now seemed an illusion, more elaborate than any film set. It was as if time had caught a fever. Days became indistinguishable from nights, she didn't sleep or eat for forty-eight hours straight and felt absolutely fine, rinsed and clarified, better than she had in her life. Actually she felt like someone else, as if an identity had been gifted to her. Until now she had been living her life in the illusion that she was Joanna, before understanding that she was actually involved in some sort of relay race, and another self had just accepted the baton. Then the funeral, the texts and phone calls to Samantha to secure Elliott and the other talent, locking key crew, rehearsals, shooting.

She bolted out of bed into the heat of the summer night, driven by an intense anxiety that felt not so much like fear as a reverse euphoria. The house closed in around her, a python squeezing her lungs — that had been her recurring nightmare as a girl, after she'd watched a documentary about Brazil on

PBS. She would be sleeping in her bed and the snake would insert its nose beneath the sheets and coil itself around her body. She would wake with its blunt head on her chest, waiting to swallow her.

The watery light of dawn soaked the edges of the curtain. Richard had always loved these shallow nights of midsummer. Yes, the house was on Richard's side. Now, in the dead of night it gathered its courage. *What are you still doing here?* it interrogated her. "Bugger off," she said, out loud. "I paid for you too."

Her phone pinged with her own reminder to call Anton first thing in the morning. The deadline for wrapping the shoot approached. On the 12th of August Elliott would go to New York to begin rehearsals in a Broadway play, a new work by Kenneth Lonergan and so a major coup, his first stage role in America.

Next up was Norwich. They would film in Norfolk for five days before going to northern Spain to shoot the end of the film in early August. Norwich was the stand-in for Benjamin's childhood in Berlin. It had certain things in its favour: 365 churches, or nearly ("a church for every day," the tourist leaflets said), intact medieval cobblestoned streets that look convincingly like pre-bombed Berlin, weepy alleyways. Meanwhile Elliott is staying with his mother in some moneyed corner of countryside, Devon or Dorset. She does not miss him, or not consciously, but when she thinks of him she feels as if someone is pulling on her breastbone.

In the dark she went to sit at Richard's desk, untouched since his death, other than to extract the shooting script of *Benjamin* from his laptop. The photographs of their children he kept within his sightline stared at her. Nathan's was taken on a school trip to France two years before. He stood in a gorge in whitewater rafting gear, a tall, dusk-coloured boy with an unconvinced cast to his face, as if he knew already the provisional nature of existence. Lucy, intense, intellectual, a Goth spread out on a towel, a smear of the palest butter, on the lawn of the house they had rented in Tuscany that same summer, scowling into the camera.

Where were they? She knew where they were physically her children, asleep in their beds, but she had lost the thread that held them to her. Possibly this had been severed some time ago, long before Richard's death, and she just hadn't noticed. She'd become a facilitator, a caretaker, the producer of their lives. On some level they knew she had abandoned them emotionally. They didn't seem to want to speak to her these days. They had deciphered the clatter emerging from the Enigma machine that used to be their mother and deciphered the message: *Save yourselves.*

She stayed at Richard's desk until morning thickened in the house. Yet somehow it failed to completely chase away the blue nocturnal light Richard loved so, and which hovered in corners, shadows or eyes, watching her.

◢

She came upon Elliott smoking beneath a *NO SMOKING WITHIN TWENTY METRES OF THESE PREMISES* sign outside a café. He was perched on the curb, his long legs thrown out ramrod straight in front of him.

"Why are you smoking?"

He gave the cigarette in his hand a suspicious look. "I'm not really smoking. I'm just getting into character."

She lowered herself onto the curb to sit beside him, limbs creaking — she was not as flexible or as fit as she liked to think. "I had to do twelve takes for the last shot," she said. "Wedge is letting them 'cool,' as he puts it."

"Good luck finding a cool spot."

They watched pedestrians pass. Women, their upper arms pink with heat, filed past in tank tops. Children slumbered, heat-stunned, in buggies. The temperatures were predicted to hit thirty degrees all week, presenting certain logistical hurdles for the filming of the Berlin interiors. Unfortunately for them, in their film it was December. Wedge had to procure three air conditioning units at the last minute and have them driven up from London — air conditioners not being exactly thick on the ground in Norfolk.

Elliott passed her the cigarette. "Want a puff?"

"Why not? I haven't smoked since film school." She inhaled. "Hmm. It's more pleasurable than I remember."

"Yeah, shame it's death on a stick."

She squinted into the rigid midsummer sun. "I've decided to film the evening scenes in day and underlight them. It's called day for night."

"I love the name in French, la nuit américaine. The American night."

"Very romantic," she agreed. "Although America has certainly lost its romance, at this juncture in history. I want to do it for texture," she explained. "Richard always loved its submarine light. He revered Truffaut's film. He said Truffaut established the emotional tone of an entire decade with it. That would be the 1970s," she clarified.

They fell into a momentary silence. It was odd, how she never felt uncomfortable during these silences with Elliott.

Anton appeared, his bald head tanned, gleaming, wearing aviator sunglasses; he looked like a gangster or a pilot. "Joanna," he called. "We're ready for you."

On July 24 she wrapped the Berlin/Norwich sequences and returned to London in a flotilla of people carriers. The fields had taken on a Van Gogh yellow. As they drove the Essex corridors of the A12 she went over the shoot in her mind. She might just be getting the hang of filmmaking. The rushes looked better. They lacked the brittle overdeterminedness of simulated actuality. There was a granular, immersive element to the footage. Elliott's performance was so naturalistic and fresh she found herself holding her breath, wondering what he would do next. He never quite played it the way they had discussed. There was always some element — a frown, a sidestep, a nervous fiddling of his fingers. She didn't know how he did this. It was magic.

She would have only a few days at home in Draft Manor before they went to Spain to shoot the final scenes of the film. In these evenings she took to sitting on the balcony by herself, a glass of white wine her company. Actually it was an unfinished roof terrace, behind what used to be their bedroom and which was now hers alone.

Many days and nights she had wished for a room of her own, she admitted to herself. At times Richard had been hard to live with. He had the monomania of the artist. He wouldn't give a thought to what time she might have to get up to corral Nathan and Lucy into their school routine or speak to a line producer in New York. He would flop into bed at 4 a.m. after a writing session and mumble lines of dialogue at her. In retaliation she would stuff earplugs into her auricles.

Now, some nights she can't sleep in their bed at all. She lays down a blanket and decamps to the floor. There, she falls asleep immediately, comforted by the floor's intransigence.

From the balcony-terrace she had a fine view of the landing track to Heathrow. She rummaged in a cupboard and found Richard's birdwatching binoculars, a long-ago present from his father. Planes appeared, arrows shot out of an unseen bow, with soothing regularity. They were far away, but the binoculars identified them: a Lufthansa A320, a humpbacked Emirates A380, a British Airways 777.

In those intermezzo evenings between location shoots she felt calmer, almost resolved. She had cultivated a renewed respect for their subject, Benjamin. He had the foresight to leave Germany not long after Hitler was elected chancellor in 1933. He did not hang on to his grief-stricken dog, his Turkish rugs, his routine, familiarity, language and country, as she was doing. Even so, why did he wait so long to try to get out of Europe? He could have gone to the United States before war broke out. It would have been possible to sail there, at least until summer 1939. Why did he stay in Paris until the very morning of the German invasion on June 14, 1940? The Nazis had taken everything from him by that point except his liberty. But they were closing in on that too.

She was not ready to go into exile, but she wondered how much longer she could stomach being the pawn of mendacious arch-manipulators. She was not built for victimhood: she had been the citizen of a liberal democracy all her life; the recipient of the gains of first- and second-wave feminism; she had been able to achieve her goals and educate her children to supersede her.

But now she was living in the residue of a dream world, one that had been her home, her country, before it was held hostage by the right wing of the Tory party. She cannot bear to look at her British passport, which now looks like a grenade. *You have hijacked my country, my country!* she screams inwardly, when one or other of the gargoyles appears on *Newsnight*, where they are subject to "balanced" BBC questioning.

This is what she will do: she will turn the key to Draft Manor for the last time on March 28, 2019, the EasyJet boarding passes she has had the foresight to purchase in October fluttering in her hand, shepherding Nathan and Lucy onto a train packed with other Brexit refugees, the airports overwhelmed, flights overbooked. No one knows for sure if they will get out of the country. No one knows what will happen tomorrow, or the day after it. "It's like the war again, innit," an elderly man on the Tube will say. He is going nowhere, he will tell her. "Too old and too poor. I'm done for, anyway." From his rheumy eyes will stare Richard's gaze. She will say, "You've come back, thank Christ, just in time to deport ourselves."

Yes, she will pluck Richard out of the lair of the dead. She will walk flanked between her husband and Benjamin, both dressed in dark overcoats, a bohemian Praetorian Guard. They will pass her wads of euros and warn her of the great reckoning to come, when the suspicious, lazy Britons who muttered in pubs against the Polish and Romanians would be delivered their fate, which they themselves had voted for, and her — Nathan, Lucy, Elliott, all blameless, but living amongst them — would be sacrificed too.

She is becoming not someone, but something else. She feels herself taking on new characteristics — maybe Richard's, maybe some unknown person's whom she has not met yet but who nonetheless shares her skin. By making a film she will make the future: hers, Elliott's, Neil's, Richard's, but also *the* future. Men's natural grandiosity is installing itself inside her. She never realized how much she had held herself back.

At six in the evening it is thirty-two degrees. Soon Nathan will call for her from downstairs. *What's for dinner, Mum? Mum, are you there?* She will say, *Yes, I'm here,* as she lifts the binoculars to her eyes and watches as an American Airlines 757, unmistakeable in its stars and stripes livery and its dipped nose, floats ever downward into a lemon haze.

VI

They met for a coffee at the town's only café. A crater-faced waiter who bore more than a passing resemblance to Javier Bardem came to take their order with only a grunt uttered in welcome. The café's placard announced *Happy Hour, 7–9*. Elliott peered at the sign. "Unhappy Hour, I guess. How is your Airbnb?"

"An Airlessbnb."

They smiled. Their collusion was now complete. Richard had been right. Making a film really was like being a family, albeit a temporary one. Just after a shoot finished, Richard's actors used to ring him in the middle of the night. She remembered that now, another piece of information her mind had conveniently deleted. She would wake, foggy with sleep at four in the morning, and Richard would be muttering to one of his actors. When she asked him what they wanted, he told her they'd rung just to hear the sound of his voice again.

At the time she'd thought it odd, and not a little suspicious. But she understood now. To be torn away from a film shoot, well, if people didn't despise each other and the shoot was going to plan, at least, was a terrible rupture. She could not believe they would all soon take up their separate lives, like collecting luggage left in an airport locker and flying to their separate destinations.

In tandem they turned their eyes to the wide, mussel-shaped bay. To the west the Pyrenees prowled its perimeter, rimmed in an amber halo of recently set sun. Speedboats and yachts were migrating into harbour for the evening, leaving long white scars on the water in their wake. It was high summer. They allowed themselves to be enfolded into an atmosphere of Mediterranean vernal decadence: bronze days, glossy topless sunbathers, a Bain de Soleil coconut note in the air.

Two kilometres from town they would film the final scenes of Benjamin's life. The last full day he was alive on the planet was September 25, 1940. Joanna had hoped to shoot at that time of year exactly, to capture the decrescendo of the late summer light. But it would have dragged the shoot on far too long, so she scheduled to film in the hours just after dawn and before dusk, in the hopes that something of their shallow light would hold.

"I have a confession to make," Elliott said.

"Oh yes?"

"I stole something from Richard's bedroom in Siena."

She waited.

"I wanted something of his. It was just a book — on Italian cinema. He had two, the same book in Italian and English. I took the English version. I wanted to know what he knew. I'm sorry."

"You could have just asked. Monica might have let you have it."

"No, she was far too scary. Maybe there's an element of pay-back too. I felt I needed to liberate something of him from her."

His mouth twitched and his forehead tightened.

She probed his features for a sign of the return of the bolt of lightning — rage — which had just flashed across it. But it was gone, as quickly as it had appeared.

"And have you been reading it?"

"I'm on the chapter about Pasolini. There's a quote I wanted to read to you —" He reached for his phone. No one, it seemed, carried notebooks anymore. "The writer says his films were about 'a society dominated by manipulative and sadistic power and organized around mindless consumption and exploitation.'"

"Sounds familiar, no?"

Elliott's eyes had darkened to the indigo of the mountains that peered down on their terrace, the flimsy aluminium table, the sour waiter who came and went, grumbling.

"Do you think Benjamin knew, on some level, that he was about to die?" he said.

"Why do you ask?"

Elliott's eyelashes fluttered. "I feel as if I'm about to die."

"Well, you are," she said. "We're all always about to die."

"But also I still don't believe it will really happen. I feel eternal."

"We all live somewhere in between 'I'm going to die' and 'It's never going to happen.'"

A cool breeze came from nowhere and inserted itself between them. The Mediterranean was dark now. It glittered, graphite in new moonlight.

It struck her that it might be an intelligent thing to do, to rehearse one's death, as Elliott was doing for Benjamin. Richard had been there one moment, striding across the living room floor, riddled with kinetics, a mountain spirit in her life. Then in the next instant he was inanimate. As if some higher being had hit the delete button by mistake.

"He must have been so tired, Benjamin," Elliott mused. "He can't have slept much the night before, lying on pine needles in a vineyard. He'd probably never slept outside in his life. He must have been cold, disoriented. And then ten hours' walking. And then at the border — the hotel." He shook his head. "He couldn't have been thinking straight. I wonder if he killed himself out of fatigue."

"It's possible," she said.

"I'm going to stay up all night tonight."

"I think that's taking being in character too far."

"I'll be on point, don't worry."

"I'm not worried about that — it's you I'm concerned about."

He gave her a thin plank of a smile. "I never feel I'm getting it right. Richard —" He darted a cautious look in her direction. "Richard thought I should call on my family history."

"How so?"

"He said, 'You have genocide in your veins.'"

She breathed in. "Richard felt dispossessed too. Although he'd done the dispossessing, or at least his ancestors had."

"Why?"

"Because his grandfathers were a Black man and a white man, one man displaced by the exact colonialists his other grandfather embodied. He had partition in his blood. I think he made films to explore rupture. That was his only real theme. Apart from love, of course."

The waiter clumped around them, noisily stacking chairs on tables. They rose. "What will you do, after?" Elliott asked.

"After?" Her voice sounded strange and jangly, in her ears, like a tambourine. "There'll be ADR, maybe even pickups. But essentially we're done, Elliott."

Her sentence hung between them, a hinge swinging in the wind.

They walked toward the sea. In the distance a lighthouse blared on, off, on, its restless eye panopticoning the harbour. Clouds coagulated around the peaks of the Pyrenees, now dark and bunched against the light, like blackberries.

Then she did something she hadn't intended to do. Someone inside her, not her, reached for Elliott's hand. It placed itself willingly in hers. His eyes, black with the moonlit sea, widened. "You have to believe that you are going to make it across the border. You have to believe that until the *last minute*."

She let his hand fall away. They held each other's eyes for a long time. Behind the curtain of his gaze, an essential element of Elliott shuttered itself away. She knew he did not want to be seen, except as the character he was playing. This evasiveness was one of the reasons why the camera was so seduced by him.

"You know," he began. "Richard was in awe of you. He said you were the smartest person he knew."

Her heart sank. She could actually feel it plummet in her chest. She hoped it would not fall out of her altogether and sit at her feet, a bleeding, adipose lump.

"Have I said the wrong thing?"

She closed her eyes. When she opened them they were rimmed with tears. She was seized by an impulse to ask him, Who do you love? She had not asked if Elliott has a girlfriend, or boyfriend. Her private supposition was that he would choose someone cruel, whatever the gender, who did not love him back, who drew him in only to push him away, much as Asja Lacis did with Benjamin. There was a note of self-critique in Elliott's person that made him vulnerable to misuse, but which was also the key to his subtlety and range as an actor.

The moon cut a path across the water in a perfect, almost technological, viaduct. She found she liked this hook of the Mediterranean where France becomes Spain, its rugged, volcanic beauty. Although for Benjamin it had not been that at all.

She had a sudden image of Richard sitting on flat rocks at the edge of an inner sea. Where he was now, would he be steeped in a soup of anguish, without agency? He was at his equinox when he died. He had been parrying a sluggish aortic valve surprisingly well for years without knowing it. The doctor who did the autopsy told her with a heart like that he should have been dead years ago.

I didn't take enough risks, Richard said through her, now.

You should have risked *everything*, she replied.

She walked toward the sea. For the first time since Richard's death, she allowed the misery in her, her enslavement to it, full rein. Such pain elicited in her an old, structural fear, like seeing a demon or confronting the law.

Elliott was running after her. "Where are you going?"

She looked down to find her feet were in the water. Elliott's too. He had followed her into the shallows.

He grabbed her shoulder. "I have an idea."

"I hate ideas."

"It has cost implications. And time. We probably can't do it. It's a kind of fantasy."

His expression was urgent. A wave slapped against their shins. "And?"

"Well," he began, "it would have to be a dream . . ."

VII

No longer does the dream reveal a blue horizon.
The river was further below the city than she'd
thought it would be. Before arriving on the shores
of the country — or better said, the city, which would become
an entire country for her — that would come to be her home,
Hannah had the bizarre expectation that its hard, rational streets
would end in sandy beaches.

Soon after she first arrived she was shown an illustration by
a colleague at Columbia, of Manhattan before Henry Hudson
sighted the island in 1609. The drawing was conjecture, of
course, but it fascinated her to see a blueprint emerge, of a
narrow, arrowhead-shaped island, verdant and dotted with hills
and ponds, chestnut trees, red maple swamps, grasslands and

saltmarshes where osprey and salamanders and the Lenape peoples had once flourished.

Four lanes of traffic on Riverside Drive barred her from the Hudson's dull brown waters, the exact colour of the black market stockings she had worn while interned in Gurs.

Gurs: even the word is ugly. If she thinks it now, she sees a pool of scorched black lava. It was an internment camp, later an extermination depot. Only women and children were sent there. From 1942, long after she "escaped" — in truth she just walked out of the gates in the confusion that surrounded the capitulation of France in June — the women who remained were shipped to Auschwitz-Birkenau.

The camp was hell, but at least you knew where you were — this thought had occurred to her many times since, although not while she was actually there. It was chilling, how tied humans were to certainty. Anywhere outside the rickety barbed wire perimeter of the camp presented a forest of obstacles. In the towns and cities she passed through after she left Gurs — Montauban, eventually Banyuls, and Portbou — every time she went to the bakery or the bar she tried to buy bread or a pastis without opening her mouth but still a word or two would slip out and they would hear her sawdust accent; every time someone stopped her on the street to ask her for a light, her heart was in her throat.

By then the Gestapo were everywhere. An innocuous moment sitting in the sun on a park bench, or walking down a country lane to reach the next, larger town and its train station, could be your final moment of freedom, the moment that led to others, more labyrinthine than the Minotaur's lair, possibly even to an encounter with the creature himself. For years afterward, entering a bakery, even the Hungarian-run exilic shops that dotted the Upper West Side, had made her heart pound as she shuffled words of French in her head.

The camp had been hastily constructed to house refugees from the Spanish Civil War. The Vichy government resurrected it instantly, throwing a switch. The walls were plywood, their beds bales of hay; there was no floor, only wood chippings, like a giant stable. It was run by Alsatian nuns. That was what surprised her most, to walk into its arcade of barracks and see them in their crow habits, moustaches ruffling their upper lips. She laughed. The women around her, not all Jews by any means, looked relieved, as if they had been waiting for years for someone to burst out laughing at the sight of nuns.

The women were batched away with the various factions — women like her, a ressortissant allemande, an enemy alien, netted in like fish; also French women who didn't know they were German, having been born in a border town speaking both languages; and the feared indésirables — women under suspicion of collaborating with the Nazis, of being spies.

By late May the temperature was already thirty degrees. The heat that summer never abated. The forests surrounding the camp thickened with creatures — bees, crickets, birds, but none of them ever ventured into camp, as if obeying an invisible cordon. The latrines overflowed. In the heat the women were dispatched with shovels to clear them out. She remembered dry-retching on her knees, her shovel covered in excrement, her headscarf pulled uselessly over her nose.

When she left, she was one of two hundred women who had the temerity to walk out of the camp, hearts in their throats. When no camp guards or Vichy officials came to snag them back on the road, she had an intuition: she broke away from the group and melted into a farmer's field, walking through towering grass left to grow for hay, the sun passing through its mesh, a cooling balm. It was not the first time she had simply walked out of a trap; four years earlier she had fled internment by the Gestapo by walking over the Erzgebirge Mountains. There, she and her mother, with whom she had escaped, walked into a house whose front door was in Germany but whose back door was in Czechoslovakia.

Hannah put her pen down. Her eye was drawn to the space between her index and third fingers, sallow with nicotine. Now, her months in the camp appeared to her as a hiatus, a fog. Gurs seemed in retrospect not to be inhabited by people but by violent spirits strolling through the avenues of the living. The low New Jersey shore comforts her, with its promise of the bulk of the country behind it, stretching far into the west, the antithesis of Europe.

No one had told her how the skies would be different in the New World: monumental, scrubbed clean. Heavy-moving thunderstorms roll over the city while unfamiliar birds call, ragged and raw, in the park. Memory caught hold of its objects at their most worn, frayed junction. Her mother's apron, hung on the door next to the woodstove, her father's briefcase, its once-black leather greying through purpose. The off-copper colour of his eyes.

She would soon have another comrade to fetch from the docks in Lower Manhattan. Walter had made it to Lisbon, arriving in early October. There, he had marvelled at the slant of narrow autumn light in the streets that nurtured the poetry of Fernando Pessoa. He spent a week awaiting passage on a ship, holed up in a hotel, and wrote to her, one of his terrifyingly cogent letters. He carried it in his pocket, all the way across the Atlantic. When they met again at the pier on the East River he thrust it at her with faintly trembling hands.

In Lisbon the streets were lined with azulejos which make the city a giant echo chamber, voices ricocheting off porcelain, he told her. He took a streetcar to the port and boarded a freighter that had seen better days. On the voyage he tipped into wretched seasickness, so bad he forgot his fear of the torpedo. She smiled at the image of Walter with a life preserver slung around his neck as he and the other passengers are mustered into safety drills.

He arrived just as New York slid into winter. The first thing she did was to take him to the Hungarian pastry shop on Amsterdam, with its walls the colour of dried blood and white-coated doctors elbowing each other in the queue to buy strudel.

This is where the pencil hovers over the paper, trying to decide: dream or reality? Dreams have their own convictions. For years she has failed to remember anything of hers; by the morning the dreams had vanished, although like the cigarettes she is fatally addicted to, there was a residue of their smoke in her mind.

She has been mistaken many times in her life, but she has survived. She has seen so many people finished. That is how Hannah thinks about the human existence: a disembodied hand is drawing a likeness of a person. The person thinks they are the engine of their own shape. But the pencil is lifted from the page, and the person being drawn, one moment so in motion, dynamic and alive, unaware of the retreating hovering hand, expires, unfinished. Unfinishable.

The Lincoln Center plaza was oddly empty. A few scattered figures sat facing the malachite-coloured fountain and its monumental Henry Moore. Joanna had become so accustomed to the crowds everywhere in London, or in Europe for that matter, their apocalyptic density, that she almost missed them. But then it was August, she reminded herself, and thousands of people had cleverly fled the sauna of Manhattan's streets.

They trailed through the glaucous heat, past the fountain, past gaping glass mouths of auditoria and atria. They took the walkway to the Walter Reade Theater and settled into its seats with so much more leg room than in Britain. A trailer came on for a retrospective. Before the first frame appeared — of a line of medieval peasants, or their heads at least, an overhead shot — she turned to Elliott and mouthed, *Tarkovsky*. Further frames revealed the unmistakeable balefulness, the mystical framing. Sure enough, the title appeared on the screen in spindly medieval letters: *Andrei Rublev. Coming Soon.*

"How did you know?" Elliott asked her in the darkness.

"There are no shadows in Tarkovsky," she said. "Or the ones that are present have the density of black sun. That's Richard, of course."

In the last few days she'd begun to let Richard's voice roam freely around her mind, searching for a door or window. She felt its panic as it realized it would be locked there forever. But somehow she could contain it, and her sorrow, better here on the other side of the Atlantic. Distance was not merely space but a kind of spiritual buffer.

They had walked thirty blocks south to the Lincoln Center in the woollen late afternoon humidity, passing innumerable Hopper-esque vignettes: slim Asian girls sweeping up inside nail bars, a bank of recliner chairs where clients sit like pashas amid fake ferns, a palette of burgundy and green; Zabar's deli, brashly over-lit, rank with its banks of cheese; the cataclysmic dimensions of the avenues and their incipient parks, the canyon junctions. Dogs everywhere, thrilled to be liberated from their apartments. People on Tinder missions, clutching their phones like totems. She remembered the appeal of the ghostless New World: to feel freed from history, merely by standing on its landmass.

She'd forgotten just how different North America was, from Britain, from Europe, from London. She was caught, paralyzed even, by a sense of the familiar in the unfamiliar: a note of gravel and destiny in the air, the rubbery newness of everything, the massive trucks that prowled the avenues like discontented beasts, the jagged sundown sound of American crows and blue jays. All of these lurked somewhere within her, they belonged to her twelve-year-old self. Of course she'd been back since many times for pitch meetings, but the feeling of her loss at being pulled out of this country was more acute now.

"This is a bit nuts," Anton said, when she revealed their plan to him. "It's a good job you're the producer so you don't have to explain it to yourself. Any other producer would pull the plug."

As for Neil, for the first time in nearly two decades of working together he would not look her in the eye. "You're playing with history, Joanna. I don't think the audience is going to like that." To which she'd replied, at least in her mind, *The audience can hang.*

Elliott would stay in New York to begin rehearsals for his role in the Lonergan play. She had ten days in the city and three scenes to shoot. They were filming lo-fi: this tail end of their film involved only her, Elliott and her Panasonic Lumix GH5, the portable film camera Wedge recommended. They were on their own. Her scenes of Benjamin's imagined resurrection will look distinct from the rest of the film, homemade yet ultra-sharp — hyperreal.

She tries to regain her equilibrium as they walk to the Lincoln Center. Blocks are longer in New York than she remembered. They pass ice cream carts, coffee vendors, warehouses, trucks, all under a vacant sky. She registers a thought she can only describe as spooky: *North America is not actually real.* What can she mean? she interrogates herself. People live unassailably real lives here, that's clear. But here she feels a sense of waiting — waiting to go back home, to be reunited with her sphere. Europe is the real continent after all, for her.

Homesickness is much more than a longing for the familiar. It means living in a place which mirrors your internal reality. She has a whiff of exile and what it must have meant, to Arendt, to Adorno, to Horkheimer and Mann and the others, to end up here, safe, but in a simulation, exiled from the stage of their lives.

Suddenly she senses a presence on the street. Where? It is not in the serried ranks of tourists behind them, nor the gawpers from the hotel terrace above, nor in the rivers of people streaming from shops and theatres. She feels the fizz of a breath on her neck and jumps. She looks around, expecting to see a tall man passing her or one of the many rigid, purposeful women the city breeds who had ventured too close to her in the melee, but there is no one.

The elevator doors opened on Robin's quarterback shoulders. He stood at the bar with his back to her, tossing cashews into his mouth. She had no sooner spoken his name than he spun around like an outsize top. He was big man, but with a narrow fox-like face.

"Joanna! You look fantastic! What have you been doing — yoga or something?"

He perceived her recoil, because his expression condensed. "Joanna, forgive me," he frowned. "I should have said straight away how sorry I am."

"Thank you," she said.

"I'm sorry to drag you up here, but I'm addicted to rooftop bars. Well, to sunsets actually."

"I know. I've seen your Instagram." Robin's photographs were all of sunsets in Manhattan or Brooklyn, taken from rooftop bars. This particular one he'd invited her to was located in a themed hotel whose corridors were lined with cloth spines, the kind of interior design books one bought by the yard or metre. It was just around the corner from the New York Public Library.

Once again she had to guide herself toward this moment, the one where she was meeting Robin. Just as with Fabrizio, she realized she hadn't thought about this meeting at all: about Robin himself, or what she wanted out of it. She really was a zombie these days, sleepwalking toward assignations for nothing other than commiseration's sake. They had worked together before, but this time she didn't need Robin or his money. But he'd got wind from Neil that she was finishing the shoot in New York and had rung her, insisting they meet.

"You really do look well. I mean, I know I should be complimenting you on your intelligence and wit, and I will, believe me."

She looked down at her body, as if to check it was still there. She was still thinner than her usual thin, and she'd had her hair cut for the first time in four months before she'd left London. In New York women looked at each other more blatantly than they did in London. On the street she'd received vaguely approving glances from other similarly attired women wearing black three-quarter-length cigarette trousers, sleeveless white tops and loafers, an army of forty-something urban mavens in uniform.

Robin put his hand, very lightly, on her back, just below her scapula. It felt heavy, as if encased in velvet. Her body leaned into it. Apart from accidental collisions with her actors or the crew and the rare shipwrecked hug from Nathan and Lucy, she hadn't registered another body's touch in five months.

He steered her out the door. "I've reserved us a table on the patio. Come on."

She trailed behind him as a hostess in a fitted black dress and three-inch heels led them onto a terrace, small but expertly landscaped, with banks of flowers and sea grass.

They ordered — her an overcomplicated cocktail with gin, him something with tequila.

"I thought you didn't drink."

"I didn't." He threw his hands in the air. "Then Trump was elected and I decided I needed to be drunk for the next four years just to deal with the clusterfuck. Cheers, here's to rehab!"

His eyes were olive-coloured. Robin was coming back to her, returning like a memory, in fits and starts. His mogul persona belied a refined intelligence. He produced award-winning independent films, somehow stumping up the kind of money a small-big-budget would normally garner. His nickname in producing circles was the Magician.

"So, Joanna, I'm not going to lie. Everyone's talking about you."

Her eyelids fluttered in alarm. "I'm not well known enough for everyone to be talking about me."

"Okay, I'm talking about you, to myself. Are you making Richard's film, or is this your project?"

"How could I make Richard's film if I'm not Richard?"

"Well it's his script, isn't it?"

"It was."

"So is this another case of reinterpreting a story with a female gaze? That's all the rage right now."

She hadn't been expecting an interrogation. Her night at the Cine Mexico in Milan came back to her, that scorched feeling of having to account for herself, and failing, because it was not her that people wanted to know about, really.

"I am female, ergo there will be a female gaze, yes. I am just making the best film I can."

Robin smiled. "I love the British. You actually say 'ergo.'"

Their drinks arrived, courtesy of the hostess who wore an earpiece, like a secret service agent. Her eye lingered on the woman's figure: snug dress, power heels, like a Fox News anchor Barbie.

Robin plunked his drink down. "Joanna, I'm so sorry. Here I am talking shop —" He shook his head. "This business is making an asshole out of me." He pulled himself taller and rallied. "So, you're here with your lead."

"Elliott. Yes, he and Richard became very close. They conceived a lot of the film together, really."

"He and Richard were friends? With, what, twenty-five years between them?"

"Richard was always very close to his actors. You know that."

Robin's only acknowledgement of her rebuke was a twist of his lower lip. "Well, I have to tell you, when I heard about Richard I was so shocked I went to the Four Seasons and downed four martinis in a row. I had to be poured into a cab home."

She wanted to say, *So? You think that's shock. I lived with Richard. I have children with him.*

A skyscraper wind ruffled their hair.

"Ah, sunset time." Robin maneuvered his bulk into a standing position and faced west. His paw-like hands dangled in front of her. "Yes, there it goes, over the Hudson. One thing I've learned from hanging out in rooftop bars is that in the moments before the sunset the wind picks up, just slightly, a last breath before dying. It's sublime, but no one seems to notice it."

He sat down. "Did Richard ever tell you the story about my great-grandfather?"

She shook her head.

"He was from southern Hungary, from a town where Jews had lived for at least nine hundred years. He came here, to New York, in the early 1930s. He sailed all the way with his brother and sister, who stayed, but my great-grandfather went back to Hungary in 1934. Do you know why?"

"I can't imagine."

"He said, 'How can I live in a country where the men on the walls are considered more real than flesh and blood men in the street?' He was talking about cinema — well, he called them moving pictures. We forget how nuts the country went for movies in the 1930s. He couldn't live in a country of unreal projections. So he went back."

"What happened to him?"

"He was shot by the Nazis in a roundup of Jews in 1942." Robin sighed. "Ironic, don't you think, that his grand-nephew is a movie producer? I often have his exact phrase ringing in my ears: *I can't live in a country where the men on the walls are more real than those in the streets.*"

The crowd around them had thinned. It was thirty degrees at sundown, yet she shivered, if only for a second.

"I like to think Richard's gone to Bali to make a docudrama about genderless shamans in Indonesian hill towns," Robin said. "He must be really, really pissed off at being dead."

She leaned across the table, faux-drunkenly and in faux-confidence: she was neither drunk nor in the mood for heart-to-hearts, but she had to tell someone. "I don't feel I can live in our house anymore. It's as if I'm living in a crime scene." She pointed to the floor. "I see Richard as a chalk outline, like when people are murdered and forensics trace the body. At night I sit there having conversations with the chalk outline, if I've had enough wine."

"I'm telling you now that anecdote is so pathetic I'm stealing it for my next movie."

They rose their glasses to each other one last time, like teenagers in a shot-drinking contest, and threw the remains of their cocktails down their throats.

They rode down in the gold-plated elevator and said goodbye on a baking nocturnal street. On the street she angled her body toward him.

Robin's face folded into seriousness. "Take care of yourself, Joanna. I know you're a tough cookie, but you've been dealt a blow."

A tingling in the bridge of her nose alarmed her. She stifled it.

"I hope this is not the last time I see you," Robin said.

She felt a rush of empathy, for him, for her, for the simulacra of Richard who had sat with them and watched them drink to the sunset he could not see.

"I hope so too."

She decided to walk for a few blocks before taking the subway uptown. The reposing lions of the New York Public Library gleamed in the heat. She walked through pools of sudden cool as doors of stores opened, then over hot subway grilles, trading squares of cold, hot, cold, hot as she drifted north, past the Flatiron Building and the giant Italian food emporium called (Richard would have loved it) Eataly.

Without meaning to, she went inside. The queue for gelato wound to the back of the building. Espresso, Amaretto, Sienese panforte, bottled artichokes — flashes of their weeks in Italy returned to her. She found her memories of filming — what angle she chose for the shot, whether she used the fixed lens camera — were indivisible from her memories of innocuous moments: with Elliott in the gelatería in Anacapri, talking about the submerged electricity of a scene; with Elliott, tractoring themselves up the island's funicular-steep paths; or the sundown feast with the crew perched high above the Tyrrhenian Sea, watching the silhouette of Ischia melt into night.

The notion hit her with a slicing force. Richard was no longer in her recent past. All the tableaux she should have inhabited with him had been bequeathed, smoothly, to Elliott.

Richard's disappearance was the most compelling demonstration of one fact: the past really was past. It wasn't circulating forever, as Richard liked to think, in the form of film. Memory is only its fiction. Even the moments she had consciously savoured at the time turn out to have been rewritten by the powerful cinematic machine that is her brain, with its full complement of scriptwriters, cinematographers, grips, best boys. But who was the director?

She whipped around. She sensed a presence, somewhere near the bottled artichokes. A dark-haired, middle-aged man in a striped shirt stood nearby, exactly like the man in the cathedral in Siena whose striated shirt disappeared him into the pattern of the marbled pillar. The man, sensing her gaze, moved away.

◢

Robin had recommended the restaurant. It was in Hell's Kitchen, on West 50th Street, a narrow neighbourhood of vegan joints and S&M members' clubs. She'd texted Elliott the address on WhatsApp: *see you for dinner?* and received two thumbs-up emojis in response.

She had spent the day running around the Columbia campus, finalizing permissions with campus security. They'd secured a room in the Pulitzer building, suitably wood-panelled and antique, at least for North America. She had cast a very reputable American indie actress to play Hannah Arendt. There they would film a scene where Arendt lectures to a room of students as yet unfamiliar with Benjamin's work. The exterior views she would get from a friend-of-a-friend's apartment. The woman was a professor at Columbia who lived in a Riverside Drive building two blocks south of where Arendt herself had lived for most of her life in New York, number 370.

She was not sure where Elliott was at that moment. A distance, slim and unobtrusive, like a delicate spider, had inserted itself between them. It might have something to do with their impending separation. The shoot was coming to an end, which meant Richard was definitively ending. They were shying away from each other in order to rehearse their loss.

The restaurant had a set menu. They ordered this and the food just kept on coming.

Elliott's eyes widened as another plate of kimchi was set between them. "So much food. I know everyone eats huge amounts in America but this is over the top."

"I have two words for you," she said. "*Doggy* and *bag*."

She felt the grammar of the future impress itself on them. Their conversation that night was anchored in the now, but their words began to lean toward the future tense. It was time to tell him.

"I had a look at Richard's phone," she said.

His eyelids flew open. "Did you know the passcode?"

"I had to take it to this guy the police told me about, with his death certificate as evidence. He sits in a small room in Bow, unlocking dead people's mobile phones — totally legally, of course."

Elliott sat back in his chair and folded his napkin in his lap. Something — an unreadable expression — flashed across his face. She thought for a second that he might do a runner and leave her with acres of Korean beef to finish.

"What did you find?"

"His contact list, the most recent messages. I can't face reading them." She sighed, and even she could hear it was a guilty sigh, too much exhalation. How could she feel guilty about looking at her dead husband's messages? Yet she did.

"I was looking for the footage, what he called *Don't Look Down*."

"Isn't that a film?"

"It was Richard's name for videos he took of everyday life — random sequences, trying out angles, techniques. Did he not show you?"

"I don't think so." Elliott's voice had changed. There was an unmistakeable note of the ruler in it. He was measuring his response to her.

"He thought he might eventually incorporate some of it into *Benjamin*, a coda of some sort, or even a parallel story of the now. He told me in January that he wanted to document 2018 as the last year the UK will be a member state of the EU, unless of course we're saved by some miracle. He thought this year could be as definitive as 1939. He thought he might have another narrative in the film, a kind of behind-the-scenes London winter, starring you, me, him." She paused. "It wouldn't have worked commercially. I would have had to talk him out of it, probably. Anyway, it's impossible now."

"Why is it impossible?"

"Because the film stops."

They sat in silence. In the restaurant young couples surrounded them. They had earnest, avid faces turned orange by the faux-tungsten light bulbs that hung above the tables, the muffled tangerine light they threw, miniature subdued suns.

Elliott had not touched his food in some time, she noticed. The expression in his eyes, when he turned them back to her, was a milky, compassionate terror.

"And me, am I in this footage?"

"Yes."

"I thought he was just — taking videos, like people do."

"Anyway, no one will see it, now. You don't have to worry."

Around them diners rose up, diners sat down, sending the restaurant's light bulbs swaying. Underneath the orange glow Elliott seemed to acquire an aura.

"What did you see, I mean, of me?"

"You and Richard at the South Bank, you and Richard walking along the river, at dinner, having drinks — somewhere in Covent Garden, by the look of it. You and Richard reading through the script. At that literary event at Sutton House, walking to Ivan's boat, the dinner party, or at least some brief clips. I haven't seen all of it. I haven't got the guts."

He gave her a level look. "What are you afraid of?"

"Of seeing my dead husband alive."

She settled on a confession, or rather a question, which is how it emerged. "Do you think realists can make films?"

"That depends on what you mean by realism," Elliott said.

"I don't have Richard's vision. He was a romantic, he had a lyrical sensibility. Actually, *metaphysical* is the better word. He saw ordinary moments as dense with rapture — I think that's a Peter Bradshaw quote in a review of *Torch Song*. Love was the only thing that interested Richard, fundamentally. And yet it's an illusion."

Elliott's look was one of benign scrutiny. She was almost prepared for his question. "What am I to you?"

"You're the bridge between Richard and me."

He blushed — he actually blushed. Roseate spots appeared on his neck. He had not wanted to hear the truth. Yet if she had understood one thing about Elliott by now it was that he was an ascetic, impassioned only by his work. Other people, even lovers, would only ever be a distraction. He was hungry for performance the way the people around them devoured sizzling barbecued beef on their tiny table stoves. With the best actors there was always something of this closed system about them, she had always thought. Away from performance, life for them was a dim paraffin lamp, burning slowly out of frame.

"He hated me, at the end."

Across from her Elliott stiffened. "Richard? I'm sure he didn't —"

"There was something he wanted to tell me. It was in March, when it was still freezing. We went to see a play at the Donmar. All week he was — electrified," she said.

What she did not tell Elliott about that evening: details engravened, unbidden, on her mind: the women with diamanté-encrusted sandals seen from the upper deck of the bus, tumbling down Old Street, the men in the theatre, hundreds of men and only her and three other women in an all-male scenario for which she was unprepared, as if they had wandered into the lower gallery of a synagogue. The men achieved a single, joint gaze: avid, hawkish, sifting through the other men in the audience, as if looking for someone specific.

No man had looked at her with the avidness she saw in the audience around her in, what? Years, decades, millennia. Maybe they never had. She had never performed for anyone's gaze. Yet something had been forfeited, and now it was too late. She ought to have been prepared for it by countless novels and films. She knew ageing women's allure could be more ephemeral than a Tory politician's promise. Yet she was taken aback by the uninvited guest of middle age.

Then the bus ride home after dinner at Belgo, Richard's unuttered confession echoing between them. Pavements slicked with neon, streaks of red, yellow, green. Trip-you-up cobblestones. Men in white shirts and white jackets careening down Old Street on Santander bikes, figures languishing in bus stop purgatory, the empty bottle of pear cider left on the seat of the 243, the garrulous clubbers who surrounded them, on their way to Shoreditch and Dalston.

"On the bus Richard said to me, 'I feel like Elliott's my son, or he's inside me. I feel like I've known him always.'"

"And what did you think, when he said that?"

"I thought it very strange, and I told him so. But I envied him."

The ice axe of grief that was lodged in her chest shifted. Grief mutated constantly, she has discovered. The only emotion the ice axe had not hacked apart was an abstract one: that she should live a meaningful life now, that she should make things that will live in the world beyond her and her lifetime. This film will be that, and also her missive to Richard. She hoped he was watching somewhere.

She stood. "Let's walk off some of those ribs."

Out on the sidewalk the white plastic takeaway bag dangled from Elliott's hand, billowing like a jellyfish in the night. The corner of 7th Avenue and 52nd Street came upon them. The glassy stalks of the condominiums that had sprouted all over Hell's Kitchen, pollinating lawyers and film industry executives, peered down.

At 59th Street they flagged and descended into the subway. Some carriages were air-conditioned, in others the aircon was in various stages of failure. In these, sweat coated the floor and shoes left footprints in their slick, like indoor rain. From a refrigerated carriage they were released onto a station platform so hot she felt the top of her head sweat and wondered if menopause had at last arrived. What would Benjamin have made of this city, she wondered as the heat poured through her. How would he have rendered it in his dense vignettes? Radiance. Varnished, scarlet interiors. Too much phenomena, too much happening all the time.

They emerge at on the corner of 103rd and Broadway. Traffic streams by in four lanes. They stand in the central median. She has received a signal. She takes her camera from her bag.

Elliott whirls around. "What are you doing?"

"I'm taking your picture."

She can't tell him about the message. She cannot say if it came from inside her or somewhere else. A voice not her own had spoken to her just as they had emerged from the station into the sodium night, surfacing into the real. It said: *Stop. Look at him.* She musters an internal response. *Who are you?*

But then the lights are about to change and Elliott will be crossing the southbound lanes of Broadway. She — or the voice — is worried he might disappear.

The moment coalesces around them. Elliott turns around. From underneath his baseball cap he gives her a frenzied, bashful smile.

She presses the button on her phone camera. In that moment a car tears through the red light, its velocity that of another machine — a spaceship, perhaps. The sear of a siren follows, upon them so quickly that people crossing the road barely have time to scatter, but they do, in ragged synchronicity, and the police car in pursuit of the bullet car passes them, a red-white-blue streak.

The lights change to green. On all four corners of the avenue people rub their arms, their legs, as if to check they are still there. No bodies lie in the intersection. There are no screams. They may have hallucinated the car.

"Did you see that?" Another woman who looks very much like her, thin, middle-aged, turns to her, addresses her like an old friend, her voice casual but shaken at once. "He's so lucky." The woman's gaze strays to Elliott, whose expression has become fixed with shock. "He would have been in the middle of the street. I mean, this is New York, anything can happen, he's so lucky . . ."

Joanna approaches Elliott. Her hands find his arms. It is not the first time she has touched him, by any means — she is his director after all — but her hands are suddenly hungry for the density of him, the dimensionality. She feels their lack of charisma as they alight on him. They may never touch another body in passion, as long as she lives.

Elliott's arm yields. His hand rises to meet hers. His fingers are cool and commanding in her palm. They stay there for some time as the traffic courses past, a frozen duet.

VIII

There is something leonine in the red of our kitchen. I've never noticed this before but now I see gums of predators, the hungry embers of fires, in its walls. The camera devours this, then swims to the living room and its Victorian colours. Through the window we see the silver leaves of the Japanese maple outside our house on Navarino Road.

"Nathan, Lucy, come on, get off YouTube would you? I can't get my emails to download and you're both supposed to be studying so you can take your place in the obsolete industrial-manufacturing economic model before the robots get here."

"We're watching Netflix, Dad."

"Whatever!"

Joanna presses pause on the laptop, to where she has downloaded the footage from my iPhone. We intuit, rather than see, that she is in a different space from the one in the video. A boxy apartment, a continual cacophony washing upward from the streets below. Is there a riot? A national emergency? No, it is the Manhattan night, ravines of streets, sluggish rivers tugging at its hems, the tinny grunt of hyena as the bus changes gears, the whippoorwill of siren.

"Do you want a frozen yogurt? I'm just popping out." Elliott has become addicted to the Pinkberry shop at 112th and Broadway. It's so hot here they may as well live on the stuff. He and Joanna eat sushi every day. They're probably going to get mercury poisoning.

"No thanks," Joanna says. "But I'll have a spoonful of yours."

There is only one scene yet for us to film, or two, depending on how you count them. In the meantime we have become an Oedipal threesome. We are better at being a family than our actual family is, but perhaps that is always the way it goes.

To recap: Elliott and Joanna return to the apartment after Elliott's close-shave crossing of the street. Joanna goes to her laptop and pulls up footage I shot the previous autumn, before either of us had met Elliott, when we were still trying to draw together financing for our Benjamin film. Joanna and Elliott watch me rove around the city. I shoot the park at night when I walk Mabati, careful to slip my phone into my pocket when hooded youngsters pass by too closely on stolen mountain bikes.

We hear the door close as Elliott leaves. Instantly Joanna's eyes darken. She does not like to be alone these days. She is thinking of getting another dog or a cat when she gets home, ostensibly to keep Mabati — who has taken my absence very badly and rarely eats or wants to go outside now — company.

I see in Joanna's expression the duel between forces she has yet to take the measure of. She had come to take me as given, a permanent fixture in the world, like the Matterhorn. Her love for me had sunk into an unconscious stratum, the same dimension where her love for herself — if that is how she could call it — abided. There, the two loves lived as married twins. She understands now why the surviving partner in long-married couples very often die soon after. They have not lost their partner, or not only, but themselves. They will spend the rest of their time on the planet as living ghosts, the haunted and the hauntee.

Now we have no secrets from each other.

It is so hot in the apartment, even with air conditioning, Joanna's forehead is lined with a thin sweat. We hear the wail from the streets and moans from the skies as planes on the landing track to LaGuardia slice open their bellies and their entrails fall out.

Neither Joanna nor Elliott speak to me anymore. They have their own rhythm now, they are collaborators. Elliott is walking the hot streets of Broadway, eating his pomegranate yogurt. Tomorrow Joanna is meeting Robin again, who may be able to help with festivals once the film is made, even if he personally dislikes meta-headfucks (his term): films within films, stories within stories.

Framed by the marine light of her computer screen, Joanna is fingering her relief at temporarily not being in a country with a "cliff edge." She finds herself thinking of the night before the referendum. She was watching a history documentary presented by Bettany Hughes, something on Herculaneum. She was trying to quell her anxiety that the vote would not go the way she wanted, or needed, it to. I was at a screening of a friend's film at the Arnolfini in Bristol. I would take a late train to Paddington to be back in time to vote the next day.

All night thunderstorms lit up the sky. Joanna tossed and turned in bed, so much so that I got up and went to the study to write, saying to her half-awake body as I went out the door, "It's like *King Lear* in here." We were both so on edge, even Nathan and Lucy felt it. The morning the result was announced Lucy cried.

Joanna knew we were embarking on an elongated trauma then, so drawn out it would qualify as something else. *Empathy with the past serves not least to make the past seem present*, Benjamin writes. For the first time in her life she felt grief for her country, or for the version of it she had thought she'd been living in. She had always felt British and European both, as much as I had, but now, having been very likely blocked in the future from one identity, and cut adrift from the other via disgust, she found that she belonged nowhere. She was homeless, maybe even stateless. They are so nearly the same thing.

It would be awhile before she became enraged by the fact that something precious had been stolen from her, by nefarious means, and that the country had been neutered for generations to come. For the first time in her life, her principles and values have been violated on a mass scale. Joanna considers that depriving millions of people of their citizenship and right to exercise freedom of movement on the premise of a bogus referendum immoral, and likely criminal. She hopes the architects of Britain's demise will be tried in a court of law for it in the future. They've swapped day for night, and for what?

What can we do? We are only filmmakers. We can only record the moment. We are witnesses to the now-moment that Benjamin considered the only real time. All others — past, future — are history's dressing rooms where we try to annihilate ourselves.

Now, the two people I loved are living together in some profound way that has nothing to do with shared space and electricity bills. *We live to love.* The thought sprang to Joanna's mind a few days after I left. It is an unusually sentimental thing for her to think, but she was in shock. She was anxious about taking on the mantle of the story, about directing Elliott, about being responsible for the shoot. As for me, I found myself in Kenya, of all places. Is it possible death really is a homecoming? It was strange: on the flight there I was no longer afraid; the fear that we would crash to earth had left me.

Joanna may have forgiven me, at least for the moment. *We live to love.* She will say this line in the penultimate scene, which we will film tomorrow, here in this room or on the street or in a café in this riotous city.

Joanna goes back to watching my videos kept in the folder named *Don't Look Down*, a nod to Roeg's eerily plasmic *Don't Look Now* and also a direct quote from my father, who gave me few nuggets of advice, but that was one of them: "Keep your head up in life, Richie. Don't think about what could go wrong. If you look down, you'll fall." Usually I hate simplistic physical metaphors for the too complex experience of actual living, but I made an exception for that one.

The camera shuffles around our London house. In it, Joanna roves on motherly missions, picking up one of Lucy's incomprehensible textbooks, my iPad, brushing Mabati's hair from the Sienese cushion, a rare gift from my mother.

The purpose of this particular video is to record what would usually be temps mort, cinematic dead time, a Tuesday night in the house we bought in 1993 at the height of the recession for £78,000 and which is now worth, if the estate agents are to be believed, £1.5 million. Tonight the scene is: Richard and Joanna will have a working supper, which means they will eat too quickly, despatch Nathan and Lucy upstairs, leaving them to their own devices (certainly the digital era has brought a new ring to the phrase), then start wrangling about narrative through-lines and money.

All this time I have been making two films, essentially: *Benjamin*, about the life of the great intellectual Walter Benjamin, killed by his own hand but in actuality hounded to death by the Nazis, but also the making of this film, our lives in the course of one definitive year near the end of the second decade of the twenty-first century. I am not sure yet how I can stitch them together, but I will.

Richard, Joanna says to me now, her voice still in residence inside me. *Why would anyone want to watch two middle-class filmmakers drink their flat whites in Hackney while they worry about Brexit?*

But it's the truth. The word, its bronze ring, hangs in Richard's — in my — mouth.

We see the fear in Richard's eyes reflected in Joanna's, a fear she can only equate with desire. He had tried very hard not to betray her, she understands. He had fought with himself, but he was up against something extraordinary in Elliott, who is what Hegel or some other philosopher had referred to as a beautiful soul. There really are souls of special luminosity circulating on the planet. If you are lucky you encounter one and it is like meeting an astonishing racehorse — Red Rum or Shergar or Nasrullah, those names Joanna instantly loved when she was a child and growing up in a horse-obsessed shire of the New World.

Richard had fought against it, she will come to understand, but it was too much for him, the power this young man has been invested with, and which probably has no name.

◥

The Manhattan night is punctured with shouts, drilling sounds, distant rumblings. Manhattan is like being on a ship at anchor.

Their rooms always adjoin. Joanna imagines she hears him breathing through the walls. Only plaster and breath separate them.

The streetlight, more feeble than in London, drifts through her window. She has never been so aware of someone's existence. She expects to carry on directing Elliott long after they are no longer shooting, through the scenes of his life. She knows what he will do before he even does it. She is not sure she even had this instinct with me.

We cut to Elliott saying, *I want to act in the space between the idea and the ideal.*

Richard says, *I felt we were chosen, not by each other but by a higher power.*

The rugged cliffs of Capri come into view, followed by the Pyrenees looming over the bay of Port de la Selva, near Portbou, where Benjamin died.

Richard's voice, disembodied, projected from the left side of the screen only, so that it seems to be entering or exiting, we are not sure. *The what-has-been and the now are united in the present as image.* Memory is imagistic, jump-cut: telluric seams of minerals, golden ribbon through rocks. Now they are in New York to break the laws of history and biography and film the impossible.

In his last published essay, Benjamin writes a short section in response to Paul Klee's *Angelus Novus*, a drawing Benjamin owned. When he died, his friend Gershom Scholem, who was living in Palestine, inherited it. *The angel would like to stay, awaken the dead, and make whole what has been smashed. But a storm is blowing from Paradise and has got caught in his wings; it is so strong that the angel can no longer close them. The story drives him irresistibly into the future.*

Benjamin's own intuition is that he is dogged by a dark star, that the geometries of fate lean toward him at a slouching angle, like an isosceles triangle. He is constantly aware that ecstatic reunions are taking place in other dimensions, his peers and colleagues and friends hugging émigrés at the bottom of gangplanks in Palestine, in New York City harbour. Holed up in Paris or, when the city was overrun by the Germans, in distant Lourdes, he lives his friends' existences faithfully as if they are happening to him. He can almost smell the chalky scent of the New World.

Bild, the word for image in German, does not distinguish between *image* and *picture*. For Benjamin, image was concept and metaphor and meaning. The image delivers the shock of awareness. Our thought crystallizes around it. In retrospect, when we try to remember what we thought, we see the image.

Here, images refuse to cohere. I live in an aftermath, drifting temperatureless between day and night, hot and cold, the sea and sky. I have dreams-within-dreams in which I am dead and at Heathrow trying to take a flight to Ljubljana (of all places, I can't even spell it) but no one will let me on board.

Eventually I board an Avianca plane to Cusco but once inside the seat I hold a boarding pass for does not exist. There is decay, and latency, and dusk. Films of the now are beamed to a council of lavish sentient trees who, together with amber-eyed wolves, scroll through the future. The sun hums in these creatures' veins. Everything is more robust. There are mountains and plains and oceans which morph into each other, joined by seams of skin-like lava. Here, there are no borders.

I'd give anything to be let out of this black circus; I can feel the proximity and impossibility of an antidote: it would be something simple — a pint of lager, a snog in a carpark, to be able to touch something, anything. But I am closer to myself now, to the engine of my own exposure.

Joanna is alone now. I cannot help her, from where I sit in the corner of this rented apartment on West 114th Street and to which I have followed her, acting on the murky agenda of the newly dead. I can only watch. Now she is speaking to Neil on FaceTime, recounting her meeting with Robin. Now she goes to the fridge and takes out the Hercules-sized American carton of orange juice. She looks thin, and lonely, but committed. What will happen after this film is done? Her life will not substantially change now, she thinks. The entropy of middle life has taken hold. But life will take her somewhere yet. She is still in the river. I can see her destination but she cannot.

Elliott's life, on the other hand, is a supernova, expanding, gaseous. Through this film, and other projects, he will achieve that rare state of siege: fame. He will experience more in a day than Joanna or I ever have in a year, or possibly ever.

Morning, August 17, 2018. It is sunny and the light is good. Joanna has been up since six, when she went for a run on the track at Riverside State Park in Harlem. She gathers the Lumix. She and Elliott leave the flat in a soundless collusion. They are so used to each other's electricity now they do not need to speak to communicate. It is time for the penultimate scene.

◥

"Okay, that's the scene."

Joanna's skeleton crew disperse onto the summer lawns outside the Butler Library. For once, crowd wrangling is not the problem. August has spread a glaze of stasis over the city. The quadrangle and buildings of Columbia are empty and stentorian in the heat. Joanna's main problem will be sound: the constant sirens of the neighbourhood, courtesy of Mount Sinai Hospital, will have to be digitally scrubbed.

Joanna drifts to the café, where they offer her three varieties of brewed coffee. The staff recite these in their robotically friendly voices. "Whichever you think," she says. "I'm English and unused to having a choice."

She is beginning to become a filmmaker. She is shooting moments of arrival as if they are really moments of departure.

As for me, I am starting to be able to remember myself. Only a few months ago I was levering myself out of that always-dark time of year, a humpback whale resurfacing after a long refuge in darkness. But my time in the dark has been well spent. Things impossible in the blare of day become, at night, evasive but necessary commandments.

In March I couldn't know that my own cliff edge was approaching, although I sensed it. This was why I gave in (my own term) to Elliott. All my life I have ignored American motivational propaganda — life is not a rehearsal, etc. — because for me *life* has not been the point. It is only the raw material. Real life is the holograms I project onto screens.

With Elliott's body I was curious, like a statistician, exploring, measuring rivers of data. In sex it would seem we can finally be direct, we can know the city of the other, walk its occluded alleyways, build a picture of the body's matrix. Finally, just before I turned mid-century, I understood we are attracted to spirits as much as genders. Benjamin wrote of the transiting character: everything is changing shape and role all the time. As Klaus Mann wrote in his autobiography, *The Turning Point*, "There is only one face you love. It is always the same."

◪

My turn at the camera, once more, for old time's sake.

I get signed waivers from everyone in the Hungarian pastry shop. Joanna and Elliott sit near the door. I hire a Columbia graduate student to vet the endless flow of doctors and nurses from Mount Sinai coming through the door.

From the window they can see St. John's Cathedral. It really does look as if it is being filmed in Europe — Budapest, maybe, or Prague.

                    JOANNA
        Have you ever had a relationship with
              someone your age?

                    ELLIOTT
        I'm not attracted to people of my own
              age. I don't know why.

Elliott hesitates. He is not sure where
he will arrive, if he is heading toward a
territory of confession.

                    ELLIOTT (CONT'D)
                  What about you?

                      JOANNA
            I've always been with Richard.

                      ELLIOTT
                    (incredulous)
            You've never slept with anyone else?

Joanna's lips make a tiny movement, like a
nod, some latent acknowledgement.

                      JOANNA
            I was late to lose my virginity. When I
            did it was to him. Then we got married,
            and — and you know the rest.

                      ELLIOTT
            Did you ever want to sleep with anyone
                        else?

                      JOANNA
            I'm not sure I can tell you that.

                      ELLIOTT
            You feel you're betraying Richard.

                      JOANNA
            Even if he betrayed me with you, yes.

The panic in Elliott's eyes is instant. She has come to know his
face better than he does, and she is alarmed for him, how poorly
he can hide what he truly feels.

"Don't worry. I'm not going to berate you."

He spoons foam around his deserted coffee cup.

"You thought I didn't know."

He doesn't answer.

She overrides her instinct, which is to hurt him.

"I've shocked you," she says.

His eyes are hidden behind the curtain of his fringe. "No, I knew," he says. A long pause. "I just didn't want to admit it to myself. How did you know?"

She understands that what Elliott really wants to ask is *when*. "It was a gradual realization. I kept looking for clues in the past, in Richard's last weeks. And then when he died I stopped looking, or thought I did. What did it matter? My discovery of whatever was happening to him emotionally wouldn't make him any less dead."

She pauses. "But I kept thinking about his birthday party . . . I'd forgotten, actually, because of what happened. I saw you both standing out on the patio. It was still cold, then, but you both looked so . . . warm. You were just standing together, talking, looking at all of us in the living room and I thought I could see a light around you. It was not an ordinary energy. I felt so abandoned. By myself as much as by Richard. I felt, *Here we are, us lesser beings inside the house, warm and supposedly safe, talking about money and schools and houses and you two were outside and on another plane. Another planet.*"

She stops. "I forgot about it until recently. I've forgotten everything since Richard died, including myself. I'm living my life now as someone else. I don't know who yet."

The café door opens constantly, clouds of heat billowing into the café. Each time it opens their eyes flick toward it, as if they are expecting someone in particular to enter.

"Last night I finally went through the pictures on his phone and —"

"And you found one of me."

"More than one. There was a picture of you sleeping."

She witnesses a strange event. All the youth drains from Elliott's face. What has been buoyant was now stale. The sleek muscles in his neck become as gnarled as the roots of a tree.

"I looked at the date of the photograph. It was taken the night of the snowstorm, when he stayed with you."

"I didn't know he took that picture."

She fishes in her pocket and finds my phone there. She passes it to Elliott.

We see a very slight widening of his eyes and a flutter of eyebrows. "I don't feel substantial," he says. "I never did. "I feel my life is on loan to me from something or someone else. Since Richard died I feel I could really disappear."

"We're all in that position, Elliott."

"I hear his voice all the time."

"Yes, I know. I do too. We're possessed."

He drops his gaze to the table. Doctors and nurses keep coming in the door, badges and lanyards sashaying in the blast from the air conditioner. They banter loudly with the barista, energized from their recent brushes with other people's deaths.

Elliott's youth returns, flooding his face. She will have to try not to let her anger and jealousy, if that is what she feels, mark him.

"Do you love him?" She cannot use the past tense.

His eyes widen, until they are more whites than iris. "Of course."

This time she can't resist the temptation to irony, to demonstrate to him the real mastery age brings, which is to position yourself in response to pain so that pain becomes your plaything, your weapon.

"Well, that's alright, then."

His eyes fill with tears. Outside the heat presses against the glass box of the café, a solid force.

She says, "You can't know what a marriage is. But maybe you will, someday."

We live to love. She rolls the words around in her mouth as if she is learning to digest marbles. She has changed her mind. She used to think it possible to will yourself not to be in love, not to fall into that particular trap. Now she is ready to accept her shadow life or, better said, the life of the shadow self that lives inside her and which has been kept in the darkness, hungry for light.

We see Elliott and Joanna from outside the café, their reflections superimposed with Broadway traffic and, if you look closely, an image of a tall man holding a hand-held video camera trained on the window while New Yorkers stride by without batting an eyelid. Inside Joanna and Elliott are silent. Air conditioning maintains a temperature of eighteen degrees; on the street where I stand it is nearly twenty degrees warmer. We have escaped one overheated megacity to come to another. *Frying pan* and *fire* come to mind. One upside of death: I won't have to live through the climate change apocalypse blockbuster we are all directing.

Joanna and Elliott look out of the window. I wait for their eyes to acknowledge my presence, but their gaze passes straight through me and falls on the street, where a crosstown bus has come to rest on its haunches at a red light. It throws a field of heat around it, a visible convection. The light changes, and the bus shudders forward.

The deed done, he lays down. He is overtaken by a leaden feeling in a part of his body he has never registered before now. He could not say where it is — halfway between the heart and the stomach, perhaps. A slender ball of mercury settles there.

He is so tired. He expected the hike to be difficult, but it has finished him. Yet it was so remarkable, at times: the lordly blue of the September sky, the drone of autumn bees as they perambulated from cork oak flower to cork oak flower — this was all that grew at the summit, where the wind stunted everything and no birds, even, ventured.

The drone intensifies in his ears as the morphine washes through him. His struggle will soon be over. Yet the resistance inside him builds — not to death, or not exactly. The fury that builds, so quickly, is the life force not of organs or platelets but ideas. He had always taken them personally. They were never abstractions for him but separate appealing lusts.

The hotel is silent, for a hotel. Few noises of gurgling taps, of doors abruptly shut. No ghosts. It is so small he has a sense of the whole establishment being a theatre set — it could be collapsed into a cardboard box at any moment.

The morphine will take much longer than it should to kill him. Henny Gurland, who has made the crossing with him, and who comes to visit Benjamin in his room at 7 a.m. the next morning, will find him semiconscious. What note of bullishness in his spirit insists on keeping going? This is wholly unexpected. From the beginning he was the verwöhntes Kind, the spoiled child with a delicate constitution, lace doilies for hands, a machine in his mind that moved in directions and revolutions more unique than most. He had seven governesses and had aspired to nothing more than sharing a maroon, toffee-scented library with Theodor and Max in benign, cosmopolitan Frankfurt, steins of beers in the Zur Sonne after robust debates about the falseness of false consciousness.

For most people he suspected ideas were conveniences or obstacles to be overcome. Why were they so visceral to him? In the idea he saw the ideals and he also lived in that space, seeking, searching. Surely, here was a better world, a better way to live? His passion for Asja had been constructed from such an idea, which she embodied: modernity, solidarity. He needed her rigidity, her conviction. Where was she now? Would she survive this Black Death other people called war?

Outside his hotel window, the pollarded plane trees of the Rambla point their stumps into a lacquered sky. A line he has written spirals back to haunt him: *Revolution always comes too early.*

The future still feels accessible. He will live in New York for a few months, perhaps even a year, but will soon join Adorno and Horkheimer in "German California," Pacific Palisades. This is his dream, softened by morphine: he is swimming before breakfast in a hot country. Strokes across a pool, his eye studded with bougainvillea. Overhead a large nameless bird, black and silent as a surveillance plane, passes across the sun.

Today, the 26th of September 1940, sunrise takes place at 7:36 and sunset at 19:38. The length of daylight will be ten seconds short of twelve hours. Astronomical twilight will begin at 6:04 a.m. and end at 21:12. Solar noon will be at 13:38 and the sun will tilt at 46.4 degrees in the sky. Seconds after dawn, an internal ocean washes over him. Two hundred metres away, small waves ripple through the Mediterranean, caused by the solar winds that accompany the dawn, unwitnessed by anyone. Unwitnessable.

◪

The final scene. Hannah Arendt is at her desk in her apartment at 370 Riverside Drive. The apartment overlooks a narrow park, wintry even in summer. Beyond it, the Hudson is sluggish and dour.

In between her eighteenth and nineteenth cigarette of the day it occurs to her: Walter saved himself from the ennui of exile. That is not a tragedy.

Arendt's dream, the one Elliott formulates in Spain, is of Benjamin in New York. Alive, he is teaching at Columbia. Arendt has invited him to give a lecture in the building that will become the journalism school, a classroom of mostly young men, but a smattering of women too. Benjamin walks along 114th Street between Broadway and Amsterdam, smoking. He passes a bookshop. In the window is *Buddenbrooks*. A map of Germany provides the backdrop to a display of contemporary authors, released from their slumber now that the war has been won. His eyes focus on an ink blot on the map, located on the bridge of his country's nose. Berlin. He has not been to the city of his birth since 1932. He will likely never see it again.

The line comes to her: *No longer does the dream reveal a blue horizon.* The future, having been stolen, does not restore itself, even if more favourable conditions emerge. That is the great triumph of fascism. She writes this down.

Joanna's camera pans out. We will see the city as Benjamin might have lived it, as it was, in 1947: smoky, unacquainted with history. We will see the widening sky of the Atlantic as evening arrives from the unknowable west, and day becomes night.

ACKNOWLEDGEMENTS

This novel arose in part from a collaboration artist Diego Ferrari and I began in 2016, about Walter Benjamin's relationship with the Mediterranean landscapes of his life and death, and which culminated in an art exhibition titled "Day for Night: Landscapes of Walter Benjamin," exhibited at the Peltz Gallery in London in 2018.

Day for Night the novel was written between January and September 2018. Its events, although fictional, follow some of those of my life as they took place, so it is written more or less in "real time." For example, I travelled to Naples, Capri, Siena and Bologna in the late spring of 2018 to deliver lectures and to do research for our exhibition. In the summer I returned with Ferrari to Portbou in northern Spain, where Benjamin died, then travelled to New York City in August to research Benjamin's possible after-life at Columbia University and the New School.

The long lead times of fiction publishing mean that this book is being published in May 2021. Three and a half years later we are living in a vastly changed world. Walter Benjamin himself lived in accelerated times and was ultimately over-taken by history. His presence is threaded lightly in this story. I did not want to write a novel that critically interrogated his work, reinterpreted his thought or otherwise wore its interest and respect for him as a thinker heavily, a cloak of knowing-ness. Rather the novel investigates how us Britons and European citizens share something important with Benjamin and his generation. Just as Joanna, in the novel, expresses, with the theft of our European citizenship in the name of the political gambit of Brexit, we have been deprived of some-thing valuable and precious in order to plump up the ill-gotten fortunes of plutocrats most of us will never meet. The result is a kind of statelessness, and a dangerous precedent that citizen rights can be fraudulently deleted. I hope history will return what is rightfully ours, although history may advance too slowly for me, personally, to be vindicated, nor does it always right wrongs.

◢

I would like to thank the following people for their friend-ship and support in the writing of this novel: Diego Ferrari, Julia Bell, Margie Orford. Henry Sutton, my colleague at the University of East Anglia, who has been a steadfast sup-port throughout the years we have worked together, read an earlier draft of the novel and gave me valuable comments. Screenwriter Samantha Collins read a draft of this work and gave me necessary insight on the film industry and the process of financing and shooting a film. Sincere thanks also are due to Elena Egawhary for loaning me her apartment at Riverside Drive and 116th Street, an invaluable base for my research in New York, and to Anya Schiffrin and students on the PhD in journalism at Columbia University for receiving me so warmly. I would also like to thank Laura Ferri and Carla Comellini in Siena and Bologna; and Koke and Sandra Valls in Port de la Selva; Catalunya, Luigi and Alfonsina at Agriturismo Del Sole in Anacapri, Capri. Various drafts and rewrites of this novel were completed in Watamu, Kenya, and I thank Andrew McNaughton for his friendship and support.

I would like to acknowledge that the title and the premise of one of Richard's (fictional) films, *Everyone Is Watching*, is taken from Megan Bradbury's exceptional novel of the same name, which I had the pleasure to read when she was a Fellow at the University of East Anglia. Like all of Richard's fictional films, it would make the basis for a fantastic film which I hope one day someone will make. *Day for Night* also harbours a statement that belongs to a valued and talented UEA colleague, playwright and author Steve Waters. In his *My Life in 16 Films* (forthcoming from Bloomsbury) astute observations abound, including the one attributed to Richard near the beginning of the novel: that film is about, essentially, figures in a landscape.

Finally I would like to thank my agent Veronique Baxter at David Higham Associates in London; my editor at ECW, Susan Renouf, for her support of my work; and all the talented publishing, production and publicity team at ECW Press: David

Caron, Jen Knoch, Susannah Ames, Elham Ali, Emily Ferko, Shannon Parr, and Turnaround Distribution in the UK.

◥

The following books have been consulted in the writing of this novel:

Arendt, Hannah, *The Human Condition*. The University of Chicago Press, 1998.

Benjamin, Walter, *One Way Street*. Harvard University Press, 2016.

Benjamin, Walter, *Reflections: Essays, Aphorisms, Autobiographical Writings*. Harcourt Brace Jovanovich, 1978.

Bondanella, Peter, *Italian Cinema: From Neorealism to the Present*. Continuum, 2001.

Eiland, Howard and Michael W Jennings, *Walter Benjamin: A critical life*. Harvard University Press, 2014.

Eiland, Howard and Michael W Jennings (eds), *Walter Benjamin: Selected writings, Volume 3, 1935–1938*. Harvard University Press, 2002.

Eiland, Howard and Michael W Jennings (eds), *Walter Benjamin: Selected writings, Volume 4, 1938–1940*. Harvard University Press, 2003.

Fittko, Lisa, *Escape Through the Pyrenees*. Northwestern University Press, 1991.

Potter, Sally, *Naked Cinema*. Faber and Faber, 2014.

Stonebridge, Lyndsey, *Placeless People: Writing, Rights and Refugees*. Oxford University Press, 2018.

Purchase the print edition and receive the eBook free!
Just send an email to ebook@ecwpress.com and include:

**Get the
eBook free!***
*proof of purchase
required

- the book title
- the name of the store where you purchased it
- your receipt number
- your preference of file type: PDF or ePub

A real person will respond to your email with your eBook attached.
And thanks for supporting an independently owned Canadian
publisher with your purchase!

Tarkovsky, Andrey, *Sculpting in Time (Reflection on the Cinema)*. Faber and Faber, 1989.

Wenders, Wim, *The Logic of Image*. Faber and Faber, 1991.